The McHenry Inheritance

"I really enjoyed reading this story and getting to know the characters. In a very short time, I found myself caring what happened to them. I am a mystery fan, and this definitely was a fun ride."

—*Mountain Mom*

Wash Her Guilt Away

"The fly-fishing descriptions were amazing. I was thoroughly engaged. I couldn't figure out who dunnit until the very end, and even then could only narrow it to two folks. Great story."

—*Lovedrama*

Not Death, But Love

"Perfect for summer vacation reading. Good character development and plot, with some nice surprises."

—*Doug Simmons*

The Daughters of Alta Mira

"As a lifelong devotee of good mystery novels, I can testify that the Quill Gordon mysteries are really fun. And in my opinion, they keep getting better."

—*Mike Milward*

I Scarce Can Die

"I really enjoyed it, from the punchy, bloody opening to the mutedly positive conclusion ... Although I've never gone fly fishing (or any kind of fishing for that matter), I'm entranced by the rivers and streams depicted and want to at least watch them flow."

— *Andre Neu*

Also by Michael Wallace

Quill Gordon Mysteries

1. *The McHenry Inheritance*
2. *Wash Her Guilt Away*
3. *Not Death, But Love*
4. *The Daughters of Alta Mira*
5. *I Scarce Can Die*

Nonfiction

The Borina Family of Watsonville (California history)

The Slaves
Of Thrift

A Quill Gordon Mystery

Michael Wallace

Cover Design: Deborah Karas, Karas Technical Services

Map: Nancy Ruiz DePuy

**In the spirit of Father Knox
and Charles McDermand**

*For John, a.k.a. Tigg,
fishing buddy since junior high*

Long-expected one-and-twenty,
Lingering year at last is flown:
Pomp and pleasure, pride and plenty,
Great Sir John are all your own.

Loosened from the minor's tether,
Free to mortgage or to sell,
Wild as wind and light as feather,
Bid the slaves of thrift farewell …

If the guardian or the mother
Tell the woes of willful waste,
Scorn their counsel, scorn their pother:
You can hang or drown at last!

—**SAMUEL JOHNSON,**
A Short Song of Congratulation

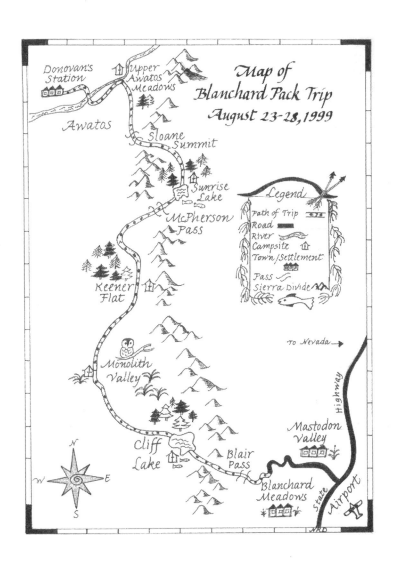

Map of
Blanchard Pack Trip
August 23-28, 1999

Donovan's Station

Upper Awatos Meadows

Awatos

Sloane Summit

Sunrise Lake

McPherson Pass

Legend

Path of Trip
Road
River
Campsite
Town/Settlement
Pass
Sierra Divide

Keener Flat

Monolith Valley

To Nevada

Highway

Mastodon Valley

Cliff Lake

Blair Pass

Blanchard Meadows

State

Airport

N
W   E
S

Watcher with a Knife

THE FULL MOON DOMINATED the cloudless eastern sky. Here, at 10,000 feet above sea level, the air was so clear and pure there didn't seem to be a particle of dust or grime between moon and earth. Every feature on the moon's surface stood out in sharp relief. Its light was amplified as it reflected off the still water of the small lake, the white boulders that circled the water and the granite faces of the mountains to the northwest.

A hundred lanterns could scarce have illuminated the campsite any better. Six two-person tents were pitched on a grassy verge by the southeast side of the lake. The campfire that had been burning robustly 45 minutes earlier had been doused, and not a hint of smoke remained in the air. The pack horses, tied up at the south end of the campsite, were largely still and silent.

Well concealed behind a clump of boulders 20 feet above the edge of the lake, the watcher with a knife sized up the situation for what must have been the tenth time in the last half hour. Cradling the knife in sensitive hands with long, thin fingers, the watcher went through a mental checklist point by point.

The campfire had been doused half an hour ago. In another 15 minutes, everyone should be asleep.

The moon was bright enough that no flashlight was needed.

There was no wind at the moment, and the stray breezes of the past half hour had come from the west to southwest. The watcher should be downwind from the horses.

The tents were laid out in a slight semicircle, and the one the watcher was interested in was second from the right. A tent at either end would have been better, but there was no helping that now. All the more reason for stealth and silence.

The luminous dial on the wristwatch indicated there were ten minutes left until strike time. Was there anything else to be considered?

Rattlesnakes.

1

The watcher jerked upward with a start. Probably not at this elevation, but there was no way to look it up now. *But I'll be stepping carefully to avoid making noise,* the watcher thought. *That should be enough.*

Ten minutes slowly ticked by.

At last it was time. Sheathing the knife, which had been painstakingly sharpened, the watcher rose and began the approach to the encampment. The first obstacle was the descent to lake level. This involved traversing several patches of loose rock, planting a foot carefully with every step. Once, the watcher dislodged a couple of stones, which rattled as they moved. To the watcher, it sounded like cannon fire, but that was nerves. Nothing stirred in the vicinity of the tents, and the horses didn't get restless, so the watcher continued the methodical advance.

The last patch of loose rock ended 120 feet from the camp, and the watcher was now on densely packed soil near the grassy verge. There was a temptation to speed up, but it had to be tamed. Every step had to be taken cautiously, and a constant vigil had to be maintained against someone coming out of a tent.

Finally the watcher reached the first tent on the left and paused to listen. No one was talking. No one was tossing and turning. Two low-level snores, distinct in timbre and cadence, were clearly audible, but it was impossible to tell from which tent or tents they were coming.

The plan had been to walk around the back of the tents, rather than in front, where the fire pit and tent flaps were. The watcher saw no reason to amend the plan and stepped cautiously to the gap between the second and third tents from the right. Only one of the snorers was still going, and otherwise all was as silent as it should have been.

Five more careful steps, and the watcher was kneeling in front of the flap of the second tent. Out of the sheath came the knife, and its blade glinted in the bright moonlight. After taking several deep, quiet breaths, trying to suck as much oxygen as possible from the thin mountain air, the watcher reached out to open the tent flap.

From behind, a hand clamped down on the watcher's shoulder.

The Concerned Attorney

QUILL GORDON SAT in a comfortable chair in the law office, sipping coffee and looking out the window toward the Bay Bridge. Halfway through this late June morning the fog was beginning to lift, and the sky behind the Oakland hills was blue. It was the first time — aside from a stray meal at the Carnelian Room — he had been this high up in the Bank of America building at 555 California Street. Gordon still called it that, even though the bank had moved to North Carolina a year earlier.

Attorney Herbert McCabe, senior partner in the firm of McCabe, Caen and Hoppe, was pacing nervously, trying to collect his thoughts. Taking another sip of coffee, Gordon idly wondered who was paying for the pacing. McCabe seemed every bit the successful, well-tailored, middle-aged attorney, and Gordon's mind shifted toward wondering what was so agitating him.

Abruptly, McCabe sat down.

"I apologize for the jitters," he said. "This is new territory for me, and I'm not sure where to begin. You're probably 20 years younger than me, so I don't imagine we read the same books when we were boys."

Gordon made a slight, noncommittal nod.

"Speaking for myself," McCabe continued, "I read a lot of British novels about gentleman adventurers: Bulldog Drummond, Richard Hannay, Chandos and Mansel — that sort of thing. I always thought of those books as entertaining bosh, but now I find myself in need of a gentleman adventurer for a confidential assignment." He paused. "You come highly recommended."

"I don't suppose one of the recommendations came from a judge?" Gordon asked, thinking of his father.

"Two of them, actually. Also a certain person at Not Guilty Northern California spoke very highly of you."

"All right. But why do you specifically need a gentleman?"

"Because what I'm about to propose is highly irregular — so much so that I can't offer to pay for it."

"Sounds intriguing," Gordon said, "but I have to admit this surprises me. I did a little looking into your firm before this meeting. You specialize in wills, trusts and estates. Very necessary, but hardly the most exciting or clandestine form of law. I can see where you might need a gentleman, but an adventurer? What's that all about?"

"Before I tell you, Mr. Gordon, I must have your word that nothing I say will go beyond this room — regardless of whether you take me up on my proposal."

"I give my word as a gentleman," Gordon said.

McCabe smiled for a second, then became serious again. He leaned forward and lowered his voice.

"I have reason to suspect that one of my clients is planning a murder."

"YOU HAVE MY ATTENTION," Gordon finally said.

"Then I'll start at the beginning. Are you familiar with the name Fred Schroeder?"

"The real estate guy?"

"That's sort of like calling Bill Gates 'the software guy,' but yes. Are you familiar with his story?"

"I know he was big. That's about it."

"Quite a legend, and he cultivated the legend well. He was born in 1917 and served in the Pacific Theater during World War II. At the end of 1945 he was flying back to California in a military transport. At the last minute it was rerouted and had to fly over the East Bay. Looking out the window, he could see that the towns on the other side of the hills were almost all country. And he said to himself, this is where the Bay Area is going to grow."

"Sometimes," Gordon said, "all it takes to get rich is one good idea."

"Give him credit for carrying it out perfectly. Within a couple of years, he'd lined up some investors and started buying land. He seemed to have a knack for guessing where the next hot spot would be. His housing developments and shopping centers were all first class and generally paid off handsomely."

"Did he ever fail?"

"Not often, and when he did, he just wrote it off and moved on. By the early '70s, he was so big that some people joked one of the East Bay counties should be renamed Schroeder County, because he'd built most of it. And he'd bought out his partners early on, so this spectacularly lucrative company was all his."

"He died young, didn't he?" Gordon said. "I mean comparatively."

McCabe nodded. "He and his wife, Lola, who he married in 1947, decided to celebrate their 30th wedding anniversary with a month in the Mediterranean. You remember when those two 747s collided on the runway in the Canary Islands in 1977? Fred and Lola were on one of them."

"And the estate?"

"Two years after Fred and Lola married, she almost died giving birth to their daughter. The doctors said another pregnancy could be fatal. So after those jumbo jets collided, the one daughter, Laura, inherited the whole thing. At 28, she was one of the wealthiest women in the Bay Area."

"Dare I ask. . .?"

"How much? Our firm didn't get involved until later, but *Forbes* magazine estimated the family fortune at $800 million last year. I suspect that's pretty close."

"And what happens to it when Laura dies?"

"She already has, and what happens next is what I'm concerned about."

"SO SHE DIED YOUNG, TOO?" Gordon said.

"Let me back up a bit," McCabe said. "Laura Schroeder was one of those people who gets excited about a lot of different things and generally loses interest in them after a while. A bit of a dilettante. And since her family could support her interests, she was free to flit from flower to flower, so to speak. In her fifth year at UCLA, she met and married Erik Matthiessen, famous sculptor in the making."

"Never heard of him," Gordon said.

"He never made it. Not even with the backing of the Schroeder money. But Erik and Laura had twin sons, Tyler and Mason, who were born — and the date is important — September 27, 1974. A couple of years later, Laura threw the sculptor out, and he sort of disappeared. The general opinion is that he died before he could drink his way through the divorce settlement, but no one seems to know for sure."

"In 1981, she married a man named David Linfield. He was a zealous environmentalist who believed in Zero Population Growth, so they never had any kids of their own. But he adopted Tyler and Mason, and they took his name. The Schroeder money supported a bunch of environmental projects that kept David busy, and Laura was involved as well with various charities involving arts and animals. They seemed to be reasonably happy. In the end, though, it was the environment that killed them."

Gordon raised his eyebrows.

"They'd gone to Costa Rica to check out an eco-lodge they were thinking of buying. This was December 1995. One of the features of the lodge was a line running above the top of the jungle canopy so you can ride the line in a pod and get a close-range aerial view. Laura and David were riding on that when the line broke and they fell 100 feet to the ground below. They lived for a couple of days but died in a Costa Rican hospital.

"And the kicker to that story is that Laura had an appointment with me the day after she was to get back. She was going to change her will."

"Any particular reason?" Gordon asked.

"She was getting worried about the boys. And not without cause. The will in place when she died left everything to David with trusts for the boys. If he failed to outlive her by six months, however, most of it, after a number of charitable bequests, went to the boys in equal parts on their 25th birthday."

"Three months from now," Gordon said.

"Correct. The boys were 14 when the will was drawn up, and at that time, the provisions arguably made sense. Four years ago, the idea of their being able to responsibly handle such a fortune wasn't looking like such a good bet. I'm afraid it doesn't look much better today."

"Bad character?" Gordon asked.

"In spades. Mason got out of his second stint in drug rehab six months ago, and I see no evidence that it took. Tyler fancies himself a painter, though from what I can tell, no one else much agrees. He also has been asking for advances on his monthly allowance, which I believe he needs to pay significant gambling debts. If he weren't coming into $400 million in three months, he'd probably be hobbling around on crutches now after taking a baseball bat to the knees.

"Over the past few months, I've been meeting with Tyler and Mason individually. They're pretty much leading separate lives, and I'm getting a sense from them that there's no love lost between them and that they wouldn't mind being sole heirs."

"I'm having a hard time wrapping my head around this," Gordon said. "Are you suggesting that someone who stands to inherit $400 million would seriously consider killing his brother for *another* $400 million? No matter how dissolute you were, you couldn't burn through half that inheritance in a lifetime."

"Believe me." McCabe said. "If anyone can do it, it would be these kids."

GORDON SHOOK HIS HEAD and finished his coffee.

"Then," McCabe continued, "last week I heard something that sent a chill up my spine. The two of them are taking a weeklong trip as a sort of fraternal bonding experience."

"Don't tell me," Gordon said. "A cruise where someone could easily fall overboard. 'Accidentally,' of course."

"Maybe worse. A pack trip in the High Sierra as part of a group of only ten people plus guides. That means five nights and six days in a vast wilderness full of cliffs to fall off of, rivers and lakes to drown in, and plenty of deserted countryside in which to permanently vanish. All of it miles away from law enforcement and medical care. It's made to order for foul play."

"Are they, the boys, outdoor types?"

"Not at all, which makes it all the more suspect. It's presented as a wilderness experience with amenities, since the company running the trip will be cooking meals and all. But it's so outside what they've done up to now that I have to be suspicious."

"And where do I come in?" Gordon asked.

"Last week two people canceled on that trip, and I bought their places. Not personally, you understand. I have to stay away from this. My sister's best friend's husband bought the trip, and I'm reimbursing him with my own money. I'm asking you and a friend of your choosing to go along on that trip, keep your eyes on the situation, and intervene, if necessary, to make sure both brothers come back alive."

"That's all?"

"Not challenging enough for you?"

"The challenge is appealing enough. There's just one potential difficulty. What are the dates of this trip?"

"Monday August 23ʳᵈ to Saturday August 28ᵗʰ."

"Then I'm afraid I'll have to send regrets. I have an unavoidable conflict."

"How so?"

"I'm getting married Saturday September 4ᵗʰ. It wouldn't be getting things off to a good start if I were to disappear for a week that close to the date."

"Is that your only objection?" McCabe asked.

"IT'S A PRETTY SERIOUS ONE," Gordon finally said.

"I take it you've never done this sort of thing?"

"Pursue a homicidal maniac through the High Sierra wilderness? No, can't say that I have."

"I wasn't talking about *that*," McCabe said. "I was talking about marriage. Is this your first time?"

Gordon allowed that it was.

"Then you need to understand that the wedding is all about the bride. All the groom has to do is show up sober enough to say two words and get a ring over her finger. Two weeks before the wedding you'd just be underfoot anyway. Do this and you'll be back in San Francisco on Sunday August 29th, in plenty of time for the bachelor party and rehearsal dinner."

"I don't know."

"Of course if you'd rather be spending that week with your future in-laws when you could be fishing for Golden Trout …"

"Golden Trout?"

"Two nights along the way, the group will be camping next to lakes that hold native Golden Trout."

"Golden Trout. The California state fish."

"But it's up to you, of course. Maybe this is all in my imagination, and no one's in any danger at all."

Gordon said nothing. In his mind was an image of a set of scales, with a Golden Trout on one side and his future mother-in-law on the other. The fish outweighed the mother-in-law.

"When I first heard about you," McCabe said, "I figured you might be the man for the job. Your interest in fishing would give you a perfect reason for going on this trip, and your record of personal investigations is becoming very well known in certain circles."

The attorney leaned back in his chair and waited.

"I'll have to talk to Elizabeth," Gordon finally said. "Maybe I *would* just be in her hair that week. And I'd have to see if Peter or Sam could come along. I'd need a trusted wingman for an assignment like this."

He looked at McCabe.

"Can I give you an answer in a couple of days?"

"Take your time. I don't have a Plan B at this point, and it's you I want. I'll wait for your answer."

"I'll let you know as soon as I can. I understand you need a decision."

"Well, thank you for being willing to consider this. Now that I've met you personally, I'm more than ever convinced you're the man for the job. Are there any other questions I can answer at this time?"

"No, I don't think so." Gordon began to rise, but stopped. "Wait. There's one more thing. You never did say which brother you think is trying to kill the other."

McCabe said nothing for 15 seconds.

"My dear boy, as far as I'm concerned, either one of them is entirely capable of it." He smiled at Gordon. "I'm counting on you to sort it all out."

Sunday August 22, 1999

San Francisco to Blanchard Meadows

THIS TRIP STARTED OUT DIFFERENTLY from the others, and that wasn't necessarily a good thing. Gordon and I have gone fishing many times over the years, and on occasion we've been drawn into the investigation of a crime (or crimes) that occurred where we were staying. In other words, it was happenstance.

Now we're setting out to spend nearly a week with ten strangers, using our interest in fly-fishing as a cover for preventing a murder. Logic would dictate that we will therefore be in the company of a murderer for five nights in the High Sierra wilderness, with no 911 to call in case of emergency. This is not an appealing prospect for someone of my temperament, which does not include a zest for courting and cheating death.

I'm Sam Akers, and I'll be telling part of this story. My brother and I are partners in a prosperous San Francisco insurance agency, I'm married to a wonderful woman, and we have two lovely daughters. I have no reason to take unnecessary risks, but I'm doing it for Gordon. He and I have known each other since we lived on the same floor at student housing at Cal two decades ago, and he's asked me to be best man at his wedding, which is less than two weeks off. I guess that means I'm his best friend, and a best friend has to be there when asked.

Oh, and one other thing. Gordon doesn't know it, but I'm sort of acting as a double agent on behalf of the bride, Elizabeth Macondray. I was there when he first met her two years ago, and in the past week she has been peppering me with emails and furtive cell phone calls urging me to keep an eye on the prospective bridegroom. Actually, I was a bit surprised that she gave her blessing to this trip at all, and at one point I asked her about it.

"Gordon comes alive when he's doing an investigation, Sam," she said. "If we're going to have any kind of good marriage, I have to support him in that. All I'm asking you to do is see that he doesn't take any unnecessary risks and gets through the trip in fit enough condition to show up at the church."

Pressure? What pressure?

And so it came to pass that at ten o'clock on a lovely Sunday morning, I was at the controls of my Cessna, approaching the summit of the Sierra Nevada, with a grumpy and silent Gordon at my right. He hadn't spoken a word for half an hour, but with the top of the range coming into sight, he blurted out:

"Do you think we could see a body from up here?"

"I don't know. I've never thought about it before. Any particular reason you're asking?"

"Professional curiosity."

"Too soon to be thinking about that," I said. Looking out the side window, I saw vast open spaces, rugged mountains and a ribbon of trail (perhaps the trail we'd be taking) below. There was no sign of human presence and plenty of room to lose (or hide) a body, regardless of whether it was being searched for by ground or air.

"I'm having second thoughts about this," Gordon said.

"By this, do you mean our mission or getting married?"

"I mean the trip. I don't have a good feeling about it. I do have a good feeling about marrying Elizabeth."

"I'm glad to hear that. I think marriage is a good thing, provided you don't botch the decision on who you're marrying. As for the trip, it's too late to back out now. We'll be crossing the summit in a couple of minutes and beginning our descent to the airport. I'll try to take it slow so it doesn't blow your ears out."

THE LANDING WAS UNEVENTFUL, and by agreement, Gordon went to look for their ride while Sam secured the plane.

Mastodon Valley Airport was located just off the highway on an arid stretch of land surrounded by boulders and sagebrush. The terminal building was a hundred yards away from where the plane stopped and was shimmering like a mirage. When Gordon reached it and opened the door, he was greeted by a blast of cold air from the air conditioning. The interior was dimly lit, with

14

a row of chairs facing the door and two vending machines (one for soft drinks, one for snacks) in the far corner to his left. The waiting room was vacant, but on one of the plastic chairs was a messenger bag with a cardboard sign hand-labeled "Gordon" resting against it. He walked to the chair, set down his duffel bag and picked up the sign.

"I see you found it," said a husky female voice coming in from his right. He looked up to see a woman in her early thirties, six feet tall, with curly reddish-brown hair dropping below her shoulders. In her left hand was a paper cup.

"Had to get some coffee," she said. "I was taking people home from the bars and parties until four in the morning. I'm Sienna from 2 Ski Bums Car Service. Are you Gordon or his friend?"

"I'm Gordon," he said, trying not to be too obvious about looking. The tight jeans and revealing tank top she was wearing showed her off to good advantage and no doubt helped her tip income. "Pleasure to meet you, Sienna."

"So you're going to Blanchard Meadows?" He nodded. "I took a fare up there yesterday afternoon. Young guy about 25, five-seven, black hair, with a mustache and goatee he was too young to be wearing. A man shouldn't try that look until he's at least 35 or 40."

That sounded like a good description of Tyler Linfield, whose photo Gordon had in his duffel bag. But he wasn't expecting the next part.

"His girlfriend was all right, but he was a pain in the ass. Sorry. Is he a friend of yours?"

Gordon's face had, uncharacteristically, given away his surprise. McCabe had said nothing about Tyler bringing a girlfriend along on the trip.

"No, they're all strangers to me," he said.

"Well, you'll want to steer clear of this guy. He complained all the way to the meadows. Too hot, too cold, not going fast enough. You name it."

"What was the girlfriend like?"

"She didn't say much, but I got the sense she was more mature than he was. Which wouldn't be hard. A real shrimp, though. Five-two at most, black hair with a green stripe, heavy black eye makeup. She told him to relax and enjoy the trip at one point, all he said back was, 'I can't believe Mason agreed to this.' "

So it had to be Tyler, Gordon thought. Sam came in, and Gordon introduced him.

"Are we going straight to the Meadows, or do you need to stop in town?" Sienna asked.

"Actually," Gordon said, "could you drop us off for breakfast and charge whatever you think is fair for the wait?"

"Not a problem."

"And could you recommend a good breakfast joint?"

"If you want a hearty bacon and eggs/omelet breakfast, go to Hansel and Gretel's."

Gordon and Sam looked sideways at each other.

"It sounds hokey," she continued, "and don't be put off by the building. But the food's really good, and if we go now, you should be able to get right in."

UNTIL 1920, MASTODON VALLEY was a flyspeck on the map, an outpost of about a dozen people. In that year, the Eastern Sierra & Nevada Railroad, anticipating a wave of postwar prosperity, decided to build a ski resort to bump up its passenger traffic. The bowl-shaped valley, a day's train ride from Los Angeles or San Francisco (via Reno) was perfectly situated and encircled by mountains with the right slopes. Mastodon Valley Snow Resort opened in 1923 and was an immediate success. Over the years a town grew up around it and now numbered just over 7,000 year-round residents.

Even within the town's mix of faux-Swiss/backwoods architecture, the Hansel and Gretel cafe was in a class by itself, with a log cabin exterior, an alpine chalet roof, and the front of the building covered with images of frosted gingerbread men and Christmas cookies. Inside, it was loud and busy, but Gordon and Sam were quickly seated at a table for two.

After they had ordered coffee, Gordon opened the leather folio he had taken from his duffel bag and took out two 5-by-7 photographs.

"There are our charges," he said, laying the pictures in front of Sam. "This one is Tyler, and he sure looks like the face Sienna was describing."

"Refresh my memory. Is Tyler the gambler or the dope fiend?"

"The gambler." He pointed to the other photo, which showed a man of the same age, with longer, shoulder-length hair and a clean-shaven face. "Mason here is the druggie."

"The faces are almost the same," Sam finally said. "Thank God the hair's different. At least we won't be spending the whole trip trying to figure out who's who."

"I thought the same thing. Either one look like a killer to you?"

Sam studied the photos again.

"I don't know about that," he finally said, "but you know what strikes me about these pictures? I don't see any character here. They look callow and unformed."

"Too much money with too little work too early in life," Gordon said. "You know what McCabe, the attorney, said? They're getting an allowance of $12,500 a month each — after taxes."

"That's a good income, even for San Francisco."

"You'd think so, but apparently they have trouble making ends meet. If McCabe's right, one of them doesn't think $400 million is going to be enough to get him through life. And now there's another complication in this assignment."

"The girlfriend?"

Gordon nodded.

"McCabe said nothing about either of them bringing someone else along. He would have, if he'd known. I'm sure of that. So she's something else to worry about."

"You think she might end up being targeted as a second victim?"

"That's one possibility, but I was thinking of something else." When Sam didn't respond, Gordon added:

"She could be an accomplice."

THE ROAD LEFT MASTODON VALLEY, wound upward past a couple of lakes, then became a narrow dirt track. It hugged the mountainside, was wide enough for about one-and-three-quarters cars, and had no guardrails on the outer edge, where the sheer drop-off could be as much as several hundred feet. I wished I was flying and was glad Gordon wasn't driving.

A bit of breeze coming through the driver's side window wafted a floral-citrus scent to me from Sienna. The scent must have been added while we were at breakfast. It reminded me of the last call I got from Elizabeth last night, in which she admonished me to "keep the women away from him," meaning Gordon. Sienna's probably just angling for a better tip, and I can't see her chasing Gordon into the mountains, like Marlene Dietrich following Gary Cooper into the desert in *Morocco*. Of more concern are the other five people on the trip (not counting the trip leaders). I guess we'll find out tonight.

It was still a bright, sunny day, with a few cumulus clouds in the sky, but not too hot. The scenery, when I could bear to look, was stunning. At length we went over a pass, and on our left I could see a small valley below.

"Blanchard Meadows," Sienna said. "Your gateway to the High Sierra back country."

It was enough to take your breath away, and I found myself wondering if this was what Mastodon Valley had looked like 80 years ago, before the railroad decided to build a ski resort.

BLANCHARD MEADOWS is an outpost and pack station, consisting of a lodge, restaurant, cabins, campground, and horse corrals. Gordon and Sam checked in at the lodge and went to the second floor, where they had adjacent rooms with a shared bath and windows overlooking the meadow. After putting away his bag, Sam came through the bathroom into Gordon's room and looked out the window.

"I wonder why they call it Blanchard Meadows, plural," he said. "All I can see is the one."

"A good question for one of the long nights around the campfire this week."

"You think there are any fish in that creek down there?"

"One way to find out. Shall we?"

"Do we have time?"

"There's a chuck wagon dinner at 5:30, where I'm hoping to make first contact with the twins. We have a few hours until then."

"And after dinner?"

"At seven o'clock there's a one-hour briefing on the plans for the trip. Then we're on our own until bedtime."

They carried their fishing gear downstairs to an area not far from the main lodge building, where three picnic tables sat beneath the shade of several pine trees. They assembled their rods there, tying on dry flies at Gordon's suggestion. Several children, with and without parents, were fishing the creek with spinning rods near the lodge.

"There's an old saying that if you walk a quarter of a mile, you leave 90 percent of the fishermen behind," Gordon said. "Let's head downstream."

A well-worn trail followed Blanchard Creek down the meadow, sometimes running within a few feet of the creek, and at other times 50 or 60 feet back from it. The meadow was at 8,000 feet, which made the sun seem brighter and closer. The lush grass was mostly brown this late in the summer and constantly rustled with the movement of unseen creatures.

They walked more than a quarter mile, and the lodge, though still visible, had receded into the distance. They stopped where the trail was about 40 feet from the creek near a horseshoe bend.

"This is far enough for starters," Gordon said. "Let me take a closer look and report back."

Before he could start for the water, two women rode up on horses and stopped. One of them had an expensive looking camera with a large telephoto lens hanging from a strap around her neck.

"So you're here for the fishing?" asked the woman with the camera.

"Just this afternoon," Sam said, stepping toward them. "We leave tomorrow on a five-day pack trip."

The two women looked at each other, and the one without the camera spoke in a mellow contralto.

"Then in that case, it looks like we're going to be campmates. We should get properly introduced."

As they dismounted and approached, Gordon did a quick size-up. The woman with the camera was five-six, with light brown hair that stuck out in a short ponytail from the back of her cap, which bore the name of a Mastodon Valley sporting goods store. He guessed she had a few more years than his 40. The other woman looked a few years younger than his 40. She was five-ten, and after getting off the horse, she removed her Stetson and shook her hair, which was short and dark brown with blond streaks throughout. On her, the effect worked. She had a more fluid and confident stride than the woman with the camera.

"Eve Bredon," she said, extending a hand with long, sensual fingers.

"And I'm Nora Robinson," the woman with the camera said.

"Quill Gordon. And this is my friend Sam Akers."

They shook hands all around, and Nora said:

"Quill Gordon. Like the trout fly?" Eve said.

He shrugged as if to say, I get that a lot.

"I wanted to get some pictures of people fly fishing," Nora said. "It looks so peaceful and relaxing. Would you mind if I take some photos of you guys here?"

"Fire away."

"We just rode down to the end of the meadow and back," Eve said. "No one's fishing down there." She sighed. "It's good to be outside and on a horse. I spend too much time reading boring reports."

"Oh, what do you do?" Sam said.

"You should know that Nora here is working for Blanchard's pack trip arm," Eve said. "She's going to be photographing our expedition."

"I'm doing it on spec," Nora said. "If they like the pictures and want to use them, I get a refund on the trip."

"And if they don't use them?"

"Then I'll still have a really good portfolio of the High Sierra and I can probably sell it off in pieces. What do you guys do?"

Gordon looked at Sam.

"Insurance," Sam said.

"I manage investments," Gordon said.

It was a deliberate understatement, one he had settled on over the years. He had, in fact, joined an old-line San Francisco brokerage after graduating from Cal in 1981, had made a modest fortune in the bull market that decade, and could, if he chose, live entirely off the income from his investments. He also managed several portfolios for people he knew, or people who had been referred by someone he knew. It brought in some money and left plenty of time for fishing.

"How long have you been fly fishing?" Nora asked.

"Since I was a kid," Gordon said. "Sam and I have been fishing together nearly 20 years now."

"We've learned to tolerate each other," Sam said.

"Well, we look forward to traveling with you," Eve said. "I need to get back now." She turned to Nora. "You going to stay and take some pictures?"

Nora nodded.

"Well, so long then. See you all at dinner." With that, Eve casually mounted her horse and rode off.

NORA PHOTOGRAPHED THEM for three-quarters of an hour, and they obliged her by catching several trout. She was surprised that they were releasing the fish. But she got a good close-up, or so she said, of a 13-inch Brown Trout that Gordon landed, before he put it back in the stream.

Eventually she thanked them and rode off. They worked downstream a short distance, catching a few more fish. Stray hikers and equestrians passed them from time to time, but for the most part it felt as if they had the meadow to themselves.

At four o'clock they took a break and sat in the shade of a pine tree 150 feet back from the creek. Sam pressed Gordon further about trying to sit with the twins at dinner.

"You really think you can get something definitive out of one dinner table conversation?"

"No, but it's a beginning. There's a pretty good chance that one or two things we hear tonight — assuming we can sit with them — will tie in with other things we observe down the road. If we can see the connections (and I'm counting on your help because two heads are better than one), we may be able to figure out what's going on."

"And do something about it."

"If there's something going on and something to do. All we're going by right now is a hunch that McCabe had."

"To change the subject," Sam said, "did you notice that the taller woman …"

"Eve," Gordon said.

"Eve. She totally dodged the question about her work."

"It wasn't lost on me."

"You don't suppose she's mixed up in this, do you?"

"Now you're letting your imagination get carried away. She probably works for a big company that doesn't like to talk too much about what it does."

He leaned back, resting his head on the trunk of the pine tree.

"Or maybe she works for the CIA," he added. "I'll bet we know by Wednesday."

BEFORE GOING TO DINNER, Gordon called Elizabeth. It was more of a production than he'd bargained for. Blanchard Meadows had no cellular service, and after swearing to himself over that, he recalled seeing a telephone logo off the main lobby. It was an ancient booth of dark walnut, with a heavy folding glass door, and three people were ahead of him in the line to use it.

When he finally got inside 15 minutes later, he realized the phone had a rotary dial and coin slots and that he had almost no coins. With a sigh, he dialed the operator and asked to make the call collect from Gordon. Elizabeth accepted the call.

"Wow," she said once he was on. "I knew you were old school, Gordon, but a collect call? That takes me back to my college days."

He explained the situation and asked, "How are the wedding plans going?"

"We're making do without you. Never fear. It'll all come together."

"And how's your mother holding up?"

"Surprisingly well. And I think she's starting to warm to you. Only once today did she tell me there's still time to change my mind and hold out for a husband with a real job."

He started to say something but checked himself. After a few seconds he mumbled, "That's nice. Please give her my regards."

"I will. How was your flight?"

"Uneventful and panoramic. I got a whole new perspective on the High Sierra."

"Have you done any work yet?"

"Starting at dinner tonight."

"Well, good luck with it." She was silent for several seconds. "I'm sorry I won't be getting daily progress reports. This sounds like an intriguing case."

"I'm sorry, too. When things start happening — if they do — I'd want to hear your take on them. I'll miss that. But this is the last you'll hear from me until I call Saturday afternoon to tell you I made it through the trip."

"And if you don't, Sam has my number?"

"On speed dial."

They were silent for several seconds before Gordon resumed.

"Elizabeth, can I ask you something?"

"Always."

"Well, I'm not sure exactly how to say this, but I'll probably have some time for reflection this coming week. And I'd really like to get on better terms with your mother. Is there any gesture I can make, anything I can work on with myself? Anything?"

She thought about it for a minute.

"Probably not."

"All right. If you think of something while I'm away, let me know on Saturday."

"Sure, but don't take it too much on yourself. She came of age in the '50s and married a man who was a senior executive at a Chicago life insurance company. Every morning, Monday through Friday, he got up, took a train to work in town, and was back home for dinner by 6:30. In her mind, that's what a husband does. She just can't wrap her head around a man who's made enough money that he doesn't have to work and can cook dinner for his wife. But *I* appreciate it, and if you give her enough time, she'll come around."

"I'm sorry I didn't get a chance to meet your father before he died. He sounds like quite a guy."

"I'm sorry too, and he *was* quite a guy, although..."

"Yes?"

"Well, if it's any consolation, Gordon, he probably wouldn't have approved of you either."

THE CHUCK WAGON DINNER was a Sunday night staple at Blanchard's. A covered wagon was brought out from behind the horse barn to serve as a makeshift kitchen, and a large barbecue was rolled up next to it. By late August, the picnic tables were in the shade of the mountains to the west, though the meadow beyond was still bathed in sunlight. The dinner was brisket, chicken or both, made on the barbecue, served with chili, Caesar salad and garlic bread.

Luck was on their side, and Gordon and Sam found Tyler and Mason at a picnic table for six, with an empty seat next to each twin. Gordon sat next to Mason, facing Tyler at an angle and Sam sat across from Gordon. To Tyler's left was a young woman with short black hair, bisected by a green streak. Eve Bredon was sitting across from her, and Gordon wondered if that was just coincidence.

The girlfriend's name, when they did introductions, turned out to be Brandi Baine. Mason asked what Gordon and Sam did, and they gave the same answer they'd given Eve and Nora on the trail.

"That sounds interesting," Brandi said. "Have you known each other long?"

"Quite a while," Sam said. "Going back to Gordon's basketball days."

Gordon shot him a don't-go-there look, but it was too late.

"That explains it," Eve said. "I knew your name sounded familiar this afternoon. You played for Cal, didn't you?"

"Go, Bears," he said.

"I went to Stanford, but I was looking at both schools and following their teams in high school. That's where I heard your name before."

Tyler became a bit more animated.

"Say, if you played college ball, maybe you can answer a question for me."

"Oh, God," Mason muttered.

"I'll try," Gordon said.

"Well, I guess my question is, what's your best advice on betting games against the spread?"

"Don't," Gordon replied. Then, seeing the reaction, he continued. "I'm serious. It's only the house that wins. I wouldn't bet."

"But where's the fun in that? Suppose you *were* betting: How would you approach it?"

A flash went off, and they looked up to see Nora standing over them with her camera.

"Don't mind me. I'm just shooting the dinner." And she was off with a wave.

"So back to my question," Tyler said. "If you had to, how would you bet?"

Gordon chewed a piece of brisket slowly. "If I had to bet, I'd ignore the spread and just bet on the team I thought was going to win. Get that right, and you're going to win most of the time. Of course, you have to be right about the winner."

"Wow, I never thought of that."

He paused, and Gordon tried to redirect the conversation.

"So what do you gentlemen do?"

"I'm a painter," Tyler said.

"A wannabe painter," Mason murmured.

"Knock it off, Mason. At least I have a place where I go to work every day. That's more than you've got."

"Yeah. Too bad you don't have any customers."

Tyler's face went straight to a sulk, and he said nothing for several seconds.

"I'm going to get a little more food," he finally said, standing up. Gordon noticed that he was heavier than he'd looked in the photograph.

"Better watch the calories," Mason said. "The waistline's growing."

Tyler headed for the service area without saying a word.

"You should get on him about that," Mason said to Brandi. "I'd hate to see him eat himself into an early grave."

"The food won't kill him as fast as what you're doing to yourself," she said. "And how do you know I'm not getting on him?"

Mason shrugged. "Just trying to help. I've only got one brother, and I'd hate to lose him." He was nervously shaking his right leg as he spoke, and Gordon realized he'd been doing it for a few minutes. Mason stood up. "Well, the meeting for the trip's in a bit. Think I'll go back to my room and rest before it starts."

He moved off, and there was a moment's awkward silence.

"Sorry about the scene," Brandi finally said. "This is supposed to be a bonding trip for them, but it's not starting out too well."

"Whose idea was the trip?" Eve asked.

"Tyler's, I think."

"And what does Mason do?" Eve said.

"He doesn't do anything. That's the problem. I guess the family has money, so he doesn't have to."

"Really?"

"Really. At least Tyler's *trying* to do something."

"Have you seen his paintings?" Gordon asked.

"They look good to me, but I don't know shit about art. At least we're not starving while he works it out."

THE PACK TRIP PARTY gathered in a conference room in the lodge at seven. They sat around a rectangular table, the head of which faced a large map of the section of the High Sierra where they would be going in the next week. Only three of the ten clients remained strangers to Gordon and Sam. Two of them entered together and subsequently introduced themselves as Brian and Emily Reed, both in their early to mid-thirties. Brian quickly came off as a bluff, affable, joke-cracking type, and Gordon guessed he might be a salesman. Emily didn't say much and frowned at some of her husband's jokes.

The last to arrive made her entrance in a fashion that reminded Gordon of the nephew who thought he was Teddy Roosevelt in *Arsenic and Old Lace*. She had an erect bearing, a purposeful stride and a voice like a bullhorn. She announced herself as Shirley Beers, retired teacher, who wanted to check this trip off her bucket list (she used those words) before her 70th birthday. Gordon guessed she might be the fittest member of the expedition.

A man and woman, late twenties to early thirties, stood at the head of the room, wearing jeans and matching dark-green chamois shirts with a Blanchard Meadows logo over the heart. He was six-one with short, dark hair and glasses. She was five-seven with a pleasing countenance and light brown hair tied in a ponytail. He projected seriousness; she projected friendliness.

"I'm Bill Snider," he said. "I'm a high school biology teacher, and this is my fifth summer leading tours for Blanchard."

"And I'm Angie Hodges. My day job is teaching English in the East Bay, and this is my third year with Blanchard, first year guiding with Bill."

"This is one of the best trips Blanchard offers," Bill said, "and we're going to do everything we can to make it one you'll remember the rest of your lives. This meeting is to go over the itinerary and procedures and to answer your questions. If you have questions as we go along, raise your hand and we'll take care of them. Understood? Good. Angie, you want to start with tomorrow?"

"WE'LL BE UP EARLY to have everything ready for departure," Angie said. "How many of you are set up for a horse already?"

Six hands went up, leaving Gordon, Sam and the Reeds as outliers.

"Good. The rest of you have given us a form outlining your riding experience. Try to be at the corrals by 8, and we'll have a few horses ready. You have meal tickets for breakfast and the dining room opens at 7. Any questions?"

There were none.

"Let's move on to the itinerary. We're going to be five days in the wilderness, with no TV, no cell phones, no internet to connect us with the outside world. That's part of the beauty of this trip. Try to slow down and take in everything around you. Smell the forest. Listen to the wind and water. Pay attention to the changing of the light. The more you involve all of your senses, the more you'll get out of this trip."

She stepped back to the map, which had a route superimposed over it on yellow tape, with several points marked along the way.

"Here's where we are now. We're going to take it easy the first day, get everybody used to riding and setting up camp. We'll start up the mountain toward Blair Pass..."

"What's the elevation?" Mason asked.

"It's 10,728 feet above sea level. Your trip booklet offers suggestions on how to minimize the effect of high altitude. Most people adjust in a day or two. Anyway, we'll stop at Pickett Lake, on this side of the pass, for lunch. It's a tiny little thing and the source of Blanchard Creek. After lunch, we go over the pass. It's the first of three times we cross the Sierra Divide, and from then to Thursday we'll be on the west slope. The first day we'll reach our destination, Cliff Lake, by about three o'clock."

Mason and Shirley raised their hands.

"That would be 9,165 feet elevation." Mason dropped his hand. "Shirley."

"Is Cliff Lake named for a person or a geographical feature?"

"The latter. The east shore of the lake has a sheer cliff that drops straight down to the water. There's a trail from where we camp to the top of it. You're 60 feet above the water, and it's deep enough that you can jump in if you're a daredevil."

"How cold's the water?" Emily asked.

"Bracing, but bearable," Bill said.

"Don't listen to him, honey," Shirley said. "It'll be colder than a witch's tits, but unless you want to go five days without cleaning up, you'll have to get used to it."

Mason smiled. "The cliff jump sounds like just the thing for you Tyler." Tyler grimaced. "I'm just kidding.

When we were kids, Tyler wouldn't go off the high board at the pool."

"Well, it's not for everybody," Bill said.

"Bill did it a few weeks ago," Angie said. "A couple of people in the group thought he was pulling their leg about it, so he showed them."

"As long as you go in feet first, you're fine. You have to be sure to go up to where you're over the deep water, though. If you jumped off along most of the trail, you'd hit rocks or hard ground below, and it wouldn't be pretty."

Gordon and Sam looked at each other.

ANGIE TURNED IT OVER to Bill for a rundown on Day Two. "On Tuesday we'll cover a bit more ground," Bill said. "We'll follow the edge of the mountain through some really pretty countryside. A good day for seeing alpine vegetation, and we generally get a lot of good wildlife views on this part of the trip. Deer and birds especially. We'll be having lunch at a meadow along the way and keep going pretty much northwest to Monolith Valley, where we'll be staying Tuesday night. It's called Monolith Valley because there's a spectacular sheer cliff that our campsite will be facing. It rises two thousand feet above the valley to an elevation of more than 11,000 feet."

"What's the campsite like?" Sam asked.

"It's a meadow by a small creek, with a lot of forested section around it. Very pretty and totally peaceful."

"Are there any bears in the woods?" Emily asked.

"A few," Bill deadpanned, "but the rattlesnakes usually keep them away."

"Bill!" barked Angie.

"Sorry. Just a little backwoods humor. You might as well come to terms with the fact that everywhere we're going on this trip is bear country. That said, it's not much of a problem. We're very careful about food storage and odor control at the campsite, so visits from bears are — well, I won't say unheard of, but pretty unusual. And they have to be pretty badly provoked before they attack a human."

"You mentioned rattlesnakes," Brandi said. "Are there rattlesnakes where we're going?"

"The bad news is that you'll find rattlesnakes pretty much throughout the High Sierra. The good news is they're afraid of people and we almost never see them. We maybe have one or two rattlesnake sightings every summer. How many have we had this year, Angie?"

"Four, actually. But three were the first week in July, when they were just starting to come out after the winter."

"I feel so much better," Emily muttered.

"This raises another point," Eve said. "You mentioned our cell phones won't work. What happens if there's an emergency? Is there any way to get help?"

"Good question," Angie said. "And yes, there is. Blanchard's insurance carrier pretty much demands it. We have a shortwave radio along on every trip, and every night from 6:30 to 7:30, someone at Blanchard Meadows is waiting for us to get in touch. We check in with them daily."

"But what if someone breaks a leg at 8 in the morning?" Nora said.

"We can quickly establish radio connection with one of the law enforcement agencies in the area," Bill said, "and they'll get the appropriate emergency response underway. It's never happened on a trip we've done, but it's always there as backup. Don't worry. We'll take good care of you."

ANGIE TOOK OVER AGAIN to outline Day Three.

"This'll be the longest ride of the trip," she said. "Thirty-one miles. But it's by and large pretty easy riding, through some beautiful valleys, past a couple of lovely lakes. We end up at Keener Flat, where we'll be staying for the night." She looked at Mason. "It's 9,547 feet, by the way. Only the second highest place we'll be camping."

"What's the highest?" Shirley asked.

"Sunrise Lake, Thursday night, 10,271 feet, in case anyone's interested. Now there are two things you should know about Keener Flat. One is that it's the only place we'll be staying that isn't next to a lake or stream."

"What do you do for water?" Brian asked.

"There's a nice little spring there. Sweetest water of the trip, and the only water so pure it doesn't have to be treated."

"The approach," Bill said.

"I was getting there. The flat is basically that — a place where the mountainside flattens out a bit. The last three quarters of a mile getting there, the trail's pretty narrow and the drop-off is really severe. Easily the dizziest ride of the trip, though you're fine as long as you keep your eyes straight ahead and let the horse move forward. Just remember, the horse doesn't want to fall off the cliff any more than you do."

"Has anyone ever fallen off?" Tyler said.

"Not to my knowledge. But some people do choose to get off and walk the horse up that part. That's perfectly fine."

Emily raised her hand.

"The long-range weather forecast said there might be thunderstorms this week."

"Chance of them Wednesday and Thursday."

"What if there was a thunderstorm when we were exposed on the side of the mountain like that?"

"Bill and I would have to make a judgment call. We could go to a protected place and wait it out. When we do get a thunderstorm up here, it's usually either light and noise and not much rain or a short, hard downpour. I wouldn't worry about it too much if I were you."

"COMPARATIVELY SPEAKING," Bill said, "Thursday should be a walk in the park. It's a short ride, just under 20 miles, but it's probably my favorite day of the trip since it takes us through the Lakes Basin. Because we don't have so far to go, we'll eat breakfast and break camp a little later than usual. You can sleep in if you like.

"Anyway, after breakfast, we go over the ridge to the Lakes Basin. We'll be riding past half a dozen stunning glacially carved lakes, fairly close together and separated by slight rises. There's Emerald Lake, Clampett Lake, Lone Pine Lake, Deer Lake, Simon's Lake and Boulder Island Lake. We'll stop by one of them for lunch."

"What makes them so stunning?" Emily asked.

"You'll see for yourselves. Bring your cameras."

31

"I'll be there with my professional gear," Nora said. "If anyone misses a picture, I'd be happy to send you what I have for your personal use."

A brief murmur of appreciation rippled through the group.

"After Boulder Island Lake, we climb over McPherson Pass, which is just over 11,000 feet," Bill continued. "That's the second time we cross the Sierra Divide, and it gets us to Sunrise Lake on the east slope for the night."

"And there should be enough time," Angie said, "to take a dip in the lake, do some fishing, or even walk around the lake on a trail. It's pretty cool."

"What's the terrain like?" Emily asked.

"The trail around the lake is pretty flat," Bill said. "Along the north shore there are a lot of big boulders. It looks kind of like the bandit hideaways where they used to have shootouts in the old Westerns." He saw Emily frown. "But I assure you, we've never encountered a bandit in these mountains."

"WHICH BRINGS US TO FRIDAY," Angie said, stepping up to the front of the room.

"If you look at the map, you'll see that this section of the trip looks like a reverse C, looping from east to west. We cross the divide again at Sloane Summit…"

She looked at Mason.

"Elevation 11,305. From there, we go down through more beautiful country. In fact, you may be sick of beautiful country by the time we're done. Midafternoon we go over a ridge and descend into Upper Awatos Meadows, where we'll be spending the last night."

"Is that *the* Awatos River?" Tyler asked.

"It is, though it's not the Awatos most people know. Awatos is a Native American word meaning 'meeting of the waters.' This meadow is where two creeks come together to form the river. Where we're camping, at 9,268 feet, it's just a big creek, 20 to 25 feet wide. But from that point on, about two dozen other creeks and springs feed into it over the next few miles. So a little more than an hour below the camp, it's a full-throated river, up to 150 feet wide in some places."

"It's a wild river, isn't it?" Gordon asked.

"That's right. No dams or obstructions all the way to where it joins the San Joaquin. You've probably heard of it as a big rafting destination below Donovan's Station, where we end up. Elevation 7,876."

"So a fairly short final day," Mason said.

"That's right. We should be at Donovan's by two, three o'clock at the latest. Some of you have arranged to be picked up there. The rest of us will get into waiting vans that will take us over the pass and back to Blanchard's, arriving about three hours later."

"Any questions?"

They looked around at each other, and finally Sam raised his hand.

"I have one," he said. "How come they call this place Blanchard Meadows, plural? From here it looks to me like one big meadow."

"It is down here," Bill replied. "But a few hundred feet up the mountain, there's a second, much smaller meadow. We'll be riding through it tomorrow morning."

AFTER THE PRESENTATION, Gordon and I held a brief strategy session in his room.

"Any thoughts, Sam?" he asked.

"An interesting group of people," I allowed. "I don't know what we're supposed to be looking for with the brothers, but I'm kind of wondering about the lady Eve."

"Wondering what?"

"Hard to put a finger on it, but I think she's up to no good. We both picked up on her being cagey about her job, and I'm wondering if it was just coincidence that she was sitting with the Linfield brothers at dinner."

"A fair question."

"And I was watching her during that meeting tonight. She didn't ask any questions, but she almost seemed to be working at taking it all in. I'll bet she went straight back to her room and wrote up notes from memory."

Gordon nodded.

"I haven't gone as far with it as you have," he said, "but there's more to her than meets the eye."

"She's doing her best not to let anything meet the eye."

"But we should probably keep tabs on her to the extent we can do that without losing sight of the brothers."

"How should we watch the brothers?" I asked. "Each of us zone in on one?"

"No," he finally said. "Two sets of eyes are better than one, so let's start out by both watching everything and comparing notes at the end of each day. We can always change tactics if it's called for."

"Whatever you say. I'm just along for the ride."

We went silent for a moment before I asked another question.

"Gordon," I said, "why do you think Mason Linfield was so obsessed about the elevation of every point along the way?"

"I don't know, but I have a theory."

"Spill."

"Well, McCabe didn't say what he thought Mason's drug of choice was, but if it's one that affects respiratory function, he might be trying to calibrate his dose according to altitude."

I FELT LIKE A BIT of fresh air before turning in. It was just past nine o'clock and getting a bit chilly, so I threw on a light jacket and went out the front door of the lodge. Two teenagers were making out on the swinging bench on the front porch, and on the other side, an older couple was rocking in tandem in separate chairs. The moon was halfway toward full and provided just enough light to see by.

In the course of my walk, I encountered a few couples and the occasional solitary stroller, but by and large, not many people were out. At one of the cabins along the way a group was singing campfire songs without the campfire. I stopped by the horse corral, where the animals seemed placidly settled for the night.

I decided to walk past the corral toward an outdoor amphitheater, where there had been a campfire presentation earlier in the evening. It was deserted now, no one occupying the five benches angled around a fire pit and slight stage. I sat at the edge of one of the benches, in the shade of pine trees, not easily visible. I had become lost in my thoughts, watching the stars, and listening to the wind through the trees.

Then I heard, just above the whisper of the wind, two voices approaching.

Swinging around so I could look up at the rim of the amphitheater, I made myself as still and quiet as possible. Two human silhouettes came into sight, and I could make out Eve and Nora. They were talking with a sense of urgency, but in a voice just above a whisper, and I could make out only a brief snatch of their conversation:

"There's nothing here. We might as well go back."

"All right," said a voice I recognized as Nora's. "But, look. About the other thing. Are you sure it's no problem?"

"Don't worry," Eve said. "I can charge it to expenses."

They turned back, and I couldn't make out any more of what they were saying. Finally, the voices themselves faded away, and a few minutes after that, I headed for the lodge myself, wishing I'd heard more of that conversation.

Monday August 23

Blanchard Meadows to Cliff Lake

GORDON AND SAM were at the corral to get their horse assignments at 7:45. It was a crisp morning, and while the rising sun had lit up the mountains behind them, the corrals were still in shadow. Brian and Emily had gotten there a minute earlier, and Angie was dealing with them, so Bill took charge and asked a few questions. Sam seemed to have a better sense of what he wanted, so Bill sent him to check out the horses in the third corral, while he walked with Gordon and asked questions.

"You said on your enrollment form that you were a 'somewhat experienced' rider. Would you say you're generally pretty comfortable on a horse?"

"Generally. I learned to relax pretty quickly once I started riding."

"Is your balance pretty good?"

Gordon had started for the University of California basketball team years earlier. His balance, reflexes and athleticism were impeccable.

"I'd say so," he replied laconically.

"Do you think you have a good rapport with horses?"

Gordon smiled. "An ex-girlfriend once told me I did."

Bill cocked his head quizzically.

"She said I had a better rapport with the horses we rode than I did with her. I guess that's why she's an ex-girlfriend."

"I wouldn't take it too personally," Bill said. "Rapport with horses is pretty general and transferable. Rapport with women is more personal and subject to unexpected disruption."

"Yup."

Bill's eyes swept over the horses in the three corrals. His right hand was resting alongside his leg, and when his glance stopped at one of the corrals, he tapped his leg with his fingertips five times in rapid succession.

"You been riding much lately?"

"Once or twice a week the last two months to get ready for this trip."

"And you feel pretty comfortable?"

"Pretty comfortable."

"Let me show you a horse and you can tell me if you think the chemistry is there or not."

They walked to the first corral where there were a half-dozen horses that had been tied up earlier in the morning for inspection. Bill held the gate open for Gordon, then led him to a handsome Palomino on the far side.

"Roy," he said to the horse, "I'd like you to meet Quill Gordon." Then, to Gordon, "Do you go by Quill?"

"Actually, my friends call me Gordon."

Bill turned back to the horse. "I think you and Gordon might get along pretty nicely for the week. What do you think?"

Roy looked quizzically in Gordon's direction. Gordon stepped up to the horse and gently put his right hand on its neck, then ran it down slowly and smoothly several times, as if giving Roy's neck a long lick with his fingers. The horse lowered his head and nuzzled Gordon's shoulder.

"I think he likes you," Bill said.

"He's a splendid animal," Gordon murmured. "Is there anything about him … ?"

"Roy's an excellent horse as long as the rider is calm. And he seems to have a fondness for tall men. The tall you were born with, and you strike me as being calm. As long as you think you can stay calm on him, it could be a pretty happy match."

"Let's do it, then."

"I don't think you'll be disappointed. We'll have him saddled for you and ready to go at nine o'clock."

They left the corral, and as they were heading to where Sam was, Gordon said:

"How did he come to be named Roy?"

"Well, when you think of Palominos, there's one that generally comes to mind, name of Trigger. You remember who owned and rode him?"

"Of course. Roy Rogers, king of the cowboys."

"There you are."

As they passed the middle corral, where Angie was with Brian and Emily, one of the horses let out a loud snort and shook its head up and down.

"I don't think this one likes me, either," Emily said.

"You need to relax a little," Brian said soothingly. "You're showing your fear, and they're picking up on it."

"You try relaxing with something that's twice as big as you are."

Bill made eye contact with Angie and gestured toward Sam's corral with his head. She picked up the cue.

"Actually," Angie said, "there's a horse in the next corral named Maggie, who has a really sweet disposition. Let's take a look. I think you'd like her."

They walked over to the next corral, where Sam was playfully petting a chestnut mare. Angie pulled up short when she saw him.

"This one's a real sweetheart," Sam said. "I'd like to ride her, if she's not taken. What's her name?"

No one said a word for several seconds, until Bill finally mumbled, "Maggie."

Angie turned to her left and pointed to another chestnut, with slightly different markings.

"And that's Maggie's sister, Annabelle," she said. "She's a real sweetheart, too. Come on, Emily, let's get you introduced."

WE SET OUT IN HIGH SPIRITS. Of course, everyone's in high spirits when the trip is just starting and nothing's gone wrong yet, so that's often the best part of the journey. Sometimes it's the only good one.

I chose Maggie because I like my horses to be as drama-free as possible. Growing up east of San Francisco, when that area was less developed than it is now, and having a mother who loved horses, I learned to ride early. I always enjoyed it, but then came adult life and responsibilities, and little by little the riding slipped out of my life. When Gordon asked me to come with him on this trip, getting back on a horse was a big selling point. We've been riding regularly for the past six weeks, together and separately, getting our minds and bodies used to it again, and it's made me realize how much I miss it. I've pretty much concluded that once this trip is over, I'm going to make a point of staying in the saddle on a regular basis.

On the other hand, I'd hoped that I'd seen the last of Gordon's adventures in the world of investigations. The last time we got ourselves into one, he nearly got himself killed. Granted, he was considerate enough not to endanger me (which hasn't always been the case), but you only have so many good friends in a lifetime, and you'd hate to see one of them check out early because he took it upon himself to do work the police should have been doing.

I'm riding near the rear of the group, just ahead of the pack mules carrying our supplies. Angie is behind me and Brian and Emily are just ahead. An hour into this, I can see that Angie's going to have her hands full with that pair. Emily barely knows what she's doing, and I don't think she could sneeze without falling off her horse. And without intending to, Brian's letting her know she's not doing it right, which I doubt is helping either her confidence or their marriage. Something's going on in that marriage, if they ended up here. And a troubled marriage is not what Gordon needs to be face-to-face with, with his own vows coming up in less than two weeks.

Gordon is riding near the front of the pack, behind Bill, who's leading the way, with Eve and Nora right with him. That means he can't see the twins and Brandi, who are in the middle of the pack, but I have a good view of them, so I suppose I'm the private eye for now. Not much to report in the early going. People are getting the feel of their horses and trying to take in the scenery. We rode through forest for about 45 minutes, then came out on upper Blanchard Meadow, which is a jewel. Now we're riding through forest again, but as we gain elevation, the trees are becoming a bit more sparse.

Wait a minute. Mason just dropped back to pull even with Brandi and exchanged a few words with her. Actually, that's not exactly right. He did most of the talking, and she just nodded and shook her head. I don't know whether she's slow, shy, or just quiet and deep, but this was the second time in an hour that Mason made a point of talking to his brother's girlfriend. It may not mean anything, but it bears watching.

PICKETT LAKE WAS BARELY WORTHY of the name —
more of a pond, really. It was rectangular, and about the
size of a football field, 50 by 100 yards. Much of its
shoreline was choked with weeds, and it was fairly open
to the sky, but as the riders circled around its right side,
they came to an area with a clump of shade-providing
pine trees and stopped there for lunch.

Still somewhat unfamiliar with each other, the
travelers stayed mostly close to those they already knew.
Gordon and Sam laid out a blanket about 25 feet from the
Linfield brothers and Brandi, and within a minute, Eve
and Nora came by to ask if they could join them.
Blanchard had provided box lunches of chicken
sandwiches, coleslaw and potato chips, and everyone
commented on how hungry they were, not that long after
breakfast.

"Beautiful ride this morning," Eve said. "I feel like
I've gotten my money's worth already."

"It was nice," Gordon said. "Hard to believe we
were on the trail for two and a half hours and didn't see
anyone."

"That's kind of the idea, isn't it?"

"Very much the idea," Sam said.

Gordon looked over at the brothers, just as Tyler
stood up and shook his head.

"Oh come on, Mason. Can't you leave it for even a
day?"

He walked over to the foursome as they looked at
each other.

"Sorry. My brother's being difficult," Tyler said. "I
thought I'd come over and ask Gordon a basketball
question."

"Always happy to talk basketball," Gordon said.

"I was wondering how you factor in injuries against
the spread in pro games."

Gordon took a bite of his chicken sandwich.

"Personally, I don't," he finally said. "It can be really
hard to figure."

He wasn't sure how to continue. No one else was
talking, and no breeze was blowing. It was utterly silent.

Before he could resume, there seemed to be music in
the air, and for a moment he wondered if he were

41

hallucinating. Then it grew louder and more distinct. A chorus of male voices was approaching, singing the "Hi, Ho" song from *Snow White and the Seven Dwarfs*. The others in the group, eating on their blankets or sitting on rocks, looked up as they heard it, too. It was coming from the trail ahead of them.

Just past where they were eating lunch, the trail curved upward and to the left, behind a rock formation. The singing grew louder, and then around the curve came a dozen young men — unshaven, sweaty, and wearing dirty work clothes. They were all in their early twenties, if that, carrying heavy backpacks, and following a tall, gaunt man in his thirties who was clearly their leader. When he saw the group, he waved to Bill and Angie, and as his entourage reached them, he raised his right hand.

"All right, gentlemen," he barked. "Water break. Ten minutes."

Bill walked up to him and extended a hand.

"Morning, Ken. Or is it afternoon?"

"I don't wear a watch out here, but I think it's afternoon."

Bill looked at his watch. "Twelve-twenty-five. You're right. Coming back to civilization?"

"Unfortunately. We've been shoring up the trail beyond Blair Pass the past five days. You can thank us now for your ride being easier when you get there later."

"Thank you," said Angie, who had just walked up.

"Looking good," Ken said, sizing her up.

"You've been in the mountains with a group of men for too long. Have you ever thought of adding some women to your work crew?"

He looked at her for ten seconds before answering.

"No."

As they were talking, two young men from the group came over in the direction of where Gordon, Sam, Nora, Eve and Tyler were. They set their packs down against nearby trees and took out their canteens.

"Come on over and join us," Gordon said.

They smiled, sheepish, genuine smiles.

"Thanks," they said over each other.

As they came over, Gordon noticed that Mason had said something to Brandi, risen from his blankets and was walking toward a group of trees slightly uphill. He wondered …

"Nice to see some new faces," said one of the young men, extending a hand. "I'm Steve."

"Terry," said the other, extending his. They shook hands all around.

"So are you with one of the youth conservation groups?" Nora asked.

"Yes, ma'am," Steve said. "We've been up here nine weeks, off and on."

"Surely not all at once?" Eve said.

"No, ma'am," said Jerry. "We go back to Blanchard's, or to Donovan's Station every week or ten days to clean up and rest a day or two. Then back to work."

"Is there a lot of work?" Tyler asked.

"Quite a bit. We've had a few hard winters, so the trails are compromised a bit. We mostly clear things up and deal with some of the erosion."

"Doesn't sound like much fun."

"You'd be surprised," Steve said. "We get to know each other, and have a pretty good little group going. And it's meaningful work."

"Not to mention the great pay," Terry said. "Minimum wage plus room and board."

"The board's a sleeping bag under the open sky. Which could be a lot worse. We have tube tents if it rains, but the rain's usually over by bedtime."

"Is this your first year?" Gordon asked. They both nodded. "Would you do it again?"

The young men looked at each other.

"I would," Steve said. "It's better than being a barista at Starbucks or making sandwiches at Subway. And there's nothing to spend the money on, so I have a good stake for school this fall."

"Same here," Terry said. "I'll probably be back next year."

"Good for you," Eve said. "We appreciate the work you're doing."

"Thank you," they said in unison.

A couple of minutes later, Ken, their leader, called them together. They quickly assembled, and were soon heading down the mountain, singing again. Mason came back from the trees as the voices faded in the distance and walked up to the group of five. Brandi, who had been sitting alone on the blanket, stood up and stretched languidly

"So who were they?" Mason asked. "Prison crew?"

"Youth conservation," Nora said. "They've been repairing trails up here for nine weeks and are just done for the summer."

"Poor bastards," Mason said. "I'll bet they're glad it's over."

WHEN THEY REACHED THE SUMMIT of Blair Pass, they dismounted to take a good look in both directions. It was a stop worth making. On both sides, the view was of mountains, with no sign of human habitation or activity whatsoever. To the west, the haze rising from California's Central Valley could be seen far in the distance, though to someone who didn't know, the haze wouldn't have looked like civilization. To the east, looking toward Nevada, it was entirely clear. In just a few hours, they had been engulfed in nearly complete solitude.

As they rode on, Gordon began to feel the pleasurable rhythm of being on a horse, and he tried to take in the surroundings as fully as possible. There was almost too much wilderness, and at one point he found his mind drifting back to a meeting with his father, Judge Gordon, ten days earlier.

They had met at Horseley's, a venerable Financial District restaurant and watering hole where deals are made. Those in the know say that half the San Francisco Waterfront was planned at Horseley's, but Gordon was there to talk with his father about this trip, not to do business. Although business was discussed.

"What can you tell me about this trip of yours?" the judge asked, after they had ordered. "It seems very mysterious, and your mother's concerned about the timing — so close to the wedding."

"If she's afraid I'll run away, she's got nothing to worry about. I'm happily in."

"Glad to hear it. We both like Elizabeth, and it's certainly time ..."

"Please don't tell me it's time to get married, Dad. Time is when it works out right."

The judge took a sip of his water. "Fair enough."

"And as it happens," Gordon said, "I spoke with Herb McCabe earlier this week. He said I could give you the bare outline of the situation — provided you sign a nondisclosure agreement."

"Tell him where he can stick his nondisclosure agreement. He knows I can keep quiet."

Gordon smiled and had a sip of water himself.

"I don't suppose he talked to you before he approached me?"

"He may have."

"Point taken."

Gordon gave his father a quick summary of his upcoming assignment, which took them to the arrival of the Caesar Salad. The judge ate his first bite before commenting.

"Pretty open-ended, isn't it?"

"Couldn't be more so, if you ask me."

"You have a strategy in mind?"

"Wish I did."

"Sam's coming, right?"

Gordon nodded.

"Glad to hear that. He can steer you away from temptation, and you can use him as a second set of eyes."

"Temptation?"

"Other people will be along on the trip. Some of them may be female. People get thrown together for a week, feelings happen. You see it on cruise ships all the time. And young men about to get married are susceptible to the idea of a last bit of freedom, if you know what I mean."

"I know what you mean, but it doesn't apply."

"That's what they all say."

"So any ideas about how I should try to carry out this job?"

"You don't even know there is a job. McCabe could be worrying about nothing. Estate attorneys deal with families, and families are weird. Some of the weirdness is bound to rub off on the family retainer."

"So you think it could be nothing?"

"I didn't say that. Herb McCabe's as solid as they come, and if he thinks something may be up, I'd have to credit it. You have good eyes and a good mind, Quill. If I were you, I'd work them both hard and keep them both open."

"That's pretty general."

The judge shrugged. "When you get into a situation like this, where there aren't any rules or guidelines, keep it simple. I'm afraid that's all I can say."

They spent the rest of the meal discussing the wedding plans and family matters. After the judge had picked up the check and they were ready to go, Gordon leaned across the table.

"One last thing, Dad. Any advice from the old married man to the prospective groom?"

His father stood up and looked at his son for several seconds.

"Be good to her."

THEY ARRIVED AT CLIFF LAKE shortly before 2:30, allowing them plenty of time to walk around and explore before dinner. Bill and Angie unloaded six tents from the pack horses and assembled the group, showing how to set up the tents, which turned out to be surprisingly simple. Each tent easily held two people, and the six tents were set in a slight semicircle around a beach at the south end of the lake. The arrangement of the tents and the pairings of their occupants would remain the same throughout the trip. From left to right:

1. Bill Snider and Mason Linfield
2. Quill Gordon and Sam Akers
3. Brian and Emily Reed
4. Shirley Beers and Angie Hodges
5. Tyler Linfield and Brandi Baine
6. Eve Bredon and Nora Robinson

It was a beautiful afternoon — temperatures in the mid-70s, mostly sunny, with large white clouds floating intermittently overhead, creating occasional shadow but holding no hint of rain. A slight breeze ruffled the waters of the lake from time to time.

"I'm surprised there are no mosquitoes," Gordon said to Bill, after the tents were up.

"You should have been here three weeks ago. They almost ate us alive. But it's later in the season, and the ground where they breed has dried up. We just may be lucky here."

Gordon scanned the lake. The jumping cliff that had been alluded to at the previous night's meeting was about a quarter-mile north of the campground. A little trail led up the cliff, and another trail went partway around the lake, clockwise from where they were camped. No fish were rising, but it certainly looked like a lake that held fish. About 75 yards down the perimeter trail, there was a small cove in the lake, and it looked to Gordon like a place where the fish might come near shore to feed. As the others scattered in their various pursuits, he took out his fly rod and began to set it up.

It was a nine-foot, four-piece rod, designed to break down into a small tube for easy travel and to be carried onto a plane. Gordon had been meaning to get a travel rod like that, if he ever flew somewhere on a fishing trip, and had been happy to use the occasion of this trip to make the purchase. He even used the justification that it was a wedding present to himself, as if that was necessary.

Savoring the look and feel of the new rod, he carefully put the four pieces together in perfect alignment, attached a reel to the butt of the rod, strung the line through the ferrules, attached a leader to the end of the fly line, and tied a size 16 Pheasant Tail nymph at the end of the leader, below an indicator that would float on the surface and be pulled under if a fish took the fly.

He took a quarter hour to do the job, even though he was experienced enough to do it five minutes faster. He wanted to enjoy his new toy. When he had finished, he decided to forsake waders for the time being and try fishing the cove from the shore. Perhaps this would be the day he'd catch his first Golden Trout.

He'd taken three steps toward the cove when Sam ran up behind him, panting.

"Not so fast," Sam said. "I just saw the heirs starting out toward the trail up the cliff, and it's just them — not even Brandi. I don't think it's a good idea to let them go up there alone."

Gordon blurted out an expletive.

"Neither do I." He leaned the assembled fly rod against the tent, and they headed for the cliff.

NOT WANTING TO ATTRACT ATTENTION, they walked briskly, rather than running. Brian and Emily, the married couple, had started around the lake on the path heading the opposite direction; Brandi had stretched out a towel on the sand and was sunning herself. Shirley, Eve and Nora had found a flat rock to sit on just up the shore from the campsite and were happily talking. With the tents set up, Bill and Angie were getting out the gear to cook dinner. It was all placid and normal.

The brothers had a good hundred yards or more on Gordon or Sam — close enough to be seen, but not seen really well. The path up the cliff started about two hundred yards beyond the campsite, following the slight curve of the lake. It was a two-foot-wide gouge in the grass, the dirt packed hard, and it was only a couple of feet from the edge of the drop-off. On the right side of the path were a couple of small clumps of pine trees and various alpine shrubbery. To the left, nothing got in the way of the view — or the drop.

Fit as Gordon was, he was surprised by how much the altitude affected him. He quickly got short of breath and was feeling a bit light-headed. Sam, not as well conditioned, was panting heavily and struggling to keep up. Gordon tried to keep his eyes on Tyler and Mason, but had to look down from time to time to make sure he was still on the path.

Mason was in front, with Tyler behind, and occasionally, Mason would stop to say something before moving on. That helped narrow the gap to about 75 yards, and Gordon felt he could at least see them tolerably well, when he was able to keep his eyes looking forward and not at the trail or over the edge. Gordon and Sam were 30 feet above the lake now, and below them was a rocky shore that would not have made for a pleasant landing. The Linfield brothers were getting close to the highest part of the cliff, where the drop would be into deep water rather than land. Gordon was just beginning to ease up, when he saw a quick movement ahead — so quick he couldn't be sure of it — and then it happened.

Tyler's foot slipped, and he pitched slightly forward and toward his left. Before he even had a chance to try to regain his balance, he was over the edge, letting out a loud, blood-curdling scream. As he dropped through the air, his arms and legs flailed so violently that it seemed as if there were a dozen of them, rather than only four. From where Gordon stood, it looked as if Tyler was going to hit hard ground below. Gordon's heart pounded furiously.

Tyler landed in the lake, ass and legs first, and immediately disappeared under the surface. Gordon began running toward Mason, lungs searing. A few seconds later, Tyler rose to the surface, seemingly all right.

"Ty, are you OK?" Mason shouted, looking over the edge.

"I think so, but this water's freezing."

"Get to shore. We'll get help." Tyler began dog-paddling toward the edge of the lake as Gordon reached Mason, followed by a gasping Sam several seconds later.

"What happened?" Gordon asked.

Mason was looking somewhat ashen, and shook his head.

"I don't know. He was walking a few steps behind me, and next thing I knew, I heard a scream. Scared me half to death."

Gordon looked at the area of the trail where Tyler had gone over. It seemed solid and well packed, but there were a couple of inches of rise at the left of it. Tyler could have tripped on that and lost his balance. One thing Gordon knew for sure was that Mason hadn't been close enough to his brother to deliver a shove, for whatever that was worth.

Tyler had made it to shore by now.

"Tyler!" Sam shouted down. "Can you walk all right?"

"Yeah, I think so."

"It's a bit rocky, but you should be able to walk back to camp," Gordon shouted. "Go ahead, and we'll follow you from up here."

Tyler made his way back to camp, with the other three keeping an eye on him. He changed into dry clothing and set his wet clothes down on a flat rock to dry. He seemed a bit dazed, but otherwise all right, and he had no idea what happened, except that he was adamant he hadn't tripped on the edge of the trail.

"It was like my legs just went out from under me," he said.

"Could be you got a bit dizzy from the altitude," Angie said.

"I didn't feel it, but maybe so."

Once everything was stable, Gordon drew Sam aside to a slight rise above the lake, not far from the campsite. They sat on the trunk of a tree that appeared to have fallen a few years ago.

"Not good, is it?" Sam said.

"Not at all, and it's only the first day. Did you see anything?"

"Sorry, Gordon. I was out of breath and really trying to keep my eyes on the trail. You see anything?"

"Maybe. I'm not sure."

Sam cocked his head attentively. Gordon continued.

"I can't be sure, but just before Tyler went over the edge, I thought I saw Mason, up ahead of him, slow down and do a quick squat, then keep going."

"A quick squat. Like ..."

"Like he might have been putting something on the ground. But I can't be sure."

"Well, there was nothing on the ground when I got there. I can tell you that because I could hardly breathe and was looking right at the ground to keep from getting dizzy."

"It was just an impression, and I could be wrong," Gordon said. "But it's too much of a coincidence that this happened the first day. I think we have our work cut out for us."

"Was there ever any doubt?" Sam said.

DINNER WAS SERVED EARLY, and between the stimulation of the day's ride and the high altitude, no one complained. Bill and Angie assembled a portable grill and made steaks to order, along with sautéed mushrooms, boiled red potatoes in butter, and a green salad with tomato, avocado and an oil and vinegar dressing. It was a sumptuous and simply elegant meal.

"We'll have fresh meat the first three days," Bill said as the food was being served. The dry ice will keep it that long. Later in the trip, we go more to pasta and flash-frozen food, but we've learned how to do that pretty well. Almost no one complains about the chow."

"Sometimes we get several people on the trip who fish," Angie added, "and the last night, we can have trout for dinner. Anybody fish here besides Gordon and Sam?"

No one so indicated.

"Maybe not this trip," she said.

They sat in small groups on camp chairs while they ate. There were three folding tables that seated four. Gordon and Sam were with Brian and Emily, not too far from a second group that included Eve, Nora, Shirley, Tyler and Mason, and Brandi, gathered around two tables pushed together. Bill and Angie sat apart from the guests for the time being, apparently talking shop and making plans for the following day. Gordon could hear the second group talking about Tyler's fall, which was growing in the retelling, and it seemed to him, from the snatches he heard, that Eve was asking specific questions about where and how it happened. She was being effectively nonchalant about it, but Gordon got the sense she had a purpose, even though he didn't know what it might be.

"So you're getting married, soon, Gordon?" Brian asked. "Good for you."

"A week from this Saturday."

"Tell us about the lucky woman," Emily said.

"She's a very independent and high-spirited woman with a strong sense of humor," he said. "We seem to suit each other well."

"What does she do?" Brian said.

51

"She teaches English at City College, and she paints. She's quite an accomplished painter, really. She had a show at a gallery in San Francisco this time last year. Everything sold."

"What sorts of things does she paint?" Emily asked.

"Landscapes mostly. She has a really good eye for light and a way of seeing and depicting things that isn't strictly accurate but that feels right. If that makes any sense."

"I'm not sure I understand that," Brian said.

"You wouldn't," Emily said. "It's perfectly clear."

There was an awkward pause, and Gordon continued. "I can't help wishing she were here. She'd be inspired by these landscapes."

No one picked up the thread of that offering, and Brian finally said, "So, Sam, are you involved in the wedding at all?"

"Last I heard I'm going to be best man."

"You don't have a brother," Brian said to Gordon.

"Nope. Two sisters."

"My younger brother was best man when Em and I got married. There wasn't any choice about that."

"Too bad," Emily said. "You could have picked someone sober."

"Oh, come on, honey. He did fine."

"I was afraid he'd keel over during the ceremony."

"Well, he didn't. That was almost five years ago."

"And his toast ..."

"So how did you guys decide to come on this trip?" Sam quickly asked.

"We've been car and tent camping," Brian quickly said. "We thought we'd try something different. This has been really interesting so far."

"If you like horses," Emily said.

AN HOUR AND A HALF OF LIGHT remained after dinner, and Gordon decided to try his luck at the cove. He made sure that the brothers were at the campsite with other people around and concluded that he could leave them for a while. He was surprised that Sam passed on the chance to join the angling, but reasoned that his friend would be keeping an eye on the errant heirs.

The sun was just above the top of the mountain as he got to the cove, and the air was becoming cooler, though still pleasant. It seemed like perfect conditions for fish to move in and feed, and he started to feel the thrill of pursuit. The lake bottom dropped off abruptly at the halfway point of the crescent of the cove, and he decided to cast from there.

He set his nymph nine feet below the indicator and cast the fly 60 feet out into the cove. He watched the indicator as it slowly drifted back toward shore over a period of five minutes, then pulled in the line and cast again with the same results. If fish were cruising the cove, one of them should have taken the fly, so he lowered the indicator and tried fishing seven-and-a-half feet below the surface.

A minute after the third cast, the indicator twitched on the calm surface of the lake, and Gordon raised his rod. He had a fish on. He quickly realized it wasn't much of a fish and began reeling it in so he could release it back to the water. As he did so, he heard voices approaching.

The fish was a handsome Brook Trout, but only five inches long. As small as the nymph was, it looked large in the trout's mouth. He pulled the fish out of the water, cradled it gently in his left hand and removed the barbless hook just as Shirley, Nora, Brandi and Emily arrived on the scene, talking loudly and happily.

"Let's see the fish, Gordon," Shirley bellowed.

He held the fish up for them to see, then leaned over and set it in the water, where it quickly swam back into the depths of the cove.

Shirley let out a belly laugh.

"Is that all you got, Gordon — less than six inches?" The other three women cracked up.

"I can get the fish to bite," he said, "but I can't control which one takes the fly first."

"Well, we need to wash off the grime and sweat of the trail," Shirley said, so the four of us are taking it all off and going in. You can watch if you want, but try to keep your hook away from us."

His heart sank. If they went into that cove, it would be ruined for fishing for the rest of the night, with all the noise and commotion they'd make. And he could think of no way to stand his ground decently.

"Go ahead," he said after a minute. "It doesn't look like the fishing's too good, anyway." He hooked his fly into the loop at the rod handle and raised the rod in their direction.

"Enjoy!" he said, and began trudging back to the camp.

As he walked back, it occurred to him that Eve Bredon was the only woman from the group, other than Angie, who wasn't there for a dip.

I'M NOT SURE WHY I DIDN'T go to the cove with Gordon, but I just wasn't feeling right. Ordinarily, it takes more time than this with Gordon to get my head out of a fishing trip, but Tyler's fall this afternoon sent things south early.

I had another idea I wanted to pursue but was waiting until things settled down and I could slip away unnoticed. When the women took off for the cove, making an unholy racket, I saw my chance. Besides which, I didn't want to have to deal with Gordon after the ladies had knocked him off his fishing spot. I remember once when some river rafters charged through a sweet hole he was beginning to fish, and it's the closest to homicidal I've ever seen him.

So when the women took off for the cove, I decided to follow my hunch. I remembered Gordon saying he thought Mason had stooped down in front of Tyler just before Tyler went over the edge. What if he put something down on the trail to make his brother slip? I recalled that there was some brush on the inside part of the trail at that area, and I figured I might as well go have a look at it.

While everyone else was standing around the campsite and waving the ladies off, I started in the opposite direction toward the cliff trail. I seemed to be getting more accustomed to the thin air, but breathing was still work. This side of the lake was almost entirely in shadow now, so I figured I wouldn't be too obvious.

It was a beautiful night to be out for a walk in any event, and as I started the climb, I was feeling grateful that Gordon had invited me to come along. This is the first time in my life I've ever been this far from human settlement, and I can't entirely do justice to the way it makes you feel. Like nothing else — that's for sure.

I'd figured I'd have the trail to myself, so I was taken aback, to say the least, when I saw some movement up ahead — just at the part of the trail I was heading to look at. Someone — I couldn't quite tell who — was kneeling on the trail and rummaging around in the brush on the inland side of it, right where I had been planning to look.

I stopped for a second to think about it, realized it had to be one of our campers, and kept walking.

Five seconds later, Eve Bredon pulled her hand out of the brush, stood up, and looked straight at me.

She was about 100 feet away, and her right hand was clenched into a fist. When she saw me, she shoved the hand into her jeans pocket, withdrew it open a second later and waved.

"Hi, Sam. What a pleasant surprise to see you here."

"Likewise." I reached her and stopped for breath. After catching it, I said, "Lose something?"

"Totally silly. I was carrying my compass in my right hand and looking at the lake, and the compass slipped out and went into the brush."

She reached into her pants pocket and took out a compass. "But I found it after a couple of minutes."

It was a compass, all right, but something else was bulging in the same pants pocket the compass had been in. It could have been something innocent, but my nasty, suspicious mind wondered if the other item was what she'd really found in the brush.

No polite way to ask.

"So how come you're not fishing with your friend?" she asked, just a bit too casually.

"Probably the same reason you're not bathing with the ladies," I said. "Just didn't feel like it. And I never got a chance to see the view from up here this afternoon, what with all the commotion with Tyler."

"Yes. That *was* interesting."

We eyed each other warily for several seconds. "I'm heading back," she finally said. "Enjoy the view."

She started back to the campsite, and I followed her with my eyes most of the way down. Several times, she patted the right pocket that held the compass and the mystery object.

AT 7:30, BILL AND ANGIE started a campfire with dead wood they had picked up in the vicinity, and at eight, with only a hint of light remaining in the sky, everyone in the group gathered around. One of the ideas for the expedition was that every night after dark, two of the group members would get up at the campfire and talk about themselves for several minutes, as a way of everyone getting to know everyone else a bit better.

Eve and Nora were chosen to go first, and Nora led off.

"I've always been interested in photography," she said. "It's in my DNA. My father was a photographer for *Life* magazine for years, and you've all seen his photographs — even if you didn't know they were his. I grew up around cameras and images, and I probably had a pretty good visual sense to begin with, but it really became well developed through the environment I grew up in."

Gordon looked around the fire. Eve and Shirley were listening intently. The Reeds were listening politely. It was hard to tell if Mason, Tyler and Brandi were really paying attention at all; their faces showed nothing. It occurred to Gordon that the twin brothers were born two years after *Life* stopped publishing weekly. If they even knew what the magazine was, or how important it had been, it had certainly never been any real part of their lives. Gordon, on the other hand, grew up in a house with a subscription and looked at it every week from the time he was eight or so. Suddenly, at only 40 years of age, he was feeling old.

"For 20 years, I did a lot of portraits and commercial photography, including some fashion. But in the last couple of years, I've become more interested in nature photography, and last winter I contacted some of the pack companies that work the Sierra to see if I could take pictures of their expeditions, as a way of getting out into the wilderness and taking some pictures for myself. The

Blanchard family said yes, and this is my second trip this summer. I went along this route with Bill and Angie in early July, and I'm looking forward to how I see it differently this time around."

"Are pictures of any of us going to be used in company materials?" Shirley asked.

"Only with your permission," Angie said. "The last day of the trip, we'll ask if you want to sign a photo release, allowing us to use an image of you. If you do, any photo we propose to use will be shown to you for approval, and we won't use it unless you're all right with it."

A general murmur seemed to indicate that the group thought this was a fair arrangement.

Nora moved on. She spoke for several more minutes about her personal life. She had been married once, but it hadn't worked out, had no children, and lived on a small property her father had bought near Point Reyes Station, about 25 miles north of San Francisco. She spoke in a flat, slightly nasal voice, but with a great deal of enthusiasm and conviction. By the time she was through, Gordon thought that even the three youngsters must have taken an interest in the talk, though it was hard to tell from looking at them.

Eve then took her turn. Her voice was more lilting and compelling than Nora's, and Gordon and Sam listened carefully.

"I work in a large office for a big company in San Francisco," Eve said. "Basically, I process and evaluate information and report my findings to my superiors for further action, if needed. I suppose it's the kind of job a lot of people would find boring, but it suits me pretty well, and I like to think I'm somewhat good at it.

"I'm at my desk for a lot of the week, so I like to get out and be active as much as I can. I enjoy horseback riding and hiking, and I'm kind of surprised I never met Nora before this trip, because I do quite a bit of my riding and hiking up in West Marin and southern Sonoma counties. They're quick and easy to get to from the City."

She paused for a second, and Gordon threw out a question.

"What made you decide to come on this trip?"

She hesitated a second or two before answering, and Gordon didn't take his eyes off her before she finished her reply.

"A good friend of mine took a trip out of Blanchard Meadows the year before last, and she really talked it up. I've never done anything more than an overnight horse camp trip myself, so I thought it would be fun to really escape civilization for a whole week."

"Well, you got that all right," Mason muttered under his breath.

She continued another five minutes, talking about herself without really revealing much of anything. When she finished, Gordon and Sam turned and looked at each other and Gordon shrugged.

They sat around the fire a half hour longer, making pleasant, if superficial, conversation, mostly about the beauty of the area and how much they'd enjoyed the day's ride. If the group wasn't exactly intimate, the various members were getting to be a bit at ease with each other at the end of the first day. At five minutes to nine, Mason, who had been sitting at the outer edge of the group, slipped off toward the darkness by the tents. Gordon found himself wondering if Mason needed a pee, a fix, or both.

Five minutes later, Mason was still absent, when Bill stood up to make an address.

"Time to put out the campfire and turn in now," he said. "If you're not sleepy, feel free to sit around and talk a bit more or go for a little walk. But if you do step away from the campsite, be sure to take a flashlight with you, and don't go too far. We don't want to lose sleep to being a search party the first night of the trip."

"Or any other night," Angie added. There was a slight group chuckle.

"Sunrise tomorrow is about 6:30," Bill said. "Our commitment to the people on this trip is that hot coffee will be ready at sunrise every day."

"Thank God," murmured Emily Reed.

"Breakfast will be served at 7:30 sharp," Bill continued. "At 7:20 we'll bang on a tin plate and keep on banging until everybody is up. It should take us an hour or so to clean up and get the horses packed, and we expect to be on the trail by nine o'clock. Are there any questions?"

Apparently not.

"It's going to be a beautiful ride tomorrow," Angie said, "and the weather's supposed to be perfect. We're looking forward to it. Good night, and sleep well."

Mason slipped back into the circle by the campfire just as people were beginning to stand up.

AFTER THE FIRE WAS OUT, Gordon and Sam walked to the infamous cove, and sat down leaning against a large rock above the beach. The moon, which would be full in three days, was large, bright and high enough in the sky to illuminate the area reasonably well, and an hour and a half into the darkness, the temperature had turned decidedly chilly. Sam had just finished telling Gordon about his encounter with Eve on the trail earlier that evening.

"I suppose you noticed," Gordon said, "that during her talk tonight, she never said where she works or exactly what she does."

"That wasn't lost on me," Sam said.

A loud, smacking sound came from the cove, as a fish rose to take an insect on the surface. In the moonlight, they could see the ripple spreading outward across the calm surface of the water. Gordon sighed.

"We're just getting started, and already there's more going on than we realized," he said. "I would very much like to know who Miss Bredon really is."

"I don't believe she's some drone working in an office, do you?"

"Nope."

"Well, we're not going to solve it tonight, Gordon. And whatever or whoever she is, I don't think her presence changes our situation. One of the brothers has already had a close call of the sort you were brought in to prevent."

"You could say we instead of you."

"All right. But the point is, we didn't stop it. Now what happened to Tyler could have been an accident, and it could end up being the only untoward thing that happens on this trip."

"Wouldn't it be lovely to think so."

"I know. I don't believe that either. Listen, Gordon. I sell insurance, and watching what happens to my clients, I've come to believe that there are a handful of people in this world who simply attract trouble."

"And you'd put the Linfield brothers in that category?"

"Absolutely. If I'm not mistaken, they're heading for something bad, and you — we — need to do better than we did today if we're going to keep it from happening."

Gordon considered the point for a moment.

"For starters," he said, "I think we have to come up with a system to make sure one of us is keeping an eye on them all the time. It doesn't look as if I'm going to get any fishing in on this trip, but so be it. When we're on the trail, one of us needs to be riding behind them so we can have them in sight, and when we're in camp, we have to divvy it up somehow. It's not rocket science."

"No. And it somehow doesn't seem like enough. It's a version of 'try harder.' But I can't see anything else we could be doing at this point."

"Perhaps inspiration will follow a good night's sleep."

Sam yawned.

"Makes as much sense as anything." He stood up. "Shall we retire to our tent?"

"Go ahead. I want to fret over it for a few more minutes myself. I'll be along soon."

"Remember I'm on the right side of the tent," Sam said, and off he went.

Gordon stared out at the lake, trying to make sense of things but getting nowhere. Another fish rose to take an insect in the cove, and that didn't improve his mood any.

Off to the side, he thought he saw a light flicker.

He stiffened, his senses becoming more acute. He could hear quiet footsteps heading in his direction. He saw only a flashlight at first, and not until it got much closer could he tell that it was Eve Bredon carrying it. She stopped ten feet away and turned off the light.

"Evening, Gordon. Hope I didn't startle you."

"Only a little."

"Mind if I join you for a minute?" When he didn't immediately reply, she added, "But if you want to be alone, I understand."

"Sorry, I'm a bit slow right now. Please sit down."

She sat three feet to his left, pulling her knees up to her torso. The sleeves of the parka she was wearing partly covered her legs, which were bare below a pair of shorts. Gordon had noticed earlier in the evening that they weren't bad legs.

"I'm not quite ready to sleep," she said. "This has been a stimulating day."

"It has. I'm looking forward to the rest of the week."

"Same here. I wasn't sure if I'd like this, but after just one day I know I will."

Gordon looked out at the lake, thinking about how he could draw her out.

"By the way," she continued. "I was wondering if you knew the twins from some place before. They seem to be taking a shine to you, like an older brother."

"Never met 'em before yesterday at Blanchard Meadows. And I think Tyler is viewing me as a personal gambling adviser, not as an older brother." He laughed.

"What's so funny?"

"He did remind me of something that happened a long time ago, when I was playing at Cal. Something I'd forgotten until now."

"Tell me."

"Do you really want to hear my basketball war stories?"

"I'll bet you have some good ones."

"All right, then. Sophomore year at Cal, early in the season, first week of December, so school was still in session. Cal State Fullerton had come up to play us on Thursday night and then Stanford on Saturday. It was a pretty meaningless game, and Harmon was only about a third full, what with finals coming up."

"Harmon was Cal's gym, right?"

"Right. Anyway, 18 seconds left in the game, we're up 70-68, CSF is inbounding at half court after a timeout. During the timeout, Coach switched us from man coverage to a 2-3 zone. The thinking was that CSF had a guard — shoot, what was his name? — anyway, he was quick as lightning and loved to drive to the basket. So we figured he'd probably try to do that and either score or draw a foul. We put three of our biggest men down low, and I was one of the two up top. Not because I could keep up with that guy, but because I had five inches on him and it would be harder for him to shoot over me. Are you following this?"

"I get to a few Warriors games a year. The company has season tickets."

"So, down to eight seconds left, he's dribbling at the top of the key in front of me, and I'm just trying to stay close enough to go up if he takes a jump shot. Then, shazam! A quick move, and he's past me on the left. But that's OK. We got three guys back there to stop him. I look back to see if there's anybody he can pass to that I should be guarding, but their guys are all heading for the hoop to try to get the rebound if he misses.

"He went right into the middle of our zone, and he had nothing, but he tried to take a shot anyway. Fred Baker, one of our big guys, got all ball and swatted it over my head all the way to midcourt, heading toward our basket. I took off after it, with everybody else under the basket behind me, grabbed it at the free throw line, dribbled once, and made a layup with two seconds left. Final score, 72-68.

"No heroics there. I could have just dribbled out the clock and we'd have won anyway. But when I went to my 8:30 class the next day, three people came up to me before it started and thanked me for making that layup, even though it didn't matter in the game. Then two more people stopped to thank me as I was walking across Sproul Plaza after the class. I asked the second one why he was thanking me for a play that didn't matter, and that's when I learned what was going on.

"Apparently, the betting line on that game was Cal minus three points. So if the final score had been 70-68, the people who bet on us would have lost. But when I made that layup, we covered the spread by one and our bettors won their bets. Without knowing I'd done it, I determined how probably tens of thousands of dollars changed hands that night. Crazy, huh?"

"It's a great story. I'm glad I got to hear it."

They made small talk and looked out over the lake for a few more minutes, then Eve rose to go.

"Good night, Gordon. Sweet dreams, and thanks for humoring me."

"My pleasure."

She switched on her flashlight and started back toward camp, but stopped after five steps and turned around.

"You know, Gordon, I'm sorry I never had a chance to see you play."

And then she was gone. After a few minutes of trying unsuccessfully to figure out her last remark, and wishing he'd been able to draw her out instead of letting her get him going on basketball, he stood up and started back to camp himself.

Tuesday August 24

Cliff Lake to Monolith Valley

ASIDE FROM BILL, Gordon was first out of the tents. It was cold — he guessed in the low 40s, maybe high 30s — but once the sun came over the mountain, it would warm up quickly.

"Coffee's just a minute or two away from being ready," Bill said. "Did you sleep well?"

"Very well." As Gordon moved around, he realized he was merely the slightest bit stiff from the previous day's ride. His riding regimen before the trip seemed to have done the job.

The mountains on the other side of Cliff Lake were half-bathed in light now, and the light crept lower as the sun kept rising. He could smell the brewing coffee, which mingled with the scent of pine needles, the faintest whiff of dung from where the horses were tethered, and the overall damp cleanness of the air. On his fishing trips, Gordon tended to sleep indoors, and encountering the rawness of a new day straightaway after wakening was a different and bracing experience.

Bill took the coffee off the burner of the portable stove and poured some into two large metal cups.

"How do you take it?" he asked.

"Black, please."

"A man after my own heart." He set the cup on one of the folding tables and gestured to it. "Those cups heat up fast, so be sure to hold it by the handle."

Gordon picked up the cup and took a sip. The coffee was almost scalding, and its flavor could charitably be described as ordinary, but in this setting, at this time, it was sublime. He waited a couple of minutes, then took another sip, looking across the lake and seeing that the sunlight was now nearly down to the shoreline on the other side.

Quietly and easily, Angie emerged from her tent and got a cup of coffee. She and Bill engaged in a brisk, businesslike exchange that established who would be doing what in the preparation of breakfast. She set about getting the food together.

"Can I ask you a question?" Gordon said to Bill, who nodded. "I was just wondering. Tyler's going over the edge of the cliff yesterday. Has anything like that ever happened before?"

Bill thought for a moment.

"This is my fourth year, and I've never heard of anything like that. And I'm sure I would have. The Blanchards make a real point of safety, and if anyone had been injured or killed at that cliff — ever — we'd have been told about it as part of our training."

Gordon nodded and took a sip of coffee.

"Funny thing about that cliff," Bill continued. "A lot of people think they want to do the jump into the lake. From here it doesn't look like that much, but when you get to the top, it suddenly seems like a long way down. Nine out of ten people bail, and a couple of times each summer, someone has to go up there when a client gets stuck halfway up and freaks out over the height. There was one guy, bigshot executive at a brokerage in Los Angeles, who froze so bad it took me an hour just to talk him into starting back down."

"But you've done it. The jump, I mean."

"It's no big deal if you have any head at all for heights. Once you get past the rocky shore below, the water at the bottom of the cliff is 40 to 50 feet deep. As long as you go in clean, head or feet first, you're fine." He paused. "Or ass first, like Tyler."

There was a rustling from the area of the tents, and momentarily Tyler emerged from his, looking half-awake, disheveled, and slightly disoriented, like a groundhog trying to get a sense of things on Feb. 2. He remained in a squat for half a minute, then ambled over to Gordon and Bill.

"Morning," he said. "Coffee ready?"

He took a cup and stood slurping it. His eyes were focused on the coffee, and he seemed not to be taking in the setting or relating to the other two men.

"Brandi up yet?" Gordon asked, conversationally.

"Sort of," Tyler said. He shook his head. "She can't get started in the morning until she's had a cup or two of coffee, but she can't get out of bed to get it until she's had a cup of coffee. Sort of a catch-22."

Gordon and Bill looked at each other.

"Why don't you take her a cup of coffee in the tent?" Gordon said. "That way she'll have the cup she needs to get up and get going."

Gordon could see the wheels spinning inside Tyler's head.

"Hey," Tyler finally said, "that's a good idea." He looked at Bill. "Would that be all right?"

"Absolutely. Want me to pour one for her?"

"Sure. Let's do it."

Bill poured a cup and set it on the table. Tyler took it, thanked him, and started for his tent. Gordon was shaking his head.

"Tyler!" he hissed.

Tyler stopped and turned around. Gordon beckoned him with a finger gesture, and Tyler came back.

"Does she drink it black," Gordon asked, "or does she take it with cream and sugar?"

Tyler thought for a minute. "You know, I think it usually has cream or milk in it, but I'm not sure about the sugar."

Bill picked up a container next to the stove. "Let's get the milk in it, and I'll give you a packet or two of sugar, just in case."

He added some milk, pouring from high enough up that the milk mixed with the coffee from its descent into the cup, and handed two sugar packets to Tyler, who ambled back to the tent with coffee.

"How'd you think to ask about the cream and sugar?" Bill said, when Tyler was in the tent.

"I saw her put cream in her coffee at the lodge yesterday morning," Gordon said. After a pause of several seconds, he added, "Apparently her boyfriend didn't."

I WOKE UP WHEN GORDON slipped out, and was coming out of the tent myself just in time to see Tyler gallantly taking a cup of coffee to his lady love in her tent. Funny, but I wouldn't have expected him to be so thoughtful. You never know.

We were still in shade, but the sun was hitting the water on the far side of the lake. Five minutes after I was out, more than half the others were, too. I decided to spend my breakfast doing some people watching. Last night, after Tyler's fall into the lake, I hadn't been in the mood for that.

The three folding tables were set up separately this morning. At one table, the Reeds were joined by Eve and Shirley; at another, Bill, Tyler, Brandi and Nora settled in, though Nora was getting up to take pictures a lot.

Mason came over to our table after getting his bacon and eggs (over easy), and Angie, after finishing the serving, took the last seat. Mason looked as if he hadn't slept all night and seemed taut as a violin string.

"How'd you sleep?" I asked, as he sat down. I couldn't help myself.

"Took me a while to fall asleep, but once I did, I slept pretty well," he said. "Is the altitude bothering you guys?"

"Yeah," said Gordon, "but it's better today. You'll probably notice."

"I hope so."

We ate for a couple of minutes.

"So it must be nice that you and your brother could take this trip together," Gordon finally said. "How long have you been planning it?" He knew the answer, of course. He was just trying to get Mason to talk.

"Since May," Mason said, biting off a piece of bacon.

"That's nice. Do you and your brother do a lot of things together?"

"Not really."

I made a wager with myself that Gordon could get him to say three words with the next question.

"But you decided to spend a week together in the back country. That must mean you wanted to be together, right?"

"Yeah."

"Great way to do it. Beautiful place and lots of free time."

Mason grunted. "I didn't know he was bringing her." Gordon and I exchanged glances. Apparently we weren't the only ones who hadn't known Brandi would be along. "It complicates things," he added.

"She seems to be very fond of your brother," I said.

"That's what it looks like, I guess."

"Whose idea was the trip?" Gordon asked.

"It was Tyler's. You see," he looked around and lowered his voice, "he and I are coming into a little bit of family money next month, and the attorney who's handling all that thought we should try to be a little closer. I don't know why. We each get our own share."

He left it there, and Gordon turned to Angie.

"The food's really good," he said. "You and Bill have a talent for this."

"Uh huh," Mason said.

"I don't know about talent," Angie said. "But the mountain air is a chef's best friend. Everything tastes 20 percent better at Cliff Lake."

"How about where we're staying tonight?"

"Monolith Valley? Twenty-five percent better."

Gordon and I laughed. Mason didn't. He shoved a forkful of hash browns into his mouth.

"How are you liking the trip so far?" Angie asked Mason.

"It's good. Different."

"You mean different than what you're used to?"

"I suppose."

"So what do you do? I mean back where you came from?"

"I don't have a regular job," Mason said. "I mostly do deals." Give him credit for a clever line, though I suppose he gets asked enough that he had to come up with something.

"Like financial deals?"

"There's always money involved in a deal," Mason said.

Gordon cut in to steer the conversation in another direction.

"I was meaning to ask, Angie. The valley where we're camping tonight —does it have a stream?"

"Thinking of the fishing, aren't you? There's a small stream, and some of the people on our earlier trips have caught fish there. Not real big ones, but 6 to 9 inches. And there's enough stream I don't think you'll have to worry about the ladies who skinny dip."

We ate for a minute or two.

"It's nice that you and your brother could do this trip together," Angie said to Mason.

"That's what everybody keeps saying."

"You all right with the horses?"

"Just a little sore. Tyler and I rode a lot as kids, so it came back pretty quick."

"Glad to hear it. It's no fun when one of our campers gets seriously saddle sore."

Just then, Emily Reed stood up. Slowly and gingerly. She walked stiffly back to her tent, and squatted deliberately before crawling in.

"Don't look now," I said, "but I think you have one on this trip."

WHEN BREAKFAST WAS OVER, Bill and Angie took down the campsite with an efficiency that was a marvel to watch. As Bill washed and put away the cooking utensils, stove, chairs and tables, Angie went from tent to tent showing everyone how to take down the tent and fold it for packing. In less than half an hour, the horses were packed and ready to go. Mason couldn't get the hang of folding the tent, and Angie had to do it for him, explaining as he watched. Tyler and Brandi needed three tries to fold theirs, but Brandi eventually figured it out.

The air had gone from chilly to cool by the time the party left, and in open areas with direct sun, it was almost warm. They rode over a slight saddle to the ridgeline, then followed that down to a small but lovely meadow and began climbing the ridge again. Gordon was taking in the scenery, but also thinking back a couple of months.

When he accepted attorney McCabe's assignment, the first thing Gordon had done was call his friend and fishing companion Dr. Peter Delaney to arrange dinner. They met at a Chinese restaurant they both liked in the Richmond District. Peter had performed a hernia surgery and an appendectomy that afternoon and was ravenous.

Over spring rolls and Oolong tea — while waiting for the cashew chicken, mushu pork and Mongolian beef to arrive — Gordon filled Peter in on the situation and asked him to be his partner in the investigation.

To Gordon's dismay, Peter said no.

"It's not that I wouldn't like to," Peter said, "but it's just not going to work right now. So many doctors in my practice are gone in August that there's been a ban on any more vacation time that month. Plus, I promised to take Stella to Hong Kong for ten days in November, and that'll use up more than half the vacation time I have left." Stella Savoy was the acerbic nurse with whom Peter had been in an on-again-off-again relationship for over four years. Having been married and divorced five times, Peter was in no hurry to rush to the altar again, though he had cheerfully (for him) agreed to be a groomsman at Gordon's wedding.

"There's nothing I could say that would change your mind?"

"Sorry, Gordon. That month is just off limits. Not a thing I can do about it."

They each picked up a spring roll and took a bite.

"Have you asked Sam yet?" Peter said.

"Don't tell him, but you were my first choice."

"Sam might be a better one," Peter said, taking a sip of tea. "His personality is more suited to getting along with a small group of people for a week. If I went, and the people were irritating me, the group would probably vote to tie me to a tree, slather me with honey, and leave me for a bear to eat."

"I'm not asking you because of your sparkling personality, Peter. Give me credit for more awareness than that. I'm asking because you have a gift for looking at a situation, seeing what's really going on, and articulating it. In a job like this, where we have to size up a vague set of changing circumstances with almost nothing to go on, that would be extremely valuable."

"That's very flattering, and you're starting to make me feel a bit guilty. But I'm stuck. Ask Sam."

"I will. But since I have you here now, what's your take on the situation as I described it?"

Peter finished the second half of his spring roll and poured himself another cup of tea before answering.

"I'd probably start by looking at two things," he said. "Do you know which of the brothers suggested the trip?"

"No. I asked McCabe, and he didn't, either."

71

"Try to find out. Odds are the one who came up with the idea is the one who has other ideas."

"But couldn't it be that the one who *didn't* suggest the trip was the one who saw the potential for using it to get what he wants?"

"Sure. But the odds are on the one who planned the trip. Start there, and change your mind if the evidence points elsewhere."

"And the second thing you'd look at?"

"See if you can figure out which brother is more amoral and irresponsible, then keep a careful eye on him."

"From what McCabe says, the two of them are partners in a sack race when it comes to being amoral and irresponsible. He seems to think either one is capable of just about anything."

"And I suppose they could both have come up with the same malign intent, independent of each other, in which case you'll really have your hands full. But one of them is bound to have fewer scruples than the other, even if just by a little bit, and that's the one I'd take a good look at."

The main dishes arrived, and both men spooned portions of all three on their plates, along with rice.

"Thanks, Peter," Gordon finally said. "I appreciate your insights, as always."

"No charge for insights. Speaking of which, I'd like some insight as to why you're vanishing into the High Sierra wilderness a week before your wedding. Anything you'd like to tell me?"

Gordon shook his head. "Elizabeth's mother. She can't wrap her head around the fact I don't go to work at an office every day, and it's maddening."

"Does she know you can afford not to work?"

"I believe Elizabeth has been trying to explain that, to no avail."

"Well, just remember, you're marrying her, not her mother. And the mother lives in Indiana, right?"

"Illinois. Near Chicago."

"Illinois. Either way, it's a manageable distance. You'll have a couple of bad weeks a year, but otherwise, you'll be fine."

"Thanks, Peter. You're a pal."

They ate in silence and pleasure for several minutes.

"You know," Peter said, "that got me to thinking. I just realized that in all five of my marriages, I never had any mother-in-law problems to speak of."

"Really? I'm surprised."

"Not so surprising if you know me and think about it. All my wives could come up with enough against me on their own. They didn't need their mamas to tell them what a shit I was."

EVE BREDON WAS MORE AND MORE on Gordon's mind as the morning went on. The party rode through stunning scenery, taking in sheer, rocky peaks, forests and meadows. They crossed clear, free-flowing creeks, saw alpine flowers that bloomed for only a few weeks in the summer and observed deer, hawks and beaver in their natural habitat. Just after eleven o'clock, they passed a stunning jewel of a lake, its water a rich blue-green that reflected the peaks around it and the scattered clouds in the sky. Gordon found himself regretting that they didn't stop by the lake for lunch. There would have been no chance of fishing it during the short lunch break the party took, but he could have imagined how he would have.

And for all the glory of the scenery, his thoughts kept coming back to Eve. He was attracted — no, intrigued was a better word — by her and increasingly curious as to who she was and with whom she was affiliated. As they drew nearer their lunch spot, he resolved to take one more stab at cracking her façade.

They rode through a small valley and started up another grade. Part way up, the trail began to parallel a small stream that was never more than ten feet wide, and Bill and Angie stopped the procession when they reached an area where there was a large enough flat space next to the running water for the group to spread out for their meal.

"Can you watch the brothers for me?" Gordon asked Sam as they stood in line for sandwiches. "I want to try again to get a fix on the mystery woman."

Sam nodded. Eve and Nora had been served, and had moved down to a small rocky beach by the creek. It was only a few feet wide and ten feet long, but Gordon figured it was big enough for a third person and approached.

"May I join you?" he asked.

"By all means," Nora said. She was removing her boots and socks and putting her bare feet into the creek. Gordon dipped a hand in the water and found, as he had expected, that it was ice cold.

"You're tougher than I am," he said. "My feet wouldn't last five seconds in that creek."

Nora smiled. "I grew up by the beach," she said. "I'm used to cold water, and I'd rather go barefoot than not."

"Looks like another nice day," he said. "Wonder if the weather will hold?"

"They said there was a chance of rain tomorrow," Eve said. "But we can worry about it tomorrow."

"And they said the rain probably wouldn't amount to much," Nora added.

"We can hope so," Gordon said, "but I've seen enough Sierra thunderstorms to know they can be pretty intense."

"Do you come up to the mountains often?" Eve asked.

"Several times a year, usually between May and October."

"And does Sam generally come with you?"

"Sometimes he does. Sometimes another friend, a doctor, comes along. And lately, my fiancée, Elizabeth, has been coming with me more often."

"Does she fish?" Nora asked.

"No, but she paints. I think she'd really be inspired by some of the country we've been seeing."

"What's her name?" Eve said. "Her last name, I mean?"

"Elizabeth Macondray."

"You're joking," Nora said.

"Not at all."

"I saw her show at the Shaughnessy Gallery last summer. There was some really good work there."

"Coming from a visual artist like yourself, that's quite a compliment."

"Seriously. There were a couple of paintings I would have considered buying, but I got there when it was almost over, and someone else had already bought them."

"Could have been me," Gordon said. "I loaned a couple of works for that show."

"Well, I hope you realize what an accomplished woman you're marrying."

For an instant, Gordon thought it was his future mother-in-law talking, but he let it go, and said only, "Very much so."

They kept a fairly good conversation going for the next 15 minutes, and Gordon finally felt that the ice had been broken enough for him to take a direct approach. When Nora got up and went to the horses, he took a sip of his soft drink and looked directly at Eve.

"Do you mind if I ask you something, Eve?"

"You can always ask."

He took a deep breath and proceeded. "Well, you've talked a bit in general terms about the type of work you do, but you've never really said who your employer is, and I'm kind of curious."

He let it hang, hoping it had come across as casual, not aggressive. Eve put the last bit of her sandwich in her mouth and made it last more than two minutes before swallowing it. She took a sip of her drink to wash it down, then stood up.

"They'd rather I didn't say."

And she walked back to the horses.

THE AFTERNOON RIDE was pleasant, but Gordon didn't enjoy it as much as he should have. He was still fuming at having struck out with Eve, and not until they reached their campsite for the night was he finally able to let it go.

In the last hour of the ride, they had passed Horse Thief Lake, so named because over a century ago a man engaged in that line of work had been tracked there and shot. Multiple times by multiple trackers. After passing the lake, they went over a rise of about 500 feet and descended into Monolith Valley, named after the sheer granite wall that rose above its north side. They stopped to make camp at a large grassy area next to a small, clear stream, three feet wide in most places.

Gordon and Sam quickly got their tent up, and Gordon strolled over to Bill to see if he needed any help with dinner. He said he didn't, and after their brief exchange, both men turned to the monolith and stared at it silently.

"It's really something," Gordon finally said.

Bill nodded. "I think it's every bit as spectacular as Half Dome in Yosemite, but because it's out here, hardly anyone ever sees it. Or knows about it."

Gordon looked at it again for several seconds.

"Lucky us," he finally said.

They became aware of a noise that sounded like human activity, coming from the trail ahead of where they had stopped. By the time the Boy Scout troop responsible for the noise arrived at the camp three minutes later, Gordon and Bill had been joined by Sam, Angie, Mason, Tyler and Brandi.

The scoutmaster, a tall, fit man in his mid-forties, with straw blond hair under his hat, wearing khaki shorts and a regulation Scouting shirt with the troop number embroidered on it, ordered a halt as they reached the camp, and the boys behind him stopped.

"All right, men," he said. "Ten minute rest break and try not to bother these folks."

The boys, 15 of them in all, moved downstream a hundred feet and sat down chattering. Bill took a step toward the scoutmaster.

"I hope we didn't take the place you were planning to camp tonight," he said. "I'm Bill Snider."

"Martin Wallander," the scoutmaster said, shaking hands. "Don't worry about it. We can set up far enough away from you that we won't be in your hair."

"Oh, you wouldn't bother us," Angie said.

Wallander looked at the boys downstream. "You wouldn't say that if you heard these guys singing at campfire. They're not great singers, to tell the truth, but they make up for it with enthusiasm and noise. They can get pretty loud."

Shirley, Nora and Eve had moved downstream to talk with the Scouts. The Reeds were sitting by a tree at the opposite side of the camp, engaged in what looked to be a serious discussion.

"Let me ask," he said. "Was there anyone at Horse Thief Lake?"

"Not an hour ago," Angie said.

He looked at his watch. It was 3:20 p.m.

"We could make it by dinner time. Maybe that's what we'll do."

"Please don't feel you have to go on account of us," Angie said.

"No, no. Just that it's good for them to be alone."

"Where are you from?" Sam asked.

"Orange County."

"And how long have you been on the trail?" Brandi said.

"We left Monday of last week, stopped at Donovan's Meadow last Thursday so everybody could get a shower and a night on a bed, and we've been on the trail again since then."

"That's a long trip," Gordon said. "Is this your first time doing it?"

Wallander shook his head. "I started doing it six years ago, when my son was in the troop. He's out now, but I've kept on going." He paused and looked at the Monolith. "He starts at UCLA this fall."

"You must be proud," Angie said.

"He's turned out well so far."

"I don't understand," Tyler said. "Why do you keep doing this if your son's out of it? Doesn't that use up a lot of your vacation?"

"Nearly all of it, but I can't think of anything I'd rather be doing. The first time I did this, I realized it was magic. You can actually see these young men getting more mature as the trip goes on and they learn to do more things themselves. And what else could they be doing at this age that they'll remember 70 years later? No, I can't think of a better use for my vacation time. This recharges me completely."

No one said anything for half a minute, then Brandi asked, "You said it's good for them, the boys, to be alone. What did you mean by that?"

"Nothing personal, if that's what you're thinking. I mean that if a problem comes up when we're camped by ourselves, the guys have to figure it out. They can't just run down to the next campsite to borrow something or ask for help." He looked around. "And on that note, I think we *will* keep going to Horse Thief Lake. Thanks for the information."

He moved into the shade of a tree, took a long swig from his canteen, looked at his watch, and bellowed in the direction of his group.

"All right, gentlemen. We hit the trail in two minutes, so assemble."

The boys got up and walked past the encampment. As they did, Gordon studied their faces. They looked a bit tired, but happy and confident. As they marched off in the direction of Horse Thief Lake, it struck Gordon that he would probably remember this trip the rest of his life, as the Boy Scouts would remember theirs.

I'D BEEN WANTING to get Gordon alone ever since we stopped for the night, so I could pump him about how it went with Miss Bredon at lunchtime. Not well, I'm guessing, based on the way he was glowering when he came back to the horses afterward. But I want all the juicy details. I suspect the woman is up to no good, but whatever that might be, it probably has nothing to do with our mission. Still, she clearly has Gordon flummoxed, and I don't see that too often.

After the Boy Scouts left, Gordon and I headed upstream on the pretense of checking fishing possibilities. Given the size of the creek, it was a barely credible cover, but it got us out of earshot of the rest of the group.

Gordon was looking carefully at the water as we walked along the creek, and it took me a while to realize that he wasn't just acting. He really was trying to calculate whether there might be decent fish in it and, if so, where they would be. He can't help himself.

We sat down on an old fallen log, lying parallel to the creek.

"Doesn't look too promising," Gordon said, making a head gesture toward the water. "But on the positive side, it'd be pretty hard to drown someone in this and make it look like an accident."

"So," I said as nonchalantly as I could, "did you find out where Eve Bredon works?"

He swore and told me what she had said.

"That's too bad," I said.

"She's beating me every which way, Sam. And it's getting under my skin. We set out to see if we could figure out which brother might be trying to kill the other one, and now we have a mystery woman and a cryptic girlfriend to deal with, too. There's too much going on here."

And then it hit me. Gordon's a competitor. You don't get a basketball scholarship to a major state university unless that's part of your makeup. And so far on this trip, Eve is out-competing him. He has to find that galling.

And, if I'm not mistaken, he's finding it a bit sexy as well. One more thing for me to keep an eye on.

For as long as I've known Gordon, he's gravitated toward strong women, and the shortest of his relationships were with women who were too clingy or fawning. That would not be Miss Bredon, and while she may be getting the better of him now, his annoyance is more at himself for not figuring it out, and he probably has a grudging respect for her.

"Enough about her," I said. What are you making of the brothers?"

"You know, while we were on the trail, I was thinking about what Peter Delaney said when I had dinner with him a while back." It was news to me that he had discussed this with Peter, but I kept my mouth shut. "He suggested two things to look for. Number one, find out which brother proposed the trip. And number two, figure out which brother is more dissolute and amoral."

"Those are pretty good suggestions," I finally said, "but I don't see that they get us anywhere. We know now that the trip was Tyler's idea, but I'd have to say Mason appears to be the more dissolute and amoral of the two."

"I agree."

"So they cancel each other out."

"Yes and no. There's the fact that Tyler took a nasty header over a cliff last night and was lucky to get out of it without much more than a soaking. Nothing's happened to Mason."

"Yet," I said.

"Such a pessimist."

"Such a realist. So any idea of what to do tonight?"

Gordon thought about it.

"If they get apart," he said, "let's each take one and strike up a conversation. See if we can get a bit more information out of them."

"You mean, like, 'Mom always liked you best.' That sort of thing?"

"Anything. We need to know more about them, but we don't know what we're looking for. So get 'em talking and see what we can find out, and then see if we can recognize the importance of the information in time."

"Are you going to try to fish tonight?"

He shook his head. "Creek's so small I doubt if there's anything over six inches in it."

"Really? Didn't you tell me once that you can often find a decent fish in a really small body of water?"

"Probably I did. But it's low odds here, I think, and we should stick to the job at hand."

We watched the creek for a couple of minutes. No fish materialized to rebut Gordon.

"You have a point," I finally said. "We really don't know that much about the twins yet."

"No. But there's one thing I feel pretty certain about."

"What's that?"

"It's scary to think of either one of them in complete control of four hundred million."

"Or eight hundred," I said, after a pause.

AFTER DINNER, THE BROTHERS decided to take a walk upstream together, leaving Brandi behind. She moved downstream to the grassy area within view of the camp, where the Boy Scouts had rested earlier. She sat down cross-legged on the grass and produced a paperback book, which she began to read part-way in.

Gordon took stock and quickly huddled with Sam.

"I'll give the twins a couple of minutes' head start and go after them. Why don't you see if you can chat up Brandi? She hasn't said much so far, and maybe you can draw her out."

Sam hesitated as if to say something, then finally said, "All right."

Three minutes after Mason and Tyler started upstream, Gordon followed them. Monolith Valley, surrounded by high peaks on all sides, was entirely in shade now, though the sun was still hitting the upper part of the Monolith and the sky was entirely bright. The cool damp of evening was beginning to come on now, and it was bringing out the meadow smells — grass, stream water, pine trees. Gordon found Tyler and Mason sitting on the same log where he and Sam had conversed before dinner.

Before Gordon could come up with a conversational gambit, Mason called out to him.

"Gordon, come on and join us. We were talking about something you might have an opinion on."

With a slight sense of dread that Tyler might be about to hit him with a new round of questions on betting against the point spread, Gordon headed over to the log.

"Always happy to talk," he said. "Are you enjoying the trip so far?"

"I'm a city guy," Mason said, "so this is different for me. It's interesting, but a few days of it is probably going to be enough."

"Actually," Tyler said, "we were just talking about investments. And you're a stock broker, right?"

"I used to be, with a firm in San Francisco. Right now I'm managing my own investments and those of a few clients."

"So you *do* know something about it. You see, Mason and I are coming into some money next month, and we're talking about what we should do with it."

"Well, I'd be happy to talk with you in general terms, as long as you understand that I'm not offering you any specific advice, and that you should see a certified financial advisor for that, probably sooner rather than later."

"So we're just shooting the shit, here, right?" Mason said. "Understood. Ty, why don't you tell Gordon what you're thinking."

"My feeling," Tyler said, "is that when you get a windfall like this, you don't want to just spend it or let it sit. You want to try to grow it."

"And you're wondering how," Gordon said.

"Actually, I have an idea. I think you'd want to put a fair piece of that money into dot-com stocks. They're the wave of the future, right? What do you think?"

What Gordon really thought was that Tyler might as well bet the money on football and basketball games, but he took several seconds to come up with a measured and diplomatic response.

"It would depend on how much money you have, what percent of it you're talking about, how much you need to live on — a lot of different things. That's why you need a financial advisor. But for whatever it's worth, I'd be careful about the dot-coms if I were you. My own opinion — and I should say that a lot of people don't agree with it — is that they're due for a correction in six months to two years."

"What's a correction?" Tyler asked.

"In plain English, I think their share value is headed for a drop, and in some cases a very dramatic one."

"Now why would you think that?" Tyler persisted. "The way I see it, the internet is the future, and a lot of people right now are coming up with really good ideas for how to make money from it."

"I'd agree with you on both points."

"So what's the problem?"

"The problem as I see it is that good ideas are a dime a dozen, but a successful business requires execution on a lot of fronts — sales, marketing, production, distribution. I see a lot of companies out there in dot-com land that aren't tending to those details as well as they should, and my take is that a lot of them are going to get bitten by that before the good idea can carry the company to takeoff. Also, some of those ideas, and I don't know which ones, are ahead of the market right now and could crash because of that."

"So you'd stay out of dot-coms?" Tyler said.

"I wouldn't be so absolute. But at this point, I'd be careful and not too aggressive."

"So," Mason said, "are there any dot-coms you like?"

"The one I think has a good long-term prospect is Amazon," Gordon said. "I bought a bit of it at the initial offering." (The "bit" amounted to $50,000 worth) "But if you bought it now, there's a reasonable chance the value could go down and it could take a few years to get your investment back. I do think, though, it's one company in the bunch that has both vision and good management."

No one said anything for several seconds, then Mason weighed in.

"My brother and I have different opinions about what to do with all this money. He tends to be ambitious and more of a risk-taker. As the first-born ..."

"Only by a few minutes," Tyler said.

"Nevertheless. I'm more cautious. My thinking is to invest the money conservatively and live off the income. I won't get a lot richer, but I also won't lie awake nights worrying about it."

"That's not an altogether bad philosophy," Gordon said. "Again, it would depend on how much you're talking about, but if you think the income would be sufficient, that would certainly be one way of going about it."

"It should be sufficient," Mason said. "At least for a while."

WHY GORDON WANTED ME to talk to Brandi, I don't know, but, ever the good soldier, I set out to do the job. As I stood at the campsite looking at her downstream, it struck me that she's closer in age to my daughters than to me, and that I don't get much from my daughters these days but lip. Since I didn't have any conversational opening, I decided to walk to where she was, slow down and see if she noticed me. If she didn't, I'd keep walking until I came up with something to say and go back past her from the other direction.

I was in luck. When I got closer to her, she looked up and closed the book she was reading, setting it down on the grass. The book was *Portrait of a Lady* by Henry James, and judging from where she put the bookmark, she's a whole lot farther into it than I ever got.

"Enjoying the book?" I asked.

"I don't know if 'enjoy' is the right word. It's not easy reading, but I'm getting something out of it. About Isobel's decision and the consequences. Have you read it?"

"I started it years ago," I said, as I sat down on the grass, "but I was probably too young to appreciate it." I paused. "It looks like you kind of got left by yourself tonight."

She shrugged. "I expect that. Tyler wanted to do this trip to bond with his brother. They're going to want me out of the picture some of the time."

"Well, I wouldn't want to bother you."

"No. I could use a break from the book, and as company goes, you seem less forbidding than your friend."

"He used to be an athlete," I said. "He tends to default to his game face."

"That's right. Somebody said that."

We watched the creek trickle by for a minute or two.

"I guess if Tyler wanted you along, he must feel like he needs you."

"I don't know what he really feels. I'm probably a security blanket in case he and his brother don't get along."

"None of my business, but do you mind if I ask how long the two of you have been together?"

"Seven months." That answered one of our questions. I was trying to think how to extend the conversation, when she moved it along on her own.

"We met at an open studio art show. A friend of mine had some paintings there, and so did Tyler. My friend's a better painter, but Tyler was cute and nice, and, I don't know, maybe a little bit lost. The kind of man I seem to fall for."

"Mmm hmm," I said.

"I worry about him a bit. He doesn't seem to have any direction and he's impulsive some of the time."

"He's young. A lot of that comes with the territory."

"I know he's young, but I'm beginning to wonder if he'll ever grow up." She stopped and looked at the creek for a while.

"If I tell you something, will you promise to keep it a secret?" she asked.

"Of course."

"Tyler's going to be coming into some money next month. Him and Mason both."

"No kidding," I lied.

"For real. And what bothers me is that he isn't really planning for it."

"Maybe he's not sure what to do or who to turn to."

"It's more than that. He wants to pay off his debts, and I don't think he's given it any real thought beyond that. He won't say how much — and I'm OK with that — but it sounds like there's enough that he could do something important with it and still have enough to live on."

"Maybe he can't decide what's important."

"I wish I could believe that. But I think he just doesn't want to think about it. I mean, how many people are lucky enough to have that kind of opportunity? It's looking to me like a lack of ambition."

"He has time to come around," I said. "I wouldn't worry about it too much if I were you."

"He may have the time, but I don't know if he has the inclination." She sighed. I realized it was getting darker and looked in the direction of the camp. Bill was assembling the wood for the fire and would be lighting it shortly.

"But at least he's a sweet guy," Brandi said. "I don't think he'd do anything evil with the money."

I had no answer for that, so we looked at the creek a bit before she finally added:

"Mason, I'm not so sure about."

TWENTY MINUTES LATER the campfire was going full throttle, and the whole group was back at the campsite, milling around. The valley seemed to hold in the evening chill, and everyone was grateful for the warmth of the fire.

Brian and Emily Reed were due to introduce themselves to the group shortly.

"Ladies first," Brian said, and Emily rose gingerly from her camp chair and hobbled a few steps toward Bill and Angie. The horseback riding was obviously getting to her more than the others.

"I'm Emily Bryce Reed," she said, "and I'm wondering how I let my husband talk me into this trip."

It seemed to be meant as a joke, but, lacking the comedian's sense of timing and nuance, she delivered the line in too quick and straightforward a manner, and it fell flat. Even Brian flinched slightly when she said it.

"That was a joke," she said. "I really am enjoying the beauty of the backcountry here and getting to know the rest of you. But right now, the horses are getting the better of me, and I'm a bit stiff.

"We live in the LA area — Glendale, actually — and I work for a large marketing and advertising firm downtown." She gave the name, and Gordon had heard of it. "It's emotionally and financially satisfying, but the hours are long and the work is hard. Brian and I haven't been able to take more than a long weekend together the past three years, so having a whole week here in the mountains, away from the cell phone and email, is a real treat. I'm still going through withdrawal, but I'll be fine in another day or two."

That generated a chuckle or two. "Brian *did* suggest this trip because he thought we needed some time together where there was no possibility of my being interrupted by the office. I'm glad he did. I just hope that by the time Saturday afternoon rolls around, I'll still remember how to use a phone and a computer."

She went on for a few more minutes, during which it came out that her work was pretty much her life and that they had no children and she had no hobbies. Then it was Brian's turn.

"I'm a property manager with a company that owns a lot of office buildings," he said. "I enjoy my job, especially dealing with people. A lot of it is taking care of problems that come up with the facilities and seeing that they're promptly dealt with. Other parts of it are seeing that routine work gets done on a regular basis — that the buildings are painted every few years, that the roofs are checked, that sort of thing.

"Most days are pretty busy, but, unlike Emily, I usually leave the job behind when I go home at the end of the day. Sometimes there's an emergency, but not too often, and I like it that way. I'm a decent enough golfer, and there's a regular group of us that hits the links every Saturday and most holidays. I'm a big football fan, but with the Rams in St. Louis now, I'm having to find a way to fill my Sundays in the fall. Also, my family's a bit more social than Emily's, and most of them live in Southern California, so we have a few family get-togethers during the year.

"I heard about these pack trips when I was on a weekend fishing trip at Crowley Lake a few years ago, and thought it might be a good thing for us to do. I'm having a blast so far."

When Brian said that, Gordon looked at Emily and saw her face grimace quickly, then return to the impassive state it maintained most of the time.

"HENRY JAMES. I'M SURPRISED," Gordon said, when Sam told him about the visit with Brandi. They had moved a slight distance away from the campsite to talk things over before turning in. The sun had been down for two hours, and the temperature had dropped into the low 40s.

"I thought you might be," Sam said. "She's not the empty vessel she seems at first, and she seems to have Tyler pretty well scoped out."

"He was pumping me about dot-com stocks," Gordon said.

"Another version of sports betting."

"That's more or less what I told him. I doubt he heard the message."

"Maybe she'll help him become a better man."

"Maybe," Gordon said, "she'll learn something from Isobel Archer ..."

"Who?"

"In *Portrait of a Lady*. Maybe she'll learn from Isobel's story what can happen when you marry the wrong man."

"Speaking of marrying the wrong man," Sam said, "what did you think about the couple who shared tonight?"

"I'm trying not to think about them too much, since we have our hands full with the brothers, and Tyler's literary girlfriend."

"Not to mention the mysterious Eve Bredon. Nevertheless, Gordon, I thought I sensed a 'but' in your last remark."

"But, I couldn't help thinking they seem mismatched. And that being the case, throwing them together for a week on a trip like this might not be the best idea in the world."

"How long do you think our friend Peter Delaney would give their marriage?"

"Three months. But that's how long Peter gives every marriage. He looks at it through a different lens."

"And were you thinking anything else as the Reeds did their little presentation?"

Gordon was silent for a minute, then spoke in a low voice.

"I couldn't help thinking that I hope that's not how Elizabeth and I are behaving in five years."

GORDON HAD BEEN ASLEEP a full hour when he became aware, dimly, of the sounds outside the tent. At first, he thought he was dreaming, but it began to dawn on him that the sounds were real and not in his head. They were thrashing, grunting, snuffling sounds of an animal nature, and he thought immediately of raccoons.

It had to be checked out. He slipped out of his sleeping bag, pulled on his jeans, slipped on a pair of flip flops, and gave Sam a nudge on the shoulder, telling him to wake up. Without waiting for his friend, Gordon unzipped the tent flap and stepped out into the night.

The nearly full moon was bright in the starry sky, and the instant he left the tent, Gordon realized how cold it was. But all thoughts of the evening chill vanished when he saw the bear. It was at the entrance of the next tent over — the one occupied by Bill and Mason — and was swatting at the zipped flap.

"Hey!" Gordon bellowed in his loudest voice. "Go away."

The bear looked in his direction, quickly judged him to be unworthy of attention, and returned to swatting the tent flap. It was hitting the tent hard enough that the tent was shaking — shaking hard enough that Bill was awake.

"Git!" he shouted from inside. "Git!"

To no avail. The bear sniffed around the bottom of the tent, and began moving to its left, around the far corner of it, away from Gordon. Judging by where Bill's voice had come from, the bear was moving to Mason's side of the tent.

Sam was out now, just in time to see the bear go around the corner. He gave full throat to a general alarm.

"Bear!" he shouted. "Bear at tent one! Everybody up!"

Angie came out of her tent just as Sam shouted.

"Holy crap," she said, then she dived back into her tent.

The bear continued sniffing along the base of the tent and stopped halfway down the far side. Suddenly and without warning, it took a swipe at the side of the tent with its right front paw, gashing a slit a foot and a half long into the side of the tent, two feet above the ground.

About a foot above where Mason would have been sleeping, Gordon thought.

Gordon clapped his hands loudly, and shouted, "Out of here! Go home!"

The bear didn't even consider him long enough to ignore him. Instead, it stuck its paw through the gash in the tent.

"It's coming in after me," Mason shouted from inside.

By now, Angie was out of her tent again, with two frying pans in hand. Also coming out of their various tents, in different stages of dishabille, were Shirley, Brian Reed, Brandi, and Eve Bredon. Angie began advancing on the besieged tent, banging the frying pans together. In the still of night in the quiet, isolated mountain valley, the noise was unholy.

The bear looked up for a minute, then reached farther into the tent with its paw.

Meanwhile, the front zipper of the tent came down, and almost simultaneously, Mason shot through the opening, scuttling along on all fours like a drunken crab. Bill bounced out immediately after him, and more gracefully.

At the same time, Nora came out of the tent she was sharing with Eve, her Canon in hand. She walked past the others to the corner of the tent and pointed the camera at the bear from a distance of eight feet.

"Smile, sweetheart," she said. "I'm going to make you famous."

And she fired off five frames, with the flash turning the area around the bear into daylight each time. The dazed bear took its paw out of the tent and turned in the opposite direction. After several seconds, it began lumbering, a bit unsteadily, toward the trees, and in half a minute it had vanished into the forest.

Bill turned to Nora after the bear was gone.

"That's not recommended, you know."

"I don't know," Nora said. "It worked better than the frying pans."

"Let's not argue," Angie said. "We need to size up the situation. Is everybody out of the tents now?"

"Not Emily," Brian said. "She said the bear has to come to her."

Angie was doing a quick count. "And what about Tyler?"

"He can sleep through anything," Brandi said.

Bill had gotten a flashlight out of his pocket and was looking at the side of the tent.

"He got it pretty good," he said. "But we can patch it when we get to camp tomorrow, or put a tarp over it if it's raining."

"The question is," Angie said, "why did the bear come after this tent in particular?"

"I might have a lead on that," Gordon said. "Just before you came out, the bear was sniffing along the bottom of the tent. Almost as if it smelled food."

Angie turned to the group. "You all know the rules. No food in the tents. This is exactly why. I know Bill wouldn't take food in there, so, Mason, I have to ask, did you?"

"No," Mason said, visibly shaken. "I'm not even hungry. No."

"Would you mind if I went in and just had a quick look along that edge of the tent, where the bear made the hole?"

Mason thought for a moment, and Gordon guessed he was trying to figure out if some things he didn't want Angie to see were in that area. They apparently weren't, because he finally said, "Sure. Go ahead."

She went in on her hands and knees, and they could see her flashlight shining on the far side of the tent. She was out in less than a minute, holding something else in her non-flashlight hand.

She held it up to the group. It was a roll of salami, with the end cut off, letting the meat smell escape.

"It was up against the tent, about halfway down your sleeping bag," Angie said.

"It's not mine!" Mason shouted in a high, shaky voice. "Salami? I can't stand the stuff. It makes me gag. Someone else must have put it there."

FORTY-FIVE MINUTES LATER, the offending salami had been added to a raised food bag used as a precaution against bears, and everyone was back in the tents. Gordon and Sam talked in low voices in the darkness of theirs.

"Do you believe him?" Gordon said.

"I don't want to but I kind of have to. Why would he put himself in danger like that? It doesn't make sense. And he was really scared."

"That seemed real enough," Gordon said. "Though he'd have been scared if he just made a dumb mistake and that bear was there."

"True enough."

"And we now have one suspicious close call involving each brother on the first two days of the trip."

"And no real evidence of any criminal intent."

"True enough. Still, with the way everybody is milling around the campsite before and after dinner, anyone in the group could have ducked in for a few

91

seconds and put that salami there. It wouldn't have been much of a risk."

"No," Sam said, "it wouldn't. But that leads to another question. If the salami wasn't Mason's, and someone else put it there, you'd think Mason would have smelled it. I mean, when Angie held it up, it was pretty pungent, even from a few feet away. And he was practically on top of it."

"Yeah, you'd think," Gordon said, "but there's an obvious explanation for that." He paused. "If Mason's drug of choice is what I think it is, his nose probably isn't in the best condition."

Wednesday August 25

Monolith Valley to Keener Flat

"I THINK NUMBER THREE is the best one. That's where he turned to the camera and you could really see his full face."

Nora was showing her bear pictures on the small screen on the back of her new digital camera. Shirley, Eve, Emily and Brandi were gathered around as they waited for Bill and Angie to put the final touches on breakfast.

"You know, now that he's gone, he *does* look kind of cute," Emily said.

"Just like an old boyfriend," Shirley said. They all laughed.

Angie came over and took a quick look.

"I don't think Blanchard's will be using that one in a brochure," she said, and went back to the stove.

Sausage, eggs, biscuits and coffee were soon served, and Bill asked the group to sit close together so he could make an announcement.

"That was a close call we had last night," he began. "We want our campers to see the wildlife up here; it's part of the thrill of the expedition. But at the same time, we do our best to keep the wildlife out of the camp area. That goes especially for bears.

"Blanchard's takes bear prevention pretty seriously. That's why we talked at the beginning of the trip about being sure there's no food in the tents. That didn't happen last night, and I think we all saw how quickly there are consequences. Now Mason said he didn't put that salami in the tent, and I believe him. It was probably a freak accident."

Gordon and Sam did their best not to react.

"But however it happened, the important thing is that it did, and we have to make sure it doesn't happen again. I'm saying this now, and I'll say it again at dinner. I want everyone to do a tent check before turning in tonight. Shine your flashlights all around the tent. Pull up the sleeping bags. Look through any personal bags you have in the tent. We'll be staying at Keener Flat, and bear visits have been reported there this summer, though not to any Blanchard group. Every tent has to be absolutely food free tonight. And don't take any food into your tents at all — even in the afternoon. You'd be surprised how long the smell can linger.

"Is that understood?"

Ten heads nodded as one, while Angie stood behind Bill and watched the reactions.

"One more thing," Bill continued. "We were going to leave at 8:30 today because it's the longest ride of the trip. But it will have to be at 9 instead. Blanchard's has a strict rule that all bear incidents have to be reported immediately, and they'll have someone by the shortwave radio from 8:30 to 9. So I'll call in at 8:30 and report."

"What's the urgency about reporting?" Shirley asked.

"They want the information themselves. They want to share it with other outfitters. They have another group leaving tomorrow on the same trip, and that group needs to know to be careful in Monolith Valley. Anyway, depending on how fast I can get through and how quickly we can pack the radio, we may be able to get out a bit before 9. And even so, we'll probably do just a 15-to 20-minute stop for lunch to make up some of the time. Any questions?"

There were none.

"Then let's take down the tents and get packed."

Everyone got down to business. Gordon and Sam were the first ones finished, with Eve and Nora a close second. Something had troubled Gordon about the bear incident the night before, and since it was five minutes before Bill had to radio Blanchard's, he decided to ask about it.

He walked toward Bill at the same time Eve Bredon did, but she had the better angle and got there first.

"Can I ask a question?" she said.

"Make it a quick one. I have to call Blanchard's in less than five minutes."

"I'll make it real quick. I was just wondering why you didn't smell the salami in your tent last night?"

He cracked a forced smile.

"I was hoping no one would think of that," he said. "It's a crazy damn thing. The last four times we've been at Monolith Valley, there's been something in the air that gets my nose stuffed up. Only place on the whole trip I seem to have that problem. And it happened again last night. Couldn't smell a thing. The one night I needed to. Can I help you with something, Gordon?"

"You just did. I had the same question."

They moved away, and Bill shortly turned on the battery-powered radio. The group gave him some distance, but they could see he was speaking intensely for several minutes. Finally, he turned the radio off, folded the table it was sitting on and the chair he was sitting on, and brought all three to the horse line. Angie helped him get them packed in a little over a minute.

Gordon was close to them, and heard her say, "How'd it go?"

"Not good. The boss really chewed my ass."

"That's his job," she said, gently touching his arm. "Don't let him get you down."

Bill mounted his horse and rode it back to the middle of the line. The others were either mounting their horses or were already in the saddle.

"All right, listen up, everybody! When I talked to Blanchard's just a couple of minutes ago, they said the forecast for this afternoon is for scattered violent thunderstorms throughout the Sierra. If we're lucky, they'll pass us by, but we need to make time, just in case.

"So enjoy the scenery this morning, and let Angie or me know if you need to stop for any reason. But we're not going to dawdle, understood?"

He rode back to the front of the line, looked back at the group, and made a forward motion with his right hand.

"Let's move 'em!"

BETWEEN THE BEAR INCIDENT and Bill's talk, it seemed to me that the collective mood had changed, and there was an edge to this morning's ride that hadn't been there the two days before. We were going forward noticeably faster than before, but Bill and Angie know the horses well enough not to push them beyond a pace that would be sustainable for a full day. The horses will definitely have earned their dinner tonight, though.

Shortly before noon we stopped at a spot where you could see a small meadow off to the left through a cluster of pine trees. Angie, apparently relieving Bill from being the heavy this time, announced that it would be a hurried lunch. The meal was sandwiches, chips and an apple, and we spread apart into groups of two and three, taking advantage of the spacing between the trees and the shade they provided.

Judging from the mean-looking clouds moving in quickly from the west, shade wasn't going to be an issue much longer.

Gordon and I picked out a tree at one end of the grouping, where we could keep an eye on everyone else and talk freely, as long as we didn't raise our voices too much. We were also facing west, with a view of the approaching storm clouds, and Gordon kept looking at them with a grim expression. I wasn't looking forward to the afternoon ride too much myself.

"What do you make of the salami?" he finally asked.

For a second I thought he was talking about our sandwiches, then I realized that he meant the salami in Mason and Bill's tent the night before.

"I don't know what to make of it," I said.

"Neither do I. But there's one thing that strikes me. We've had two misadventures in two days, one that was aimed at Tyler and one aimed at Mason."

"There's really no proof they were aimed at anybody, but I tend to think you're right."

"Let's assume it for the sake of argument. What strikes me about each incident is how imprecise it was. Supposing Mason somehow rigged up something to send Tyler over the edge of that cliff. He did it too far along the trail for Tyler to land on the rocks — though not by much, I admit — and whatever it was, there had to be some doubt it would trip Tyler up in any event.

"Then look at the bear affair last night. It was no sure thing that a bear would appear in the first place. Yeah, the mountains are full of them, but there was no telling that there'd be one in this neighborhood who'd be inclined to come into the campsite. And even if he or she did, it was a long shot that it would maul whoever was sleeping by the salami. Our California black bears aren't exactly aggressive killers. The bear was after the food, and as long as it got that, and no one interfered too much, the chances of Mason being all right were fairly good.

"In short, we had two episodes that could be considered murder attempts, but they weren't very well thought out and they weren't terribly high-percentage in terms of succeeding. What do you say to that, Sam?"

I thought about it for several seconds, and replied, "I'd say look at who was the brains behind each operation, assuming those were planned events. We're not dealing with professionals here."

Gordon nodded.

"Something else strikes me, too," I continued. "The attempt on Tyler, if that's what it was, wasn't going to put anyone else at risk. They were going up that trail alone, and we only came along later. But last night was a different story. If Tyler put that salami in the tent, he wasn't just exposing his brother to danger. It put Bill in jeopardy, too, and anyone else who came out of their tent. If the bear had been a bit meaner than it was, it could have taken a swipe at you, Gordon. Or Angie, or Nora, or Eve, or Brian, or Brandi or me. If that was directed at Mason, it was done so thoughtlessly it could have harmed, or even killed, just about anybody in the group. The perp either didn't realize that or didn't care."

"Wait a minute," Gordon said.

He was looking over at the brothers, and I did, too. Brandi had been with them earlier but had moved away, and it looked as if the two of them were arguing and gesturing furiously. We could hear raised voices, but the only sound I could make out was right at the end, when Mason barked something that sounded like "Letty" at Tyler and walked away from him.

Tyler stood there, mouth open, looking as if he'd seen a ghost. Mason had made an impression on him, and it was a good bet that their conversation was drawing on at least an undercurrent of tension from the events Gordon and I had been discussing.

"Five minutes!" Bill boomed out.

We scarfed the rest of our food and headed back to the horses. The clouds, mostly gray and black, now filled the entire sky above the mountains to the west. Bill was studying them.

"You might want to put on rain gear now," he said to us as we got there, and he went down the line repeating the suggestion to the rest of the group. Gordon and I put on lightweight jackets and draped water-repellent ponchos over them. We were both wearing hats, and the ponchos had a pull-up hood if needed.

As we rode away from the trees to the more open trail, I felt a large raindrop hit me square on the nose.

SOME THUNDERSTORMS approach with menace, then don't amount to much: A few flashes of distant lightning, scattered showers, and a low-key thunder that sounds more like a growling stomach than anything else.

Other thunderstorms burst in with both barrels blazing, and the storm the group encountered that afternoon was one of those. In a matter of minutes, they were in the midst of an epic downpour.

The rain came down in sheets, and from the back of the pack train, it was difficult to see the front. The sky lowered and closed in, creating a sensation of gray twilight. The bright, colorful palette of the High Sierra backcountry was gone, and in its place was a drab, claustrophobic view of grays, muddy browns and off-blacks. Water was everywhere on the trail, following whatever slope there was downhill.

With the clouds and rain obscuring any vistas, there was no sense of the surrounding landscape. It all looked pretty much the same, and, in any event, everyone in the party was mostly focused on the trail ahead. The riders looked identical through the heavy rain; all had been issued rain ponchos by Blanchard's, and everyone was a tented, olive-brown figure with a wide-brimmed hat.

Forty-five minutes into the storm, Gordon found himself wondering what it would have been like without the ponchos, considering how bad it was with them. He was wearing a Western-style canvas hat that had been advertised as water-resistant when he purchased it from a highly regarded San Francisco outfitter. It had served him well on a number of rainy days beforehand, but less than an hour into this storm it had soaked through thoroughly, giving lie to the manufacturer's claim. Not only was his hair drenched, but cascades of water ran off the brim of the hat. Most of the water landed on the poncho, but some of it found its way under the narrow neck opening and onto the clothing underneath. In half an hour, his shirt was soaked and clinging to his body. The jeans on his lower legs weren't covered by the poncho, and they had soaked through and were dripping water into his boots. The brim of his hat covered only half his face and neck. The other half of both face and neck were being incessantly pelted with cold raindrops, which ran under the poncho's neck opening.

About the only consolation was that everyone else had to be just as wet and miserable.

And it wasn't just rain they were getting. Every few minutes a flash of lightning would illuminate the sky, but because the clouds were so low, it was impossible to tell exactly where the lightning bolt was. The whole sky, or what they could see of it, lit up for a couple of seconds, then the twilight gloom returned. The lightning flashes were followed in reasonably short order by peals of thunder, with the thunderclaps varying in intensity from sonic boom to exploding dynamite.

Both horses and riders were edgy, yet the group trudged forward. At one point Sam came up next to Gordon, and Gordon realized he had no idea whether Sam had approached from the front or the back. Sam said something in a normal voice, and Gordon had to shout, "What?"

"I said," Sam shouted, "do you think we're safe riding like this with the lightning and thunder?"

"I've been counting the intervals between the lightning and thunder," Gordon said. I'm usually counting to ten or twelve, though occasionally eight or nine. I think the lightning's a ways off, though it would be nice to see that for a fact."

"How low does the count have to go before we pull over and look for cover?"

"That's an excellent question, and I sure as hell hope Bill and Angie know the answer."

As he said that, Angie rode past them from behind. With the hat and poncho, she was hard to recognize, but they knew her by the horse. Several minutes later, after presumably exchanging words with Bill, she rode back in the other direction.

They passed through a meadow, skirted the edge of a small lake whose surface was churning from the rain and wind, went over a ridge top, and rode through a mile of forest on either side of the trail. It was lovely scenery, and no one saw much of it.

An hour and three quarters into the ride, the rain stopped as suddenly as it had started. The air was damp and the visibility low, but the smell of earth, grass and trees was accentuated by the cleansing the atmosphere had received.

The respite lasted only a few minutes. With a flash of lightning and a loud clap of thunder, the skies opened again.

Only this time it wasn't rain that was falling. It was hail.

Pelted by aspirin-sized balls of hail, the group rode on. The ground was quickly covered by hailstones to such an extent that it looked, if one wasn't looking too closely, like an early snowfall. The air, which had been cool since the onset of the storm, was cooler yet, and the riders could see their own breath and the breath coming from the horses as they moved steadily forward.

Half an hour into the hailstorm, Bill guided the group into a large grove in the forest next to the trail. The trees were close enough together that there was just about a tree between each person and the next. Bill and Angie sat astride their horses, facing the others, and conferred briefly. The riders were out of the hail, but the rain that had fallen previously had so saturated the treetops that large drops of water were consistently splattering on everyone.

"We'll give the horses a bit of a rest here," Angie shouted over the noise of the wind and hail. "Fifteen minutes. If you want to get a snack out of your packs, this is a good time to do it. Maybe we'll get lucky and the hail will stop by the time we get back on the trail."

She looked at Bill.

"And we wanted to give everybody a heads-up now," he said. "In about half an hour, we'll be coming to the beginning of the ascent to Keener Flat, where we'll be camping tonight. It's a mile and a quarter climb up the side of the mountain on a narrow trail, and it's pretty exposed. As long as I can count to seven between lightning and thunder, it should be pretty safe.

"But I could understand somebody not wanting to make that ride until the conditions get a bit friendlier. So before we start up that mountain, I'm going to stop and ask if anyone wants to wait below until the weather gets calmer. There's a nice little grove of trees that provides some shelter, and it's as good a place as any to wait out a storm.

"If you're at all bothered by the prospect of that ride, please say so and wait below until things get better. Angie or I will stay with anyone who wants to do that, and no one will think less of you. Is that understood?"

It was even gloomier in the woods than it had been on the trail, but it appeared that there was a semi-circle of nodding heads. Almost everyone took advantage of the break to get an energy bar, apple, or other snack and eat it ravenously. Fifteen minutes later, they set out again. It seemed as if the hail had let up slightly, but it was hard to tell for certain.

BY THE TIME THEY REACHED the beginning of the ascent to Keener Flat, the hail had given way to rain again. The rain was beginning to melt the hail on the ground, but the raindrops themselves were so cold that it would be a slow process.

From where Bill stopped the procession, the view of the trail ahead was daunting. They were essentially riding north-northwest at this point, and the trail made its way up the side of a nearly sheer rock face. The trail was a narrow ribbon barely wide enough for a horse or pack mule, with a sheer drop on the left side. The trail went up the mountainside for about a quarter of a mile before being lost to sight in the mist.

"It looks as if we're on the way to Brigadoon," Shirley said.

"Or Shangri-La," Gordon said.

"What's Shangri-La?" Mason asked.

Bill asked if anyone wanted to wait below until the weather improved, and no one took him up on it, so the entire group started up the trail.

They hadn't gone more than a hundred yards before the wind kicked up and the rain began falling harder. The wind was driving stinging drops of icy water into the sides of their faces, and the clouds were descending on the mountainside to the point where it was hard to see the beginning of the pack train from the rear. Miserable as the circumstances were, there were two factors that could be considered somewhat positive: The howling wind was blowing people toward the wall on the right side of the trail, rather than over the edge; and because of the low clouds, no one could see how far it was to the ground below.

Fifteen minutes into the ride, a blood-curdling shriek rang out, penetrating the noise of the wind and rain.

"I can't go on!"

It was Emily Reed, who was riding directly behind Gordon at the time, and she had reined her horse to a halt. Gordon turned to look at her over his left shoulder, and the motion brought his full attention to how close to the edge of the cliff they were.

"What's wrong?" he shouted.

"I can't do it. I'm afraid I'm going to fall."

"What's going on?" Angie shouted from the rear.

"Altitude freak-out," he shouted back. "Emily."

"There's not enough room for me to move through," Angie yelled. "Can you get her down and walk the rest of the way."

"I'll try," he said.

"Gordon!" shouted Sam, who was riding ahead. "There's a little turnout 50 to 60 feet ahead where you can dismount."

"Wait there for me." He turned toward Emily. "Sit tight. I'll be right back."

He rode ahead to where Sam was. On the right side of the trail was an indentation in the wall of the mountain, about the length of a horse and a half and two feet wide. It offered three feet of trail for a rider to dismount on the left side of the horse, which is what Gordon did after steering Roy, the Palomino, into it. Even so, he stepped down with great care and made absolutely certain the ground was firm under his feet.

He walked back to Emily, trying not to look over the edge of the trail.

"Give me the reins," he said to her. "There's a place up ahead where you can get off."

"I can't," she said. "I can't go any farther."

"Where's Brian?"

"Back here," he shouted from behind Shirley, who was riding behind Emily. "I'd come up, but there's no room to get off the horse here."

"Give me the reins, Emily," Gordon said again.

"No. I can't do it."

"You have to, but only for a little bit. Just 50 or 60 feet. I'll walk the horse up there. Just close your eyes, turn your head to the mountainside and hang on to the horse's neck. It'll be over in no more than a minute."

"What if the horse tries to throw me?"

"This mare doesn't know how. I'll see that she behaves. Just give me the reins."

A minute passed, and he thought he'd lost the argument, but finally she whimpered, "All right," and handed him the reins. She embraced the horse's neck and leaned forward, turning her head facing the mountainside. Gordon slowly walked the horse up to the turnout. It took only a minute, but he doubted she was counting.

"All right," he said, when the horse was as close to the mountain wall as he could get it. You can get off on the left side now."

She turned her head and snapped it back toward the mountainside almost immediately.

"No," she said. "It's too close to the edge."

Gordon turned and looked behind. There wasn't a lot of room, but he moved to the edge of the trail, planted the heels of his boots six inches from it, and determined that there was enough space between him and the horse for her to get down.

"I'm standing right behind where you'll be getting down. If I'm on solid ground, you will be too. Just take it slow and keep your eyes on the mountain. I'll catch you if you fall."

She sat frozen atop the horse for a minute and a half before croaking, in a half-whisper, "I'm trying now."

She eased her right foot out of the stirrup and attempted to bring it back over the horse. The movement was stiff and awkward, and Gordon remembered that she had been complaining of saddle soreness earlier. She barely got the right leg over the rear of the horse and lowered it gingerly toward the ground. For the last 12 inches going down, she lowered the foot three inches at a time before it finally touched the trail.

"There you go," he said. "You made it."

"I made it," she said.

She eased her left foot out of the stirrup, but the toe of her boot caught it at the end, and she pitched into Gordon.

He had anticipated that possibility and had been leaning forward, but even so there was a terrifying second when he wasn't sure he could hold his balance. But he did, and pushed her back toward the horse, the two of them clutched in a lovers' embrace without a scintilla of passion amid the sheeting rain and whistling wind.

WITH SAM LEADING ROY ahead of them, Gordon walked Emily the last 25 minutes to Keener Flat. It was a long 25 minutes. He held her horse's reins in his left hand while she walked slowly, keeping as far to the right of the trail as she could and keeping her eyes on the point where the mountain met the inside of the trail. The insides of Gordon's boots had been filling with water and squished with every step. On the horse he hadn't noticed the water in his boots so much, but walking, he noticed it very much. He hoped that his athletic shoes and at least one pair of socks in his pack had stayed dry.

The rain stopped a few minutes before they reached Keener Flat, but the wind continued to blow, and the clouds remained low. The flat was a place where, over considerable geologic time, an area about half the size of a football field had been gouged out of the side of the mountain. It contained three pine trees and two campfire rings left over from previous visitors. At the back, where it ended against the mountain, a spring burbled out of the rock wall providing some of the purest water to be found in the High Sierra.

The tail end of the group rode in behind Gordon and Emily. Brian practically leaped off his horse, threw his arms around Emily and took her to one of the pine trees, where she buried her face in his chest and sobbed loudly.

The rest of the group circled around Bill and Angie.

"We should probably set up the tents as soon as we can," Bill said, "while it's not raining, though I think the storm is over or nearly over. Then we'll change into dry clothes and have a good dinner."

"Was this a particularly bad storm?" Eve asked.

"Worst I've seen in five years. It was something all right."

"Bill!" Angie said, barely keeping her voice under control. "We have a problem."

"What?"

"I just did a count. There are only nine campers."

"Nine?" he said uncomprehendingly.

"Tyler's missing."

BRANDI, WHO HAD REACHED the group only a few seconds earlier, began to shake, then advanced on Mason, who was standing 15 feet away from her. When he saw her approaching, he began to back up.

"What did you do to Tyler?" she shouted. "He was with you."

"He wasn't with me," Mason said, his voice rising and quavering. "At least not this afternoon. I thought he moved back to be with you."

Angie stepped between them, and Brandi nearly bowled her over as she pushed toward Mason. Eve grabbed Brandi by the arm to hold her back.

"Calm down," Eve said. "This is serious. Someone's missing. We need to be getting information now, not making accusations."

"She's right," Bill said. "We need to figure out who last saw Tyler and where."

"How about a show of hands," Gordon said. "Who saw Tyler when we stopped for lunch?"

Every hand but Emily Reed's went up.

"I know he was at lunch because Mason said something that upset him," Brandi said. "That's why I want to know what Mason did."

"Well?" Eve said to Mason.

"It was between us and no big deal," he said.

"Was Tyler with you when we rode out after lunch?" Bill said.

"He was right behind me when we started."

"How long was he behind you?" Angie asked.

"I don't know. Once the rain started, I put my head down and didn't look back."

"Was he behind you when we got to the forest and took the snack break?" Gordon asked.

"Can't say. We were in among the trees and half the people were behind one or partly behind one."

"Did anyone else see Tyler in the forest?" Bill asked.

"This is a wild goose chase," Shirley said. "It was so dark and wet in there, and we were all spread out. I don't think any of us could swear to seeing more than half the party."

"I agree," Nora said. "I took my camera out to get a picture, but it was so dark I'd have needed a flash, and it wouldn't have covered enough of the area."

"You're his girlfriend," Eve said to Brandi. "Were you watching him during the ride? That's what I'd be doing if my boyfriend was along."

"I usually do — watch him, I mean — but the rain was blowing into my face and I was trying to keep my head down. And everybody was wearing a hat and a poncho, so it was hard to tell who was who anyway."

"This isn't getting us anywhere," Angie said. "We need to get a search party together and go look for Tyler. The sooner the better."

"I'll lead it," Bill said.

"No, Bill. That has to be my job. I should have done a count of the group when we left the forest, but I was so caught up in thinking about whether we could get up to the flat in this weather that I forgot to do it. It's my mistake that we didn't miss him earlier. The best I can do is cover the mistake by going back and trying to find him."

They looked at each other for ten seconds without a word.

"All right, then," Bill finally said. "How many do you need?"

"I'd say three beside myself. Any volunteers?"

"I'm in," Gordon said, nearly overlapping her last word.

"Me, too," Sam said.

"I'll go," Eve said, "just to get a bit of gender equity in this operation."

THE RAIN DIDN'T RESUME, so the search party took ten minutes to change into dry clothing before setting out. They all wore their ponchos over the dry clothes, just in case.

It was shortly after four-thirty when they started out. No rain, but the wind was still blowing intermittently, and the clouds were still hugging the mountain.

The ride down was worse than the ride up. From atop a horse, the slope of the trail seemed exaggerated, and it was hard not to feel that the horses might lose their footing and begin sliding rapidly downward. Added to this was the fact that the drop-off was now on their right side, where most right-handed people tend to turn. And to top it off, the clouds had lifted just enough that they could look over the edge of the precipice and see how far a fall it would be to the hard ground below. Until nearly the bottom of the grade, it was a long enough fall to kill anyone for certain.

When they reached the bottom of the grade, Angie stopped them. She was breathing heavily.

"I've never gone downhill on that trail before, and I never want to again," she said. A series of slight nods confirmed that she spoke for them all.

"At least we could see," Eve said. "It doesn't look like Tyler fell."

"Even with that storm," Sam said, "I don't think he could have gone over the edge without someone noticing."

"I don't think so either," Angie said. "I think we lost him before we ever got to this point. Let's keep going."

They rode slowly, scanning the terrain in all directions, and calling Tyler's name every 30 seconds or so. The lack of response merely reinforced how utterly alone they were.

By the time they reached the forest where they had taken the snack break, the wind had mostly let up, though an occasional gust still rattled the treetops.

"I think we should give these woods a good look," Angie said. "He might have gotten away from the group and gotten disoriented."

No one objected. They rode into the trees about 50 feet and secured the horses.

"I'd say two of us should go left and two of us right," Angie said. "Look around carefully and call his name. If we don't see anything, meet back here in 20 minutes."

"I'll go with Gordon," Eve said, gesturing right.

"Lead the way," Sam said to Angie, pointing left.

THE FOREST HAD a haunting and enchanted quality to it. It was a place where one might have encountered Little Red Riding Hood (or the wolf), or even a witches' coven out of Hawthorne. It was even darker and gloomier now than it had been when they stopped there a few hours earlier. Although the rain had stopped, the saturated trees dropped large drops of icy water on Gordon and Eve as they made their way among the trees. Not even the chirp of a bird broke the primeval silence. They called Tyler's name at least once a minute, but the only answer was the occasional rustling of some creature in the brush or grass.

They had a flashlight, but it helped only in the narrow area where it was pointed, and the beam of light it cast made the surrounding gloom seem darker.

Gordon was acutely aware of Eve's physical presence. Clad in a parka and jeans, she moved smoothly and economically through the trees, and her concentration seemed unrelenting. After a quarter hour of calling out in the near darkness to no effect, he was regarding this as a fool's errand.

"Hold up, Eve," he said. "This is looking like a snipe hunt. I'm not even sure I know how to get back to the horses at this point."

She turned and waved the flashlight through the trees behind them and to the left.

"If we go in that direction, we'll get either to the horses or the trail. This isn't that big a forest."

"I'm glad to hear that," he said, "because I really don't want to spend the night here."

"I can think of worse things," she said.

From their right, and not terribly far away, came a guttural animal noise, unlike anything they had heard in the forest so far.

THE QUARTER HOUR OR SO I spent walking through that godforsaken forest with Angie only increased my respect for her. She was thorough and focused, and at the end I felt we had covered our patch of ground as well as could have been done under the circumstances. No sign of Tyler, and I realized at the end that we hadn't heard Gordon and the lady Eve calling Tyler's name in a while.

"I think it's time to head back," I finally said.

She shined the flashlight on her watch.

"Damn. You're right." She looked around the darkening forest. "If he was in this section and conscious, he'd have heard us and called back."

"Maybe Gordon and Eve had better luck," I said.

"Maybe," she said without conviction.

We walked silently through the woods for a few minutes, and eventually came out on the trail. Out from under the trees, I was surprised by how dark it was. My watch said 6:30, which meant there should be more than an hour of daylight left, but calling this mist-shrouded grayness daylight would be misleading.

When we reached the trail, I had no idea which way the horses were, but Angie decisively turned left and I followed her. We were only 150 feet away from them as it turned out, and we were the first ones back.

"What now?" I said.

"Dark as it is, I guess we have to return to camp. Bill can radio Blanchard's for a search and rescue team, and at least we've identified that they should work from here backward."

"Has this ever happened before?"

"In nearly 50 years, Blanchard's has never lost a client," Angie said. "I don't want Tyler to be the first."

We heard a rustling and muffled voices in the trees in the direction that Gordon and Eve had gone.

"Over here," Angie shouted.

"Thanks," Gordon called.

We could hear footsteps moving closer.

"Any sign of Tyler?" I yelled.

They walked into the small clearing where we were standing.

"No," Eve said, "but we found his horse."

THE SEARCH PARTY, with Tyler's horse trailing, rode into camp at last light. Bill had gotten a campfire going — albeit a smoky one, owing to the wetness of the wood — and the others were gathered around it. They jumped up and ran toward the rescuers, shouting questions.

"Hold on! Hold on!" Bill shouted, moving in front of them. "These people have got to be tired and hungry. Give them time to eat something, and then we'll all gather round the fire and come up with a plan."

Dinner that night had been a stew, flash frozen and packed in dry ice. Bill had kept the pot on the camp stove at low heat and served out generous portions, accompanied by sourdough bread. The four of them devoured it in ten minutes, and, somewhat restored, gathered around the fire with everyone else.

They told their story, and Gordon and Eve explained that when they had found the horse, they were near the edge of the forest and had canvassed the immediate area, calling Tyler's name with no result.

"There's no way he could have been there and not heard us," Gordon concluded.

"If he was alive," Shirley said.

The group flinched as one at the open expression of what they were all thinking.

"All right," Bill said. "Here's what happened on this end. I radioed Blanchard's at 6:30 to let them know a member of our party was missing and a search team had gone back to try to find him."

"How did that go over?" Angie asked.

"Not well, as I'm sure you can imagine. I'm supposed to radio back with a follow-up in half an hour. Before I do, I'd like to get a sense of what the group would like to do next."

"What are the options?" Nora said.

"Before I go into that, let me tell you what's going to happen. The sheriff's department here claims to have the best search and rescue operation in the entire High Sierra, and I have no reason to dispute that. They have two helicopters, and when I radio back that Tyler is still missing, I'd expect both choppers to take off at sunrise. Each one will be carrying four deputies, so that means eight sets of boots on the ground. And thanks to Eve and Gordon finding the horse, they have a center for the circle they'll be searching."

"Can they really get a search together that fast, starting this late at night?" Brian said.

"Jerry Blanchard has the sheriff's home and cell numbers on speed dial, and he was chair of the re-election committee last year. Trust me, they'll be flying at dawn."

"It sounds like you're saying there's nothing much we can do," Eve said.

"In practical terms, that's it in a nutshell. If we left before first light, without eating breakfast, we probably wouldn't get to that forest before the search and rescue team. If they find Tyler healthy, they can fly him back our way and deliver him to us. We have the horse, after all."

"Does the sheriff do that sort of thing for everybody?" Shirley said.

"I can't answer that question. But he'll do it for Blanchard's, and the company will probably reimburse some of the cost. Now if Tyler's found injured, the deputies are trained in first aid, and he'll be airlifted back to Mastodon Valley General Hospital, which has an excellent trauma center."

Seeing quizzical looks on some of the faces, Bill continued:

"Ski accidents. They get a lot of those. So in short, no matter what we do from this point on, the search for Tyler will be in the best possible hands."

"Could we abort the trip and just go back?" Nora asked.

"We could, but it wouldn't make much sense. At this stage of the trip, we're closer to our end point, Donovan's Station, than we are to Blanchard's. And it would mean two days of riding back over the same terrain when there's nothing we can do to help Tyler."

"So what are the options?" Sam said.

"Even though we'd be a fifth wheel in the search, we probably want to give emotional support. Especially Mason and Brandi, I'm guessing. So here's what I propose. If the two of you want to be with the search and rescue team tomorrow, we can leave at dawn, and I'll ride down to that forest with you. I'll stay with you until the choppers arrive, then head back after the group with your horses until I catch up. Worst case, I'll be at Sunrise Lake at dinnertime."

"What about us?" Brandi asked.

"One of two things is going to happen," Bill said. "They'll find Tyler well or unwell. If he's all right, they can fly everybody up to Sunrise Lake, and you can rejoin the trip there. If he has to go back to Mastodon Valley, you can go back with him.

"It's your call. What do you say? Ladies first."

"Let Mason go first," Brandi said.

It was obvious to everyone that Mason didn't want to make the decision. He fidgeted and stared alternately at the ground and the sky. Finally he spoke.

"If I kept going with the group, would we get an update tomorrow?"

"Absolutely," Bill said. "We'll know one way or another."

Mason fidgeted and looked at the ground again.

"You know," he finally said, "this trip was Tyler's idea for both of us. I think Tyler would want me to keep going, and since there's nothing we can do, I'll do what he would have wanted."

"Fair enough," Bill said. "And you, Brandi?"

"If it's not too much trouble, I'd like to be with the search party, and with Tyler when they find him."

"It's not too much trouble at all. I'll wake you a half hour before sunrise and put together some snacks to hold you through the day." He looked at his watch. "And it's almost nine. The radio's in the tent in case it started to rain again, so I'll let Blanchard's know what's going on."

Bill went into the tent, its side covered with a plastic awning where the bear had slashed it, and from time to time they could hear his muffled voice, but could make out only an occasional word. The group stood around the fire silently and a bit sullenly, considering the situation. The fire was burning down, but no one thought to put more wood on it.

Finally Bill emerged from the tent.

"It's all taken care of," he reported. "Blanchard had called the sheriff already, and not only will both of his choppers fly out on the search, he got hold of the Forest Service, and they'll be sending one as well. Everything that can be done will be done."

He exhaled, and his shoulders slumped, as some of the strain left his body.

"Three helicopters?" Shirley said. "If there's any chance of finding him, that should do it."

Angie stepped forward. "Tonight was supposed to be Gordon and Sam's turn to introduce themselves, but under the circumstances, I think that should be postponed. We've had a rough day and we could all probably use more sleep than we're going to get."

There were general noises of assent.

"Bill and I will put things away and douse the fire. See the rest of you at breakfast tomorrow."

The group began to disperse. Bill and Angie carried some gear to the opposite end of the flat, where the horses were tethered, and Gordon and Sam lingered by the fire.

"So what did you think about Mason's decision?" Sam asked.

"He doesn't want to be back there, does he?"

"Well, he wouldn't if he knows what the search and rescue team is going to find. Do you think he had something to do with Tyler's disappearance?"

"I think there's a very good chance, but I can't for the life of me figure out what he did or how."

"Same here."

"And there's something else," Gordon said. "Considering what must be in his gear bag, I don't think he wants to be anywhere near eight sheriff's deputies. Or be leaving the stuff on his horse for Bill to take back. You could practically see the wheels turning in his head, trying to figure out how to get out of going back to the forest. 'Tyler would want me to keep going.' What a humbug."

WE WENT INTO THE TENT exhausted. By all rights, I should have fallen asleep the second my head hit the pillow — or, to be more accurate, the blanket that served the same purpose. But my head was spinning from trying to process everything that had happened that day. Gordon didn't actually say it out loud, but I know he couldn't have been happy that one of the twins had disappeared, and was most likely dead, on his watch.

In a quarter of an hour, though, the warmth of the sleeping bag began to trump the racing mind. I could feel myself starting to doze off, and as I was fading out, I was aware that Gordon's breathing was becoming deeper and more regular. I had just gotten into that zone where I was between wakefulness and sleep, and the switch would have flipped in less than a minute.

That was when I heard the rustling outside.

Mindful of the visiting bear from the night before, my entire body jerked stiff and I was wide awake and listening. It sounded as if something was swatting the front of the tent. That happened a couple of times, and just as I was trying to figure out what to say to a bear, there was a noise I didn't expect.

The zipper to the tent flap went up, and I thought, no bear could have done that.

And into the tent, on her hands and knees, came Eve Bredon.

"Gordon!" she hissed in a loud whisper. "Wake up. We need to talk."

I think he was already partly awake from the noises, and he sat up groggily.

"That sounded just like Elizabeth," he said.

"You'd better get used to it."

"What's this all about?"

She looked at me. "Is your friend in on it, too?"

"In on what?"

"Don't try to be cute, Gordon. Unless I'm very much mistaken, you have an interest in Tyler Linfield. So do I. Now that he's gone missing, it's become a crisis. I've been thinking it over and decided we should both put our cards on the table and work together."

Gordon looked at me. "Sam's OK," he said. "Anything you say to me you can say in front of him."

"I'd already figured as much. Now are you in with me or not?"

"I don't know. You'll have to tell me more about yourself."

"No. I made the first move. Your turn."

"Not so fast, Eve. I've been sworn to confidence."

"So have I, more or less. If Tyler were asleep in his tent right now, I wouldn't be here. But he's disappeared without a trace, and extraordinary circumstances call for extraordinary measures. I'll show you mine if you show me yours, and maybe we can do more together than we can separately."

Gordon looked at me, as if for guidance, but I had nothing to offer.

"All right," he said, "but you go first."

"No way. I went first by coming here."

He sighed, sat up, and reached for his jeans next to the sleeping bag. Rummaging in the side pocket, he fished out a quarter.

"Only one way to settle this. Call it in the air."

"Let me see the coin first."

She took it from him, ascertained that it had both heads and tails, and gave it back. He flipped it in the air, and it seemed to turn over and over again in slow motion."

"Tails," she said.

It landed on the tent floor directly in front of her flashlight, and we could see by its glare that tails it was.

"All right," he said. "And you can assure me this goes no further than you."

"If you can assure me the same thing."

"Deal."

They eyed each other warily, like two poker players looking for a tell. Gordon took a deep breath and began.

"I'm here — very unofficially, I might add — at the request of the attorney handling the Linfield estate."

"McCabe?"

"You knew that?" She nodded. "Maybe you know that Mason and Tyler are in line to inherit a significant sum of money when they turn 25 next month."

She nodded. "The rumor mill puts it at about 750 million."

"The rumor mill's not far off. In any event, without going into too much detail, McCabe was concerned about the heirs taking a trip in the backcountry together. He'd kind of like to see them both live long enough to collect their share, and he asked me to go along on this trip to keep an eye on them and see that they made it to the end safely."

He paused and sighed.

"A job I seem to have bungled."

"That makes two of us. Was McCabe specifically worried about Tyler?"

"He was worried about both of them."

"Then he knew more than we did."

"Perhaps suspected, rather than knew, but yes."

"So we are on the same case after all."

"I'm all ears. Who are you working for?"

She waited several seconds before answering. They passed like minutes.

"Are you familiar with C&A Insurance?"

"Of course. You can't listen to a baseball game on the radio without hearing their ads. What's your connection with them?"

"I'm an investigator. Full-time staff, not contract. I'm looking out for the company's interest. Which is roughly the same as McCabe's, except we're only interested in one of the brothers. At the beginning of April, Tyler Linfield bought a life insurance policy with us. A big one."

I felt the hair begin to stand up on my neck, and I could tell, just because I know him so well, that Gordon was caught by surprise, too.

"Ordinarily, a young man buying a life policy wouldn't raise much alarm. Money in the bank for us nearly every time. But what got our attention was the name of the primary beneficiary."

She paused and looked around for dramatic effect. She certainly had my attention.

"Does the name Nick Moretti mean anything to you?"

Gordon whistled. "To me, and to anyone who follows the news. He's supposed to be running half the rackets in San Francisco. The district attorney's been after him for years, but hasn't been able to make a case."

"Not just the DA," she said. "The state attorney general has been after him, too, and so have the feds. He's been too slippery for everybody. But apparently our chucklehead agent in Burlingame didn't know who Moretti was and wrote up the policy. Somehow it got past the next level as well, and the policy was issued.

"If anything happens to Tyler, we owe Nick Moretti a cool two million. One of the auditors caught it in June, but by then we couldn't get out of the policy. I was called in to look at it, and when I found out Tyler was going on this trip, I had the same reaction McCabe apparently did. The company insisted I sign up for this and keep an eye on Tyler."

"But I don't understand." Gordon said. "Why would Tyler make Moretti his beneficiary?"

"What's he been asking you about the whole trip?"

"Point spreads. Gambling. You think he owes Moretti that much money?"

"I'm guessing he owes quite a bit and was probably trying to keep the guys with baseball bats at bay by saying he'd pay up when he inherited. But Moretti, who knows how short and fragile life can be, probably wanted a guarantee he'd be paid in case there was an accident."

"So you think Moretti was behind the insurance policy?"

"I can't prove it, but yes. And unless Tyler miraculously reappears, C&A is going to be paying two million to the mob. Not exactly good public relations, and I'll be getting some heat."

There was a long silence, before Gordon finally said:

"Well, you've got more skin in the game than I do."

"So, are we in this together?"

Gordon looked at me.

"What do you say, Sam? You've been pretty quiet so far."

"We might as well pool our resources," I replied. "We haven't exactly distinguished ourselves up to this point."

"So where do we go from here?" Gordon said.

"First we get a good night's sleep. Tomorrow we can come up with priorities and start looking into things with three sets of eyes and ears."

"I have a question, Eve," I said.

"Shoot."

"When I saw you on the path by Cliff Lake Monday night, you were picking something up from the side of the trail. Now that we're partners, can you tell me what it was?"

She reached into her pants pocket, took out an object, and set it in front of the flashlight. It was a rubber ball, about two inches in diameter.

"I'm guessing that's what tripped up Tyler," she said.

"Which would point to Mason," Gordon said.

"It's suggestive but not conclusive. Someone else could have dropped it there three weeks ago and Tyler just happened to be the one to step on it. Or he might not have stepped on it at all, though I don't believe that."

"In any case," Gordon said, "I'd say Mason should be the first person we look at."

"I'd agree with you, but he's not the only one. It's possible someone else in this group is working for Moretti."

"But that wouldn't make sense," Gordon objected. "If he wanted the insurance policy, it would be as an insurance policy. Tyler alive is worth more to him than Tyler dead. If Tyler's into him for two million before his 25ᵗʰ birthday, how much could Moretti milk him for in the next 20 or 30 years? He could end up with practically the whole inheritance."

"He could, but maybe he thinks Tyler is too unstable and he wants to take the money he knows he can get. We have to consider that."

There was another awkward silence, and finally Eve said, "This is a nice tent you boys have. If I had a blanket, I'd be tempted to curl up right here in the middle."

"I'm a very light sleeper," I said. "And I have another question. Is Nora working for C&A?"

"Not directly. She was a lucky find. I asked her to take pictures of Tyler as much as she could and said we might reimburse her if we use any."

"Maybe we should look at those photos tomorrow," I said. "Knowing what we know now, we might see something interesting in hindsight."

"Good idea. I'll talk to her about it tomorrow morning. And now I'm going to get back to our tent."

"One last thing," Gordon said. "Do you think we'll ever see Tyler alive again?"

"I don't have much hope. At this point, I'd be good with being able to prove what happened to him."

As she pivoted to leave, something in what she'd said called for a follow-up question, but I couldn't think what it was. She opened the flap of the tent and looked out.

"Looks like the clouds have broken up and the moon's out. Maybe tomorrow will be a nice day. Sleep well, guys."

She went through the tent opening, and a second or two later, we heard the zipper close, leaving us alone in the dark with our thoughts.

Thursday August 26

Keener Flat to Sunrise Lake

AN HOUR BEFORE FIRST LIGHT, Gordon was awakened by noises outside. It took a few minutes to figure out that it was Bill and Brandi saddling up to ride to the forest and meet the search party. Once he'd figured that out, his thoughts turned to Eve's visit to the tent the previous night, and any thought of going back to sleep was a delusion.

Her visit and her revelations had been so unexpected he didn't know what to make of them. His inner skeptic considered that there was no way of checking any of what she had said. It could have been a total fabrication, in which case he had been badly played when he trusted her. He believed her to be telling the truth but couldn't be sure. It was, he thought, something like getting married: At some point you have to set the doubts aside and take a leap of faith.

And, he reflected, Sam is in the insurance business, so it would be good to get his take on her story.

Eventually the darkness outside the tent began to dissolve as the sun came up in the east, behind the mountain. He waited until he heard rattling metal, indicating that Angie was up and getting a start on breakfast, before sliding out of his sleeping bag and getting dressed. He emerged into the pre-dawn cold, pulled the hood of the parka over his tousled hair, stood up and stretched.

"Top of the morning to you," Angie said.

"And to you. Is there anything I can do to speed the arrival of coffee?"

"Not really. The water boils when it boils. But with Bill gone, I wouldn't mind some help setting up chairs and tables while I get the cooking gear ready."

He did as asked, and in the few minutes it took, his hands were ice cold. He put them in the parka pockets after being told there was nothing else for him to do.

"I heard Bill and Brandi leaving," he said to make conversation. "And then I couldn't get back to sleep. I started thinking about all that's going on."

"I hardly slept a wink myself, and I doubt Bill did, either. Tyler's disappearance is bad enough in its own right, and there's no telling what harm it will do to Blanchard's. And to us."

"You mean you'd be held responsible for it?"

"Who else? It's our job to see that no one gets lost, and we fell down on the job. Big time."

"It may not be that bad," Gordon said. "Maybe Tyler just got lost and will be found this morning, a bit scared and worse for the wear, but basically all right."

Angie turned and looked him in the eye.

"Do you really believe that?"

"I believe it's possible," he said after some hesitation. "But if you pressed me on the point, I don't believe it's likely."

"Neither do I." She looked at the stove. "The water won't boil for several minutes. Come with me, Gordon."

They walked from the back of the flat, against the mountain, where the camp was located, to the trail. While the trail and the area below it for a mile out were still in shade, the sun was shining on the landscape farther to the south and west. They could see miles and miles of mountains, partially carpeted with trees, partially exposed rock.

"Pretty stunning, huh?" Angie said. "Now try to imagine the sun setting in the distance. Keener Flat was always my favorite campsite because of the sunsets, and now it'll always be associated with tragedy."

"Let's have a cup of coffee, and the world will look better," Gordon said.

"I wish. But the water's probably getting close to ready now."

Several minutes later, the first pot of coffee was ready, and Gordon and Angie each had a cup in hand. She drank it black, as did he, and for a few minutes, their moods improved. Soon the others were out, and Angie was making eggs with bacon and sliced melon. The group was more subdued than usual, and when all had been served, Angie called for their attention.

"I don't want to make anyone eat and run, but we have to get an early start today. We don't know what damage the storm may have done to the trail up ahead, so we have to allow ourselves some time."

"What about Bill?" Shirley called out.

"Bill will be about an hour behind us, and if I know him, he'll take a ten-minute lunch break and ride hard. I'd expect him to reach Sunrise Lake soon after we do, if he doesn't catch up with us earlier."

Without the normal morning banter, they finished breakfast, took down the tents, and had the horses saddled and packed quickly. By 8:40, they were ready to go. The sun hadn't yet risen high enough over the mountain to take the flat out of shadow, but almost all the vista below it was now illuminated.

"Eight hundred feet down," Angie said, pointing to the edge of the trail. "Keep your horses calm, and they'll stick to the trail. In less than an hour, we'll go through a gap and come into a beautiful alpine valley. No more white-knuckle riding after that."

No one said anything, but a sense of relief began to pervade the group. As they mounted their horses, they became aware of a buzzing sound, like a loud insect, but off in the distance. They looked back down the trail, in the direction they had come. In a minute, a helicopter flew over the mountains from their left, followed by another, then a third. The sound of their engines became more distinct.

The search for Tyler was underway in earnest.

I DON'T MIND SAYING that I was mighty glad when we got over the gap in the mountains and away from the Keener Flat trail. My personal opinion is that if God had wanted a trail carved into the side of that nearly vertical mountain, He would have put it there Himself, instead of leaving the job to whatever government agency built it way back when. And I have my doubts that God would have wanted people to ride that trail on horseback, thereby getting a more elevated and comprehensive view of the potential fall to perdition hundreds of feet below. Emily tried riding again, and without the wind and rain, and by looking to her right the whole time, was able to make it to the gap without imploding.

We rode downhill on a wider trail with a lesser grade. It took us along a brush-lined creek that apparently spilled out from a small lake above and to our right, then through a small but stunning valley, where the green grass glistened with residual drops from yesterday's storm, and the air felt as clean and fresh as if the earth had just been created at sunrise. With Bill gone for the day, Angie had asked me to ride at the rear and count the group from time to time, which I was happy to do. If I didn't know better, I'd think she felt we bonded during the search of the forest last night. In any event, on a clear day like this, with no distractions, it was easy work and I was happy to oblige.

As the riding became more routine, I gave free rein to my thoughts, especially as they had to do with Eve Bredon's visit to the tent last night. I can't help but feel that she would have preferred that I not be there for her conversation with Gordon, but I wouldn't have left, even if asked directly. And I'm pretty sure that Gordon would have backed me up on that. Two sets of eyes and ears are usually better than one, and I think I heard a couple of things during the tent talk that Gordon may not have picked up on. I'll know more when we get a chance to talk by ourselves.

When Eve mentioned the name Nick Moretti, a little bell went off in the back of my head. It wasn't about Moretti himself, but of something his name reminded me of. Whatever it was, it wasn't coming to me earlier this morning, but once we got off that death-defying trail, it hit me pretty quickly.

At lunch the day before, the last time we saw Tyler, he and Mason were having a discussion with Brandi absent. At the end, Mason barked out a few words I couldn't understand, and Tyler went white as a sheet. The only thing I could make out in what Mason was saying was that the last word or syllable sounded like "Letty."

Could it be that instead of "Letty," Mason had said "Moretti?" If so, that might have accounted for Tyler's reaction, and it would raise some questions worth pursuing further. For starters, what do those brothers have on each other, and is Mason in some way connected with Moretti himself?

There being no way of following that thread at the moment, I turned to the other issue raised by Miss Bredon's tent call.

I didn't twig to it immediately, but before I fell asleep, I remembered quite clearly that Eve had said Moretti was the primary beneficiary of Tyler's life insurance policy. Our agency doesn't do life insurance, but in the course of learning the business, I couldn't help but pick up a few things about it. The typical life insurance policy has only one beneficiary, but it's perfectly legit to have more than one beneficiary and to divide the amount of the policy between the two, equally or in shares.

The fact that Eve identified Moretti as the primary beneficiary not only suggested her bona fides for being in the insurance business, but it also meant that there was probably a secondary beneficiary on the policy as well. And if the primary beneficiary's share of the benefit is a cool two million, I'm guessing the secondary beneficiary's share is probably nothing to sneeze at.

All of which means that with Tyler missing, and the outlook for his return not so good, it would behoove us to find out as soon as possible who that secondary beneficiary might be.

We rode on throughout the morning, most of us probably not giving the scenery the attention or appreciation it deserved. At noon, we came down from a slight ridge and stopped for lunch at a small lake — more of a large pond, really. It looked stagnant and choked with weeds and fallen logs, and Angie told us it was called Gnat Lake. Fortunately, the critters from whom the lake took its name were not in evidence. There was a large, mostly flat shoreline on the side of the lake nearest the trail, and Gordon and I went to the far end of it, where we could talk without being overheard.

I brought up my two points and was secretly pleased to see that he hadn't noticed either of them and that he thought they might amount to something.

"We can get Eve aside tonight and find out about the insurance policy," he said, "and we probably need to try to get at Mason about what he said to his brother at lunch yesterday. Considering the disappearance immediately afterward, it could be really important."

"That's what I thought, but how do we approach him?"

"I don't know, and we shouldn't do it until we have a plan. We can think about the plan during this afternoon's ride."

I nodded assent.

"That was a good catch about the secondary beneficiary," he continued. "I'm glad you're here, because I never would have thought of that."

"Insurance is my business," I said. "It's easy when you know how."

THE AFTERNOON RIDE, to the extent that anyone in the party noticed it, took them through impressive scenery. The rain had scoured any hint of haze or particulate matter from the sky, and whenever there was a vista to be seen, it was clear and sharp. The vegetation, from the trees to the grass, gave off a potent fragrance. There were puddles and a few muddy patches on the trail, but by and large it had dried quickly. In the early afternoon a gaggle of puffy white cumulus clouds moved in from the west. They held no rain, but occasionally darkened the sky as they passed briefly in front of the sun. By midafternoon those fleeting periods of darkness were welcomed, as the temperature had risen to the high 80s, the heat alleviated somewhat by the bone-dry air.

For an hour after lunch, they rode through a basin of small, glacially carved lakes, each of them exquisite in its own way. On Sunday night, the lakes had looked like a high point of the trip, but now no one was in the mood to pause and enjoy them. Shortly after two, the group passed the last lake and began another ascent up a trail cut into the mountainside, but this one was wider, and the drop-off gentler. It led them to McPherson Pass, where they crossed over to the eastern slope of the Sierra after nearly four days on the west side.

From the top of the pass they could see, not too far below, a lake that sat in a bowl gouged out of the side of the mountain by a glacier eons ago. It was Sunrise Lake, where they would be camping that night. The clouds above were reflected off its blue-green waters, and the southeastern shore presented a large, flat area suitable for camping. Beyond and below the lake, they could see desert and more mountain ranges stretching a hundred miles, well into Nevada.

They were on the lake by 2:45, and most of the camp had been set up 20 minutes later, when they were hailed by a strange voice. Looking up, they saw a solitary hiker approaching from the direction in which they were heading. As the figure drew nearer, they saw it was a woman in her late twenties or early thirties.

She walked up to where Angie, Gordon, Sam, Shirley and Eve were setting up the cooking equipment and chairs and tables.

"I'm glad to see you here," the young woman said. "My name's Jessica Paisley. I'm hoping you can give me some help."

"Sure," Angie said. "What do you need?"

"You've come from the other direction. Can you tell me if it's possible to get over the pass and to the lakes on the other side before five o'clock? It looks like it on the map, but you can never be sure."

"You should be at the first lake by 4:30," Angie said. "It's not that far, and once you get over the pass, it's mostly downhill."

"How's the trail?"

"Pretty good, considering the storm we had yesterday. I expect you got caught in that."

"It was terrifying." She paused. "But exciting, too."

"So are you coming from Donovan's Station?" Gordon asked.

"I left there Monday. I stopped overnight, just to get a shower and a night in a bed for a change."

"Sounds like you've had a long trip," Shirley said.

Jessica smiled. "A long trip and a wonderful trip. I've always wanted to hike the Pacific Rim Trail, and ever since I got out of college, I've been saving my pennies to do it. Not easy when you work for Friends of the Rivers. They do big work, but they don't pay big salaries, which is all right. I lived with three other women in a two-bedroom apartment in Oakland for three years and finally had enough put aside to do this."

"You're going north to south?" Sam said.

She nodded. "I started near Mt. Shasta just after the Fourth of July, and a friend will be picking me up at Blanchard Meadows on Monday. Next year the plan is to come up to Blanchard Meadows after the Fourth of July and walk to the southern end."

"And you're doing this yourself?" Eve said. "Aren't you a bit concerned about traveling alone?"

"Not really. I can take care of myself, and I figure I'm probably safer here than in Oakland. And no one else I know wanted to do a trip like this badly enough to save the money or arrange the time off. If I waited for someone else to join me, the time might go by too fast, and I'd be too old or too tied down to do the hike."

"Well, good for you," Shirley said. "There are a couple of things like that I wanted to do when I was your age, but I never did. They'll be lasting regrets."

"Just what I don't want."

"If you want to throw down your sleeping bag and camp with us tonight, you're welcome," Angie said. "We're one short as it is and could even deal you in for dinner."

"That's very kind of you, but if I can make the lakes while there's still enough light to set up camp, I think I'll keep going."

She hitched up her pack on her shoulders, drove her walking stick into the ground, and started up the trail toward the pass. They all watched her go, including Mason, who had come in halfway through the conversation.

"Man," he said to Gordon after she was out of sight, "did I hear right that she saved for three years to take this trip with just herself and a backpack."

"That was the gist of it," Gordon said.

Mason shook his head. "I don't know about that. This has been a nice trip, I mean, except for Tyler, but I don't know that I would have put three years of effort into taking it. And I don't think I'd do it for two months either. The trees would all start to look alike after that long."

Gordon hesitated before replying, "Well, to each his own. Or her own."

THERE ARE CERTAIN LAKES that, to a discerning angler, simply look like good fishing lakes. Sunrise Lake was such a body of water, and Gordon was nothing if not a discerning angler. With time on his hands once camp was set up, he had an excellent opportunity to wet a line and perhaps catch his first Golden Trout, but his heart wasn't in it at all. The only thing he could think was that he had flubbed his assignment.

He could tell himself, with some justification, that yesterday's storm had been of such astounding magnitude that even Bill and Angie, who were used to doing it, couldn't keep an eye on everyone and had let Tyler disappear. But in his own mind, the justification wouldn't wash. He had specifically been asked to keep an eye on two people who might be in jeopardy and had allowed himself to be distracted at the critical moment.

What, then, could he do at this point? Aside from hoping against hope that Tyler would turn up safe and sound, his mission had to be to figure out what had happened and why, and to see to it that if someone in the pack group was responsible for what happened to Tyler, that person was identified and faced consequences.

He was sitting on a large boulder planning a course of investigation and was so engrossed in his thoughts that he scarcely noticed three trout rising in the lake 40 to 50 feet from shore — an easy cast for him. He was still thinking when he became aware of a buzzing sound in the background. It took him a second to realize it was the same sound he had heard this morning when the search helicopters had flown over the mountain south of Keener Flat. The boulder was nearly flat, and he stood up and looked toward McPherson Pass, straining his eyes.

A helicopter flew over the gap, barely a couple of hundred feet above the ground, and began a descent toward the lake.

Hardly daring to hope, he half-jogged back to the camp, some 50 yards away. The other campers were all clustering near the campfire pit watching it as well.

The area where they had pitched camp was on the southeastern shore of the lake, but the relatively flat shoreline extended considerably beyond it, going a third of the way around the lake toward the mountain and the trail down which they had come. The pilot veered to his left and flew over the lake, then turned back and aimed for a landing spot 150 yards away and closer to the mountains. The helicopter's engine noise was making the horses restive, but was far enough away that it did no worse.

It landed soft and sure on a sandy-grassy stretch of beach near the mountainside, with the pilot's side facing the camp and the exit door facing away from it. It sat there for several seconds, and hardly anyone in the camp was breathing.

A man jumped out the side door, followed by a woman, but the body of the helicopter shielded them from view, save for their legs.

As one, the campers began advancing along the lake shore toward the helicopter.

Head ducked down, a man came around the back of the copter. For an instant Gordon thought it might be Tyler, but then the man got clear of the whirling blades overhead and stood up. He was taller and more muscular than Tyler, obviously a member of the sheriff's search and rescue team.

The woman coming behind him, however, was definitely Brandi.

She moved forward until she was a good 20 feet outside the radius of the helicopter's blades, then stood up, looked back at the deputy, and waved to him. He waved back, circled around the rear of the copter and got back in. It took off straight up, then looped toward the campsite before turning around, gaining altitude and heading back over the pass.

The group and Brandi advanced toward each other, meeting in the middle of the flat area. There was an awkward silence when they did, as no one knew how to ask the question, and Brandi finally broke the silence herself.

"They searched out from the center of the forest for five hours and found nothing," she said. "Nothing at all.

The captain of the search party said it was as if Tyler never existed."

She was on the verge of tears, and Shirley stepped forward and embraced her with a warm hug. The thought flashed across Gordon's mind that it was exactly what Elizabeth, his fiancée, would have done.

A minute later, Brandi got her composure back somewhat and continued.

"They're going to start looking backward along the trail from the forest. The captain said there's a slight chance he got lost earlier, then lost the horse, and it kept going to the forest. I don't think he was very hopeful, but it's the best they can do."

"You poor thing," Shirley said. "But why did you come back here?"

"They offered to fly me either to Mastodon Valley or back to our camp. I don't know anyone in Mastodon Valley, so there was no point going there without Tyler."

She looked up at the assembled group.

"But you guys have gotten to be like family in the few days we've been together. I decided I wanted to be with you. And to finish out the trip the way Tyler would have wanted. It was an easy call."

AS SOON AS HE COULD break free from Brandi, Gordon stepped back, his mind racing. The fact that Tyler — or, more likely, his body — had not been found was puzzling. It was, he reasoned, barely possible that in the chaos of the storm the previous afternoon, another member of the party could have moved off the trail with Tyler and quickly dispatched the young heir. Barely possible, but highly unlikely, and there certainly would have been no time to conceal the body effectively.

What else could have happened, then? He briefly considered the idea that someone could have been waiting in ambush to abduct and kill Tyler, but that line of reasoning didn't go too far either. Absent the storm, which no one could have counted on days in advance, any such attempt would surely have been noticed.

Another explanation — and still an unsatisfactory one — was that Tyler had briefly left the group, perhaps to pee or look at something, and had become disoriented.

But he couldn't have ventured far in that storm, and Bill and Angie had been very clear in the opening night talk that if anyone got separated from the group, the thing to do was wait by the trail until they were found. Even Tyler should have been capable of that, Gordon thought. And if he had somehow been injured and unable to get back to the trail, he surely would have heard the search party and been able to call for help.

Unless he was beyond speech and recognition.

And, finally, there was the question of why Brandi had come back to the expedition, rather than returning to civilization when the search had turned up empty. And was it merely coincidence that she and Mason had both said they wanted to continue the trip because it was what Tyler would have wanted?

That was as far as Gordon's reasoning had progressed when he looked up and saw a lone figure coming up the trail toward the campsite. For a second, he thought it was Bill, then realized there was no horse and the figure was coming from the wrong direction to be Bill. Gordon moved back toward the group as the hiker approached.

The hiker turned out to be a man in his early to mid-thirties, just under six feet tall, with shoulder-length dingy brown hair, oily from being unwashed, protruding from beneath a well-worn felt hat. He sported a goatee, but the rest of his face hadn't seen a razor in days. His eyes were set together, which accentuated the power of their glare, and his mouth was slightly turned down, suggesting a hint of disgust or cruelty. It is a given that no one looks his best after a few days on the trail, but this man, even allowing for that truth, conveyed a sense of being, at very least, more menacing than average. His backpack was monogrammed "R.L." and from his left side hung a sheathed knife with a blade that was probably 10 to 12 inches long.

"Good afternoon," he said, as if he didn't quite believe it.

"Hello," Angie replied.

"Can you tell me something? Do you think I can get to the lakes on the other side of McPherson Pass by six o'clock?"

Gordon looked at Angie, and she looked at him. He thought they were both thinking the same thing: Do we really want to send this guy on to the lakes, where the woman we met an hour ago might be camping by herself tonight? And if not, what do we say?

The silence between the question and answer went on a little too long, and Mason broke it by saying:

"Sure. No problem. You should be able to make it in an hour or so."

"Thanks," the hiker said. "Good to know. In that case, I'll just wash my face in the lake and start over the pass." He took a step away from them, then turned back. "By the way, you wouldn't know if anybody else is camping at the lakes tonight, would you?"

"As a matter of fact," Angie said, "a group from Blanchard Meadows is expected there tonight. But there's plenty of room, and you should be able to find a place as close or as far away from them as you like to pitch your tent."

"I don't carry a tent," he said. "I like to sleep under the stars in just my sleeping bag. That way I can pick it up and go whenever I need to."

He turned away again, and Gordon barked after him.

"Excuse our manners, but we haven't been introduced. I'm Quill Gordon, this is Angie Hodges, Mason Linfield and Sam Akers. What's your name?"

After hesitating longer than necessary to answer the question, the hiker replied, "Randy Larson."

"Randy Larson," Gordon repeated. "An easy name to remember. A pleasure meeting you, Randy."

The hiker grunted, moved on to the lake, took off the bandana that was around his neck, dipped it in the water, washed his face, dipped it again, and put it back around his neck. Then he started up the pass. When he was out of earshot, Gordon turned to Angie.

"Is there really going to be another group staying at the lakes tonight?"

"Not that I know of," she said, "but it was the best I could come up with on short notice."

"Is there some problem?" Mason said.

"Probably not," Angie said, "but I'd rather not have sent him on to the lakes where that woman may be camping by herself tonight. I didn't like his looks."

Mason shrugged. "I know a lot of guys in San Francisco that look like that. They're pretty harmless."

Shirley, who had been back by her tent, approached the group.

"Who was that fellow who was just here?"

"Randy Larson," Gordon said. "Or at least that's the official version."

"I don't know," she said. "He spooked me. He looks kind of like Charles Manson."

"Who's Charles Manson?" Mason asked.

ONCE THE PARADE OF PEOPLE coming and going slowed up, Gordon, Eve and I retreated to the rock where Gordon had been moping earlier. It was far enough away from the campsite that we likely wouldn't be bothered, and the sun was still shining on it.

"It's not looking very good, is it?" Eve said, by way of opening the conversation.

No one contradicted her.

"Unless you're Nick Moretti," she went on. "He stands to collect a cool two million."

"Money he'd have gotten in a month or so, anyway," Gordon said. "Not meaning to be ghoulish, but could he collect if there's no body?"

"There would have to be a death certificate, and you can bet that the best lawyers in San Francisco will be making an argument for one to some judge."

I cleared my throat.

"Speaking of Moretti," I said, "Something happened yesterday that may bear a closer look."

I had their attention, so I plowed forward.

"At lunch yesterday, just before the storm hit and we were riding again, Mason and Tyler had some words while Brandi was temporarily away. We weren't close enough to hear, but at the end, Mason said something that sounded to me like 'Letty.' I'm wondering now if instead of 'Letty,' he said Moretti."

"That's right," Gordon said. "And whatever it was, it spooked Tyler."

"You could be onto something," Eve said. "Knowing you owe serious money to Nick Moretti should be enough to spook anyone."

"But what would Mason have been saying?" I said. "Do you think he's working for Moretti?"

Eve shook her head. "Anything's possible, but I can't see Moretti hiring a druggie to do any serious work for him. And it's not like Mason needs money from Moretti or anyone else, considering what he'll collect at the end of September."

"I agree with you that Mason isn't anyone's idea of the most reliable independent contractor," Gordon said, "but there may be a little something to what Sam said. If Moretti somehow heard about this trip — and with the money Tyler owes him, he probably has feelers out — he might think it wouldn't be a bad idea to have a set of eyes and ears along on his behalf. Maybe he outfitted Mason for this trip, if you catch my drift, in exchange for having someone keeping an eye on his client and reporting back."

"That's more plausible than thinking he was actually hired to do anything," Eve said. "But if that's the case, why would he mention Moretti's name to Tyler?"

"Ignorant impulse," Gordon said. "Damn. I wish we'd heard a little more of that conversation."

"Too late now," I said, "but this line of thinking leads to another question, doesn't it? If Mason wasn't working for Moretti, how would he know about him? I mean, we didn't know, did we, Gordon?"

He shook his head. "And I'm sure McCabe would have said something if he knew," Gordon said. "What do you two think about the possibility that Mason is in cahoots with Moretti?"

Eve went first, after a long pause.

"I'd say there's maybe a one in three chance he's in at a low level like you suggested, Gordon. That's as far as I'd go."

"I'm pretty dubious about going that far," I said. "But I can't rule it out."

"This raises another interesting question, though," Gordon said. "It would make sense for Moretti to have a mole on this trip. If not Mason, who?"

We looked at each other suspiciously.

"I'd go with you, Gordon," Eve said. "You're the kind of reliable and resourceful guy Moretti would put on the payroll."

"Interesting," Gordon said, looking her in the eye. "I was going to suggest you. You've been poking around the whole trip, and it might be that you're not doing it for C&A Insurance — or not exclusively for them anyway."

There was a bit of tension in the thin mountain air, and it was still there when the two of them turned as one to me.

"How about you, Sam?" Eve said.

I considered for a couple of seconds, then pontificated.

"I'd go with Emily Reed," I said. I could tell that caught them both by surprise, so I added, "Because she's the least likely."

That broke the ice a bit, and everyone laughed. Then Eve stood up.

"It looks as if Bill's riding in. Time for us to get back to camp, I guess."

So we headed back, and it wasn't until 15 minutes later that I realized we hadn't gotten to my question about the secondary beneficiary on Tyler's life insurance policy.

BILL WAS SURPRISED to see Brandi in the camp and was clearly unhappy that no sign of Tyler had been found, though he said the news wasn't entirely unexpected.

"Brandi and I did a bit of looking around this morning and called for him. Nothing. What I can't understand is what hazard might have caught him up. There aren't any big rivers, glacial crevasses, or even high cliffs to fall from. Well, unless you consider the trail to Keener Flat, but I was looking below as we rode down this morning, and there was no sign of him."

"It's a puzzler, all right," Gordon said. "If he just got lost, he should have been able to get back to the trail and sit tight until help came."

"It's almost as if a UFO came down and made off with him," Mason said.

"That's not funny, Mason," Brandi snapped.

"I wasn't trying to be funny. This whole thing is weird, and that's what I was trying to get across."

"Well, keep it to yourself."

There followed an awkward silence, which Gordon broke by changing the subject.

"On your way here from the lakes, Bill, did you see anyone going the other direction?"

Bill nodded. "Two people. A young woman by herself, and less than an hour later, a man by himself." He paused. "Almost a Charles Manson look-alike. Pretty creepy. I was glad to get him well behind me."

Emily, Shirley and Nora had been helping Angie get the dinner ready, and Bill went into his tent to set up the shortwave radio and contact Blanchard Meadows. Gordon and Sam, meanwhile, walked down the lake to get out of earshot of the campsite.

"What are your plans for tonight?" Gordon said to Sam.

"I wasn't exactly making them. It's not like I can go to dinner and a show here."

"I know that. But there's something that needs doing, and it's a job for you or Eve. I'd rather you did it."

"You don't trust her?"

Gordon paused for a few seconds.

"I'm trusting her for now, but I don't want to bet too much on that trust just yet."

"What did you have in mind?"

"I think we need to pick Brandi's brain about Mason and Tyler. What she's seen of the relationship and the tension between the two of them. You seemed to hit it off with her the night before last, so it would make sense for you to approach her now."

"I don't know, Gordon. Talking to her once was OK. If I keep doing it, I'm afraid it'll come across as a sicko."

"You're the least sicko person I know, Sam. Look for a natural opening and don't push it. And if the opportunity doesn't arise tonight, try tomorrow. Do what you can."

"I'll do what I can, but don't expect too much."

Dinner that Thursday night was grilled teriyaki chicken breast with saffron rice and zucchini topped with seasoned salt and a dash of Parmesan cheese, with biscuits on the side. Though Tyler's disappearance still cast a pall over the excursion, Brandi's return had pumped a bit of energy back into the group, and a decent, if occasionally flagging, conversation was maintained during the meal.

Afterward, the group split up by gender, with the women moving down the lake in one direction and the men in the other for a swim/bathe in the lake. There had been nowhere to wash up at Keener Flat, so everyone welcomed this opportunity. Cleaner and in better spirits, they gathered around the campfire at 7:30. The sun was behind the mountains in the west, but the last half hour of light still remained in the sky.

Bill opened the campfire session with a report on his radio conversation.

"I'm told the search and rescue people are stumped," he said. "They can't figure how Tyler could have vanished so completely. But they're not giving up. The sheriff will send two helicopters out tomorrow. Forest Service begged off on a second day. They'll work all the way back to where we had lunch yesterday."

"Is there really any hope of finding him?" Shirley asked.

"If anyone can do it," Bill said, "they can."

No one responded to that, and Angie jumped in to break the silence.

"Bill and I talked about it a bit after dinner, and decided to put it to the group whether or not you want to continue the campfire introductions, where we talk about ourselves. What do you say — yes or no?"

They looked at each other, no one willing to go first.

"How about you, Brandi?" Angie said. "What's your feeling?"

"I hadn't thought about it." She paused. "But if it's all right with the rest of you, I would like to get to know more about the people here."

"Let's do it, then," Shirley said.

"All right," Angie said. "Eve, you spoke the first night, so pick two names out of the hat." She held an old baseball cap over Eve's head, and Eve pulled two pieces of paper from it.

"Gordon and Shirley," she said.

"I WAS BORN AND RAISED in San Francisco," Gordon said. "Went to St. John Bosco High School and then got a basketball scholarship to Cal. I can't seem to get away from the Bay Area, not that I want to."

He went on to explain how, after graduation, he had landed at an old-line stock brokerage on Montgomery Street and had had a good career. He left out the part about having gotten into the market himself in 1982, right at the beginning of its big rise, and having made enough money therefrom that he didn't need to work again. Instead he said vaguely that he had gone out on his own, managing portfolios for a small group of select clients (including himself) in order to get a bit more freedom and spare time.

"I was put onto this trip by an acquaintance, who knew of it and knew of my love of fly fishing. He said it would be a good opportunity to fish for Golden Trout, California's state fish. This trip is also my last bachelor outing with my friend Sam. On Labor Day weekend, I'm going to be marrying a wonderful woman named Elizabeth, who teaches English at City College. I took my time getting married, but she's worth the wait, and Sam's going to be best man at the wedding.

"I guess that's about it. I'll turn it over to Shirley now."

She stood up and looked over the group around the campfire.

"I have one question for you, Gordon," she said. "What did you major in at Cal?"

"U.S. History, with a minor in English."

"Thank you. The teacher in me wanted to know about your academics, in addition to your athletics."

She began to talk about herself with the calm confidence of someone who has stood in front of countless classes filled with students whose attention had to be earned. She had graduated from San Jose State, gotten into teaching, married a man named Lou, set the teaching career aside while they raised two children, Bob and Alice, both of whom are married and successful in business, though a bit laggard about producing grandchildren. As the children grew older, she went back to teaching at junior high school level.

"After two years, I made a deal with the principal," she said. "I told her I'd teach seventh-graders, because they're still young enough to be interested and polite, and I'd teach ninth-graders, because they were beginning to get mature and could absorb a handful of advanced concepts. But no way was I going to teach eighth-graders. They were in between and impossible to deal with. Once we reached that understanding, I had a happy end of career.

"I retired at 62 so Lou and I could travel and, we hoped, help with grandkids. Three years later, Lou was diagnosed with pancreatic cancer and died four months after the diagnosis. It was too soon, but we had those three years, and I'll never forget them. And I never would have had that time with him if I'd worked all the way to 65.

"So if I could offer one bit of advice to the youngsters — and that's all of you — don't put off doing what you really want to do. Life is short, and if you wait too long, the chance could be gone forever."

It was completely dark now, though the full moon had risen far enough to cast its light on the lake. No one said anything, and her final words trailed off into the stillness of the mountain light.

The silence that followed her talk continued for a full minute before being broken by the sound of approaching footsteps. Looking up, they could make out a human figure coming their direction along the shore of the lake, moving like a gliding apparition. Instinctively, they stood up, and as it drew closer they parted to allow it to get in the range of the light cast by the campfire.

It was Jessica Paisley, the young woman who had stopped by their campsite that afternoon.

"Is the offer to bunk with you guys still good?" she asked. "There's a bit of a problem up ahead."

"It wouldn't be another lone camper, would it?" Gordon said.

She nodded. "He's been way too attentive, and he was freaking me out. When it got to be dusk, I slipped out as quick as I could and headed back here. Thank God for the full moon the last part of the trip."

"Of course you can stay with us," Bill said. "But doesn't it bother you being up here all by yourself?"

"I have a gun in my pack, and I'm willing to use it. The problem is, this guy was making me think about using it, and I'd rather not."

"Good call getting away from him," Angie said. "You'll be safe here."

"I'm in a tent by myself," Brandi said. "You can sleep with me." She looked at Bill and Angie. "If that's all right.:

They nodded.

"I'll take you over," Brandi said to Jessica. "Good night everybody."

With low-key good nights, the group slowly broke up. Gordon stayed until the others, except for Sam, were gone, then approached Bill and Angie.

"We need to talk," Gordon said. "I'm afraid she might still be in danger."

"You think he'd follow her here?" Bill asked.

"I wouldn't be surprised," Angie said. "He looked like a stalker, and that type doesn't give up easily."

"I'm with Angie," Gordon said. "Maybe — probably — nothing will happen, but I think there's enough chance of it that we should keep a watch tonight."

Bill ran his hands through his hair.

"Man, I really don't feel like it, but it needs to be done. All right."

"Gordon and I can do it," Sam said.

"I'm co-leader of the trip," Bill said. "I need to step up."

"You've had a rougher day than any of the rest of us," Gordon said. "Why don't I take it from 10 to 3, then you pick up after that."

"Well, I don't know."

"Don't be a martyr, Bill," Angie said. "Gordon's right. Get some sleep and take the second shift."

After a bit of grumbling, Bill agreed to that, and went to turn in. Angie left, too, after dousing the last of the campfire. Gordon and Sam remained by it as it hissed and smoked.

"Sorry, Sam," Gordon said, "but one of us is going to need to get a good night's sleep tonight. Stay fresh so you can help with the investigation tomorrow."

"All right. If that's the way it is."

"Oh, and Sam: One more thing."

"Yes?"

"I just saw Brandi head down toward the lake by herself. This could be your chance."

IT'S NOT EASY FOR A MAN of 41 to approach a woman nearly half his age without looking ridiculous. I was keenly aware of this as I walked down to where Brandi was sitting by the lake. Along the way I turned over several possible opening lines in my head, and each one sounded dumber than the one before.

In the end, I opted for bogus concern.

"Are you all right, Brandi? We saw you coming down here by yourself, and wanted to be sure nothing was wrong."

She looked up at me. Although the moon was full, I couldn't see the details of her face, but thought I detected a bit of a smile.

"That's sweet," she said. "No, I just wanted to give Jessica a little time to get set up in the tent."

"Nothing more than that?" I said softly.

She didn't answer right away, and when she did, there was a bit of a quaver in her voice.

"All right, I was thinking about Tyler, too."

"How could you not? It's obvious you two mean a lot to each other."

"Maybe you should have said 'meant.' You should have seen the search team looking for him today. If those guys couldn't find him ..."

"They're going out again tomorrow. That means there's still hope."

"I have to tell myself that. But I'm not sure I believe it."

"Do you have any idea what might have happened? How he got separated from the group?"

"I didn't, but now that Jessica is here, I wonder ... No, it couldn't be."

"What couldn't be?"

"Maybe the man she's running from got Tyler. Maybe he's coming after the rest of us."

"I wouldn't worry too much about that. We're going to be keeping a watch tonight. No one's going to sneak up on the campsite. And the man Jessica's worried about couldn't have done anything to Tyler. He was coming from the opposite direction."

"He could have doubled back."

"I suppose, but probably not." We sat, looking at the reflection of the moon on the lake for a minute.

"Could I ask you another question, Brandi? And if I'm out of line, just say so."

She seemed to nod, so I went on.

"Yesterday, at lunch, which was the last time we saw Tyler, something happened at the end. I'm wondering if you might be able to explain it."

"I could try."

"It was when you were away at the end of the lunch break, and it was just Mason and Tyler together. Mason said something to Tyler, and I could just hear the last word, but whatever it was, Tyler was shaken up by it. Gordon and I commented on it at the time."

"Do you know what he said?"

"Like I said, I only heard the last word, but it sounded like an Italian name. Canetti or Moretti or something like that."

She drew her breath in sharply. Bull's eye.

"Oh my God."

"That means something?"

"It does, and it doesn't. Tyler owes some money to a man named Moretti. I don't know all the details, but he told me it was taken care of and that he would pay it off when he comes into the inheritance."

"That might explain things. But it was Mason who said the name. Is there any way he would have known about it?"

"Tyler wouldn't have told him. They weren't on good terms."

"That's too bad. You hate to see brothers — especially twins — on the outs."

"They've been on the outs almost from the beginning. They just have really different personalities.

For all I know, Mason was pushing Tyler around even in the womb. It wouldn't surprise me."

"But Mason wouldn't have known about Moretti, whoever he is."

"Actually, he might."

"But how, if Tyler didn't tell him."

"Tyler didn't tell him, but I just remembered I did. It didn't seem like such a big deal at the time."

"It may not be a big deal now."

"Sunday afternoon, just before dinner, Mason took me aside and asked me what was bothering Tyler. I told him about Tyler owing money to Moretti because I figured it was taken care of and I didn't want Mason worrying. Do you think I did the right thing?"

"That judgment's above my pay grade," I said, "but under the circumstances, it seems like a reasonable thing to have done. And it's done, so let it go."

We looked out at the lake and up at the moon for a couple of minutes. A pity we were both too apprehensive to enjoy it as well as we should have. Finally she stood up.

"I'm going back now. Thanks for asking about me."

"No problem. And try to get a good night's sleep. No one's going to come around tonight and murder us in our sleeping bags."

I couldn't entirely see her face in the light of the full moon, but it seemed as if a quick smile flashed across it.

"They'd better not," she said. "I'm counting on you."

FOR THE FIRST 15 MINUTES of his watch, Gordon sat in one of the camp chairs by the fire pit. Looking up at the sky, he found himself wishing that the trip had been two weeks earlier, when the Perseid meteor showers were at their peak and there had been a new moon. The full moon lit up the night sky enough to dim the effect of the stars, but they were still impressive.

About the time he saw his first shooting star of the night, it occurred to Gordon that sitting in the open by the fire ring might not be such a good idea. He was clearly visible by moonlight, and, if someone happened to be watching the campsite from a nearby hiding spot, Gordon would clearly be a tempting target. He decided to take cover and watch from where he couldn't so easily be seen.

In the unlikely event someone was watching, he made a show of it. He stood up, stretched and grunted, then poked the ashes with a stick for several seconds. He walked slowly to his tent, scanned the surrounding area, stretched and grunted again, and knelt by the opening, lifting the flap.

Then, in a quick, athletic move, he rolled to his right and lay flat between the tent he and Sam occupied and the Reeds' tent next to it. On his hands and knees, he crawled to the back of the tent and looked at the luminous dial of his watch. After five minutes, he figured that anyone watching the campsite would assume he was safe inside the tent.

Thirty feet behind the tent, there were several pine trees clustered together. In their shade, in his dark clothing, he should be all but invisible. To get to that shade, he had to cross 20 feet of grass and sand lit by the full moon. Picking out a tree trunk to aim for, he scuttled, crab-like, over the ground and was in its shade in a matter of seconds. Anyone watching the camp would have been uncommonly lucky to see him. He pulled the hood of his parka over his head to keep his ears warm and drew his knees up to his chest to stay warm and compact.

From the vantage point apart from the campsite, his perspective began to change. He saw it clearly as a unit and had a good view of all six tents. To keep his brain engaged and to avoid dozing off, he kept his eyes moving. At one point he thought he saw something move on the far shore of the lake and held his eyes in that direction for several minutes. Nothing more happened, and he decided it had been a trick of the light, or perhaps his mind.

Moments later, a jet flew far overhead, en route from San Francisco to some other city. He watched it go by, thinking the people in it probably couldn't have seen the campsite, even by daylight. His group really was a speck in the middle of nowhere. From time to time he could hear a slight rustle or rattle or snap as some nocturnal creature moved about nearby, but nothing that suggested any human presence. He caught himself dozing off and shook his head. It must be nearly one o'clock by now, he thought, and sneaked a look at the dial on his watch. It said 10:30. There were over four hours left on his watch.

His mind began to drift in a different direction. With everyone else presumably asleep in the tents, the humans had essentially abandoned this part of the mountains to their usual nighttime inhabitants. All alone in this setting, he began to think of the production of Shakespeare's *A Midsummer Night's Dream* that he and Elizabeth had seen in Berkeley last month. Might there be wood sprites that would start coming out now and working their magic? It was a silly thought, but it kept his mind occupied as his eyes scanned the landscape. As he did so, looking to his right toward the boulders down shore along the lake, he saw a movement and heard a slight, indistinct noise.

His body tensed.

That's no wood sprite, he thought to himself.

Barely daring to breathe, he kept his eyes fixed on that spot, and a few seconds later saw another movement. Someone was emerging from the shadows and making for the campsite.

It looked like a man, but, like Gordon, the figure had his parka hood pulled over the head and it was impossible to see a face. He stopped at the first tent, seemed to take a long survey of the campsite, and began moving stealthily along the backs of the tents. When he reached the third one, he was even with Gordon, and Gordon stood up quickly and silently.

In order to follow the stalker, Gordon would have to cross the moonlit area of grass and sand, where he would be easily seen if the visitor happened to turn around. In a split second, he decided it was a chance he would have to take. He eased out of the shade and tried to follow the stalker, keeping behind the intruder and on the side of his left shoulder.

Walking gracefully and quietly, Gordon closed the gap on the stalker and watched as the figure paused between the last tent, where Nora and Eve were sleeping, and the next to last, where Brandi and Jessica were. Gordon made a split-second decision to go between the third and fourth tents in the semicircle. He crawled to the front of the fourth tent, where Angie and Shirley were sleeping, one of them snoring a bit, and poked his head around the corner just enough to see where the intruder had gone.

The man was squatting in front of the flap of Brandi and Jessica's tent, his back slightly turned toward Gordon as he fumbled with the tent flap with his left hand and drew a large knife from a sheath with his right.

Gordon sprang up and was behind the stalker in three steps. He probably hadn't been as quiet as he should have, but the intruder was so preoccupied with the tent flap, he never heard it coming. As he reached the man, Gordon dropped to his knees, brought his left hand down hard on the stalker's left shoulder, and grabbed his right wrist with his right hand.

The intruder let out a blood-curdling scream, dropped the knife, and turned to look at Gordon. They locked eyes for several seconds before Gordon spoke.

"Tyler. Welcome back. Your horse is waiting."

TYLER'S SCREAM woke up just about everyone, and people began to emerge from their tents — some quickly, some slowly. Once Tyler had recovered from the shock of being surprised by Gordon, he began to shout excitedly.

"Someone's in there with Brandi! I saw you go in, Mason."

Gordon looked over his shoulder. Mason wasn't among those who had come out of the tents, and he wondered if he'd missed something.

"Come out, both of you," Tyler shouted.

"Get a grip, Tyler," Brandi shouted from inside the tent.

"Who's in there with you?" Tyler shouted.

The tent flap was unzipped from inside. Jessica stuck her head out.

"Just me."

Tyler's mouth moved for several seconds, but no words came out. Finally, he said, "Who — who are you?"

"Someone who just joined the group," Gordon said.

He turned and looked at the others.

"I was keeping watch tonight, because Bill and Angie were concerned about the guy who followed

Jessica to the lakes. I saw someone come from the far shore to the tents and moved in behind him. When I saw he had a knife, I was sure it was our Charles Manson look-alike."

He turned to Tyler.

"I really wasn't expecting you, but I think we're all glad to see you back."

There was a buzz among the others, and Shirley finally spoke above the noise.

"Let me tell you something, young man. When you go calling on a lady at this hour of the night, she isn't going to appreciate your arriving with a knife."

I WAS ONE OF THE FIRST ones out of the tent — nerves, I guess — and it was interesting (though irrelevant to the story at hand) to note the variety of sleeping attire represented by the others.

Tyler was semi-hysterical and barely coherent. When pressed, the story he told about how he had become separated from the group and found his way back was spellbinding and fascinating. I believed about 10 percent of it and figured that was probably giving him the benefit of the doubt. In the end, Bill gave Tyler a sleeping pill and announced that in view of his ordeal, we'd let him sleep as late as he wanted tomorrow. I was very much looking forward to hearing what Gordon has to say about his story.

But now I was back in the tent, trying to fall asleep for the second time tonight. I had just gotten into a comfortable position, curled up in the sleeping bag, and was beginning to drift off when I heard a rustling at the tent flap, and Eve Bredon slithered in, flashlight in hand. She looked at Gordon's empty sleeping bag on the left side of the tent and turned to me.

"Where's Gordon?"

"Outside somewhere, keeping watch."

"Still?"

"Apparently he and Bill and Angie had a caucus and decided there was still a chance of Jessica's stalker paying a visit. He's on duty until three."

"Maybe I'll go out and keep him company for a bit."

"I should warn you that he's utterly single-minded when duty calls. He'd pay you very little attention."

That slowed her down a bit, and she apparently decided that for company, I'd have to do.

"So what did you think of Tyler's story?"

"I thought it was pretty preposterous."

"Which part? When he claimed he took a piss before we left the forest, then his horse ran off in the other direction, and he chased it for a while, then doubled back. Then when the clouds cleared, he followed us up to Keener Flat at night and passed us because he couldn't see the camp, even with a full moon?"

"That was a good one. But his explanation for pulling the knife at the tent flap took the cookie for being lame."

"I know. He'd seen someone else on the trail and wanted to protect himself."

"In that case, why draw the knife when he got to his own tent?"

"Well, he did say he saw someone else going into it."

"I'm guessing it has something to do with Mason and Moretti, but Mason was four tents away. Why pull the knife before going into his girlfriend's tent? By the way, what happened with Jessica?"

"She's bunking with Nora and me. Good thing the tents are big enough for three. Do you really think the other guy is going to come after her?"

"I'd be surprised. But we wouldn't want her — and you and Nora — to be surprised, even if Jessica has a gun."

"Probably best to be safe." She paused. "Can I ask you a question, Sam?"

"All right, but only if I can ask you one."

"Deal. I'll go first. How did Gordon meet Elizabeth, the woman he's going to marry? And what do you think of her?"

"That's two questions."

"No it's not. It's a compound question."

"If you say so. The first part's easy. I was there when it happened. We were on a fishing trip and having dinner in a restaurant with an old friend of Gordon's, when she walked in and he introduced us."

"What was she doing way up in the mountains? I assume it was way up in the mountains."

"Teaching at the local community college. But she and Gordon started to hit it off, then she got a teaching job in San Francisco."

"And do you like her?"

"You know, I didn't at first, but I do now. She's smart, of course, and very independent and outspoken, but Gordon needs somebody who'll stand up to him. And she has a good heart."

"Can't overestimate the importance of that."

"I don't think so either. Now can I ask my question? You work for C&A Insurance. I've always wondered what C&A stands for."

"It stands for — are you ready? — Colossal and Astounding."

"You're pulling my leg."

"I'm doing nothing at all to your leg. The company was founded at the end of the 19ᵗʰ Century when everybody believed in progress and big things. But during World War I, they changed it to the initials. Hardly anyone's alive who remembers it any other way."

"It was a smart change," I finally said.

Friday August 27

Sunrise Lake to Upper Awatos Meadows

GORDON SLEPT FOUR HOURS, until 7 a.m. It wasn't enough, but it was a sound sleep, and he was ready to begin dealing with some of the ideas that had been turning over in his head during the long, solitary hours of his watch.

Breakfast that morning was served as people woke up and made their way to the stove area. It was a concession to the fact that Tyler would be sleeping in and they would be leaving later than usual. The ride that day, to Upper Awatos Meadows, on the other side of the Sierra divide, was short enough to accommodate the improvisation.

When Gordon and Sam emerged from their tent, they saw that only Eve was up and about, talking with Bill and Angie, who had fried up a mess of bacon, made pancake batter, and were ready to cook hotcakes to order.

"How hungry are you boys?" Angie asked.

"Pretty hungry," Gordon said, casting a knowing glance at Eve. "But would it be all right if we relaxed with our coffee before eating?"

"Of course."

The three of them walked down the lakeshore to the rock where they had talked the night before. Because they were on the east slope of the Sierra this morning, the rising sun had only to clear a berm by the edge of the lake to light up the rock and was about to do so. When it did, it took away the morning mountain chill.

"You must be exhausted," Eve said, "sitting up half the night."

"Not as bad as it could have been," Gordon said, taking a sip of coffee. "So just out of curiosity, was anyone else as underwhelmed by Tyler's story as I was?"

"Eve and I were talking about that last night," Sam said. "If it were a canteen, it wouldn't hold water."

"Still, we shouldn't be too hard on him," Eve said. "I'm sure he wasn't expecting Gordon to tackle him from behind, and it probably startled him so badly he didn't have time to make up anything good."

"Anyway," Sam said, "he's back now, safe and sound. We need to make sure he stays that way for another 48 hours."

"Toward that end," Gordon said, "we need to figure out what's going on. I had plenty of time to think about it last night, and there's one conclusion that's nearly inescapable: He didn't get lost, like he said. He deliberately split off from the group the day before yesterday. If that's true, he was either afraid of something or planning something."

"I think you're right that he took off," Eve said. "But if he was planning something, he would have been better prepared than to bolt with just a few snacks from the bag on his horse. So I vote for afraid."

"I may be able to offer something there," Sam said. "I talked to Brandi last night, after campfire. I mentioned hearing Mason say something that sounded like Moretti at lunch Wednesday. She thought that was possible."

"Did she say how Mason would know about Moretti?" Gordon asked.

"She told him. A couple of days earlier."

"Let's look at it from Tyler's point of view," Gordon said. "He probably thinks Mason was behind his fall into Cliff Lake on Monday, and he knows Mason probably figured out that his brother put the salami in the tent to attract the bear on Tuesday."

"You're right," Eve said. "Tyler had to be figuring the next shoe was about to drop. And Mason probably egged him on by saying something about Moretti. That could have been enough to make him take off impulsively."

"All right," Sam said. "I'm with you so far, but what made Tyler pull out the knife right before he went into what he had to believe was a tent with only Brandi in it? That doesn't make sense."

There was a moment of silence as they contemplated the play of the sunlight on the surface of the lake.

"It doesn't *seem* to make sense," Gordon said, "but it obviously made sense to Tyler. We need to figure out why, and I have a thought."

He turned to Eve.

"Your friend Nora has one of those new digital cameras, doesn't she?"

"Two or three of them, actually."

"So she doesn't have to wait for film to be developed. She can go back and look at all the pictures she's taken so far this trip on the screen on the back of the camera, right?"

"I think so. I can ask."

"Can you get her aside no later than lunch and ask her to go back through all the photos she's taken since she got to Blanchard Meadows?"

"That would be a lot of pictures. You've seen how much she shoots."

"I know. But I'm only looking for a specific set of photographs — maybe even one picture if she was lucky enough to get it."

"What are you after?" Sam said.

"Ask her," Gordon said to Eve, "to look at all the photos that have Mason, Tyler, or Brandi in them. And particularly at any pictures of Mason and Brandi together."

"I can do that," Eve said, "but what are you hoping to find in those pictures?"

"Evidence," Gordon said. "Evidence to back up my suspicion that there's more to the relationship between *Mason* and Brandi than meets the eye. And if there is — well, it might explain a few things."

AT EIGHT O'CLOCK, Bill went into his tent, switched on the shortwave radio, and gave Blanchard Meadows the good news that Tyler had turned up safe and the day's search could be called off. He emerged a happy man, because the expedition was now back on a normal footing and he would not forever hold the distinction of being the first lead guide in Blanchard's history to lose a client.

The expedition's normal footing didn't make it through breakfast, however.

Jessica emerged from the tent she had shared with Eve and Nora to say that Tyler's stealth appearance at the campsite the previous evening had so unnerved her that she was changing her plan to hike on alone to Blanchard Meadows.

"After that," she said, "I don't think I can sleep alone — at least not for the next few nights. And I don't want to head back the way I was going, when that other guy might be out there. I'd be a nervous wreck every time there was a noise in the woods, and there are a lot of noises in the woods in any case.

"So I think I'm going to turn back to Donovan's Station and call my friend from there, and say it was a great trip, even if it didn't end the way I wanted. Would you mind if I followed you on foot to the next place you're going and just slept at your campsite tomorrow? I can eat my own food and sleep outside so nobody has to share a tent with me."

Bill and Angie exchanged glances.

"Under the circumstances," Bill said, clearing his throat, "we'd be happy to have you along. Wouldn't want it on our consciences if anything happened."

"And you're certainly welcome to eat with us as one of the group," Angie said. We have plenty of food for tonight."

"And there's no need for you to sleep outside," Nora said. "You're welcome to join Eve and me again tonight."

"Really? That's very nice of you."

Everyone made an "Oh, it's nothing" murmur.

"One thing, though," Angie said. "I'm afraid you'd get too far behind us if you walk, which would defeat the purpose of joining our group. Can you ride a horse?"

"You bet. Back in civilization, I do a lot of riding on weekends."

Angie looked at Bill.

"Are you thinking what I'm thinking?" he said.

"Bella."

"Bella. That's what I was thinking, too."

Angie turned to Jessica.

"We've gone through most of our food, so we can probably redistribute some of our cargo to free up one of the pack mules for you. If you can ride a horse, you should be able to handle a mule. I was thinking of Bella. She's very gentle."

"But do you have a saddle?"

"We always bring a spare. It may not be your style, but it'll get you there, and our ride today is one of the shorter ones."

"Well thank you. Thank you very much. I feel so much better now."

Gordon and Sam had been watching the conversation without comment, and when it was over, Gordon made a head gesture in the direction away from the camp. They went down the lakeshore far enough to get out of earshot.

"Well, that's an interesting development," Sam said.

"Isn't it? I'd like to believe it's what it looks like, but so many things have gone upside down on this trip that I'm beginning to suspect everyone."

"You know, when I talked to Brandi last night, she was concerned that the guy Jessica is running from …"

"Claims to be running from."

"… All right, have it your way. Anyway, she was wondering if he might have done away with Tyler."

"Not coming from the opposite direction a day later. But maybe he'd been planning to meet Tyler yesterday. Maybe Jessica had. Maybe they're both in it together."

"Or," Sam said, "maybe, as you observed earlier, it's what it looks like. She's a single woman, frightened of a scary looking guy. Who may or may not be dangerous."

They looked out at the lake, which was entirely in sunlight, for a moment.

"Damn," Gordon finally said. "I wish we had phones or email so we could check up on a few things. Including Eve Bredon."

"You still doubt her?"

Gordon considered the question.

"My gut tells me she's all right, but a little evidence would be nice." He laughed. "Good God, I'm turning into my father. How many times have I heard him say about a case he had, 'In my gut, I thought he was guilty, but some evidence would have been nice.' Scary."

"If getting married doesn't turn you into your father, nothing will. And there's no hope of phone or email out here."

"No, there isn't. Which means we'll have to figure it out ourselves the best we can. For starters, I think we should keep a watch again tonight. You up for taking a shift?"

"It would be an honor," Sam said.

THIRTY-SIX HOURS. Just keep anything bad from happening for a day and a half — less, actually — and we've done our job. We had one break already when Tyler's disappearance turned out to be self-inflicted. The same applies to Eve Bredon, if she is who she says she is. I wonder if, when she saw Tyler back in camp, she thought of him as a human being or whether she saw a cool two million standing on two feet and breathing.

None of my business. I need to keep my eyes on the trail ahead.

Gordon and I tossed for it, and I wound up riding at the rear this morning. That means the whole group is ahead of me, and I have to keep an eye on Tyler and Mason — not to mention Brandi, Jessica, and Eve. The forecast is for clear, sunny weather today and tomorrow, so that's a good sign.

Just did a mental recalculation. We should be at Donovan's Station by midafternoon Saturday, so it's really only a day and a quarter we need to keep the twins alive. Thirty more hours.

I can see everybody from back here, and as I look at them now, I'm thinking about how the dynamics between and among people have and haven't changed.

Bill and Angie looked a lot better this morning, as if they'd thrown an 800-pound gorilla off their shoulders. They've been capable and professional throughout the trip, and unless my eyes deceive me, there's a bit of a spark smoldering there. Certainly on her part. And I think on his, too, though he's a bit harder to read.

Shirley hasn't changed at all. She's still loud, sensible and enthusiastic. At her age, she is what she is.

Nora, I can't get a read on. She's concentrating on taking pictures, and by now, nobody's really paying much attention to her as she does it. Aside from Eve, she hasn't really connected with anyone else on the trip.

Things have been a bit strained between Brian and Emily ever since she had her flame-out on the trail to Keener Flat. I get the distinct sense that the trip was

Brian's idea, she wasn't too happy about it, and now that she's made a huge scene in front of everybody, she's blaming him for it. There's going to be a reckoning in that marriage when they get back to civilization, if not sooner.

Eve, meanwhile, is trying to make sure Gordon doesn't forget she's here. In the first half hour of the ride, she's twice pulled her horse abreast of his and tried to strike up a conversation. He enjoys attention from a woman (what man doesn't?), but I don't think he's taking it seriously enough that I'll need to consider an intervention. I do believe he's made his decision to settle down with Elizabeth. Can the wedding really be just a week from tomorrow?

And something is going on with Brandi. Considering how upset she seemed last night when I talked to her about Tyler, her joy at seeing him back safely seems a bit muffled. Or, maybe, is she emotionally wrung out? Keep an eye on that.

Mason and Tyler were distinctly chilly toward each other this morning. It's as if each one is wondering what the other one knows and what the other one is trying to do. If this was supposed to be a bonding trip for them, it's been an epic failure, and all we can hope is that they both survive it and go on to lead their spoiled, separate lives.

Only 29 hours to go now.

THEY RODE DOWNHILL until the trail took them into a small valley flanked on the east by a lower ridge of mountains. It was densely forested, and the creek that began at Sunrise Lake, fed by several other rivulets along the way, snaked through a long but narrow meadow at the valley's heart. Deer, unafraid of people this far from civilization, were feeding throughout, beginning to store up for the approaching winter.

Going over a slight ridge, they passed through another, smaller valley, this one with a small lake or large pond at its heart. The shoreline was muddy and weed-choked, and it looked like a stagnant body of water, unsuitable for fishing or swimming.

From that valley, they went uphill again, eventually following the side of the main mountain range to Sloane

Summit, where they would once again cross over to the western side of the Sierra. It was past noon when they reached the summit, and Bill stopped the caravan at that point.

"The place we'd ordinarily stop for lunch is half an hour ahead," he said to the group drawn up around him. "But we're running a bit later than usual. We can stop here, if that's what the group wants."

"The usual place is by a waterfall," Angie said.

"Keep going," said Shirley.

Several other people said the same thing, and they kept going.

The waterfall was 25 feet high and three feet wide, shooting through an opening in the rocks above as if through a funnel. It dropped into a pool about the size of a large living room before the water continued downhill, paralleling the trail for a quarter mile.

There was a grassy area large enough for them to break out in groups and sit together while they ate lunch. Gordon, Sam, Eve and Nora moved as close to the falls and as far from the trail as they could, hoping the distance and the rushing water would provide them the privacy for a frank conversation. Tyler, Mason, and Brandi were closest to the trail and horses, but well within view. Bill, Angie and Shirley sat together, and the Reeds kept to themselves, eating their meal in silence like an old married couple that had run out of things to say to each other.

Before Gordon's group could properly start up a conversation, Jessica came over.

"It's really nice of you guys to let me join your trip," Jessica said.

"It was the only thing to do," Nora said. "That guy following you on the trail was scary."

"Maybe he was harmless, but I didn't want to take the chance."

"I don't blame you," Sam said. "You figure you should be safe in a place like this, but it's also a long way from help."

"Is this the only time you've been concerned about someone on your hike?" Eve said.

"Strangely enough, yes. In almost two months, no one else really hit me the wrong way. For starters, I've been the only solo hiker on the trail. There have been several nights where there were two or more people camping the same place I was, but it was a group and I never felt any fear."

Gordon turned to Nora.

"Did you get any photos of our friend when he stopped at the campsite?"

"Several."

"When we get back, could you email me one that shows his face well? I have some contacts in law enforcement. Maybe they can recognize him."

"Sure." She paused. "Are you keeping a watch again tonight?"

"Oh yeah," Sam said. "I'm signed up for the first shift."

Jessica appeared to be taken aback.

"Is that really necessary?" she asked.

"Maybe not," Gordon said, "but why take chances?"

She shook her head.

"Fine way to end the trip," she said. "Too bad. It's been so nice. But then, it's good to meet you folks, too."

As they ate their sandwiches, she told them about some of the things she'd seen and done on her hike. Her passion grew as she spoke, and it became clear that this had been a trip of a lifetime for her, and that despite the aborted ending, she would have no regrets about it.

As she spoke, Gordon listened with one ear, and kept an eye on the twins and Brandi. Toward the end of the lunch, Mason's face morphed into a sardonic smile, and he said a few short things that appeared to upset Tyler. Brandi's back was to him, so he couldn't see how she was reacting. Before the situation escalated further, Mason stood up, stretched, and strode over to a group of trees across the trail.

Gordon wondered if he was going for a drug break or a bathroom break, and concluded it was probably both.

Jessica finished eating and storytelling and excused herself as well, heading for the horses. As soon as she was out of earshot, Gordon turned to Nora.

"Did you have a chance to look at your pictures?" he said.

"I had enough time this morning to look through the ones from Sunday."

"And?"

"In light of what you asked, there were two or three that looked more interesting than they did at the time I took them."

"Can you show us?"

She picked up one of her two cameras and began scrolling through back photos.

"It'll take me just a minute."

At that point, Jessica returned with a worried expression on her face.

"Is something wrong?" Eve said.

"I don't know," Jessica said. "I brought a gun on this trip in case I needed to protect myself, and our conversation made me think I should check the pack real quick to make sure it's still there."

Her eyes panned from left to right across their four faces.

"It isn't there."

SHORTLY AFTER THREE O'CLOCK they reached Upper Awatos Meadows, where they would be camping the last night of the trip. Most Californians have heard of the Awatos, one of the state's largest and wildest rivers, but this Alpine meadow, just over 9,000 feet above sea level, is where it properly starts. Five different rivulets (four of them originating in springs fed by the snowpack) ran through narrow gorges in the mountains above before coming together in the floor of this narrow valley to form the beginning of the Awatos, at this point a creek averaging 25 feet in width.

The meadow was largely grassy, but at the southwest was a pine grove sitting 75 feet back from the water and providing shade from the afternoon sun. After the group set up tents in the same configuration as the nights before, Gordon, Sam and Eve moved downstream and sat down on the grass at an oxbow bend of the creek, where they could be approached from only one side.

"So," Gordon said, to open the discussion, "what do we do about the missing gun?"

"Is there any chance we can figure out who has it before it gets dark?" Eve asked.

"Unlikely. You heard what Jessica said about how it was stored."

"In a pack inside your tent," Sam said to Eve. "There was a lot of milling around this morning, and anyone could have slipped into the tent, pinched the gun from the pack, and been out half a minute later."

"They'd have been taking a terrible chance," Eve said.

"Would they?" asked Gordon. "Unless they actually got caught with their hand in the pack, they could just say they spaced out and went into the wrong tent. I've almost done that once or twice myself."

"And it really could have been any of us," Sam said. "There were several minutes when you, Jessica and Nora were all eating breakfast at the same time and others were walking around. I wasn't watching them, and I'm supposed to be paying attention."

"Same here," Gordon said.

"You said it could have been anybody who took the gun," Eve said. "But there's one person it couldn't have been."

Gordon and Sam looked at her expectantly.

"Whoever took the gun," Eve continued, "had to know about it. Anyone who was at the campfire when Jessica showed up last night would have heard her say she had a gun for protection, but one of us …"

"Tyler," Gordon said.

"Tyler wasn't there. He couldn't have known about the gun."

"So what do we do?" Sam asked. "I think we have to report it to Bill and Angie."

"I'm not so sure about that," Eve said. "I think we should nose around for at least a few hours more and see if we can't find the gun ourselves."

They both turned to Gordon. After a minute of consideration, he finally said:

"In other circumstances, I might agree with you, Eve. But in this case, I think we need to go to Bill and Angie.

They're going to be held responsible for what happens on this trip, and they have to know there's a gun unaccounted for in our midst. And they, at least, have some authority to do something about it, which we don't."

"All right," Eve said after a pause. "I'll go along with you guys. Who's going to tell them? I vote for Gordon."

"So do I," Sam said. "We have a majority opinion."

WHEN HE GOT BACK TO CAMP, Gordon found Bill busy explaining the formation of the Awatos River to Brian and Emily, so he went to Angie, who was taking care of the horses and off by herself a bit. As he expected, she was not the least bit happy to hear the news.

"This is bad in so many ways, Gordon. Obviously, having a gun unaccounted for in our camp is not a good thing, but there's also the fact that Bill and I screwed up again last night."

"How so?"

"When Jessica said she had a gun, we should have immediately said she needed to turn it over to us as long as she was in our group. If you remember the contract everybody signed, Blanchard's has a strict no-firearms policy, so Bill and I had every right to ask for that. And if we had, I guarantee you there wouldn't be a missing gun right now."

"Would you have the right to search everybody's tent to see if you can find it?"

"That's a great legal question, and I'm no lawyer. But as a practical matter, I don't see that happening. You know how expensive this trip is, Gordon (actually, he didn't; the law firm had paid). Do you think people are going to take kindly to being searched?"

"Do you think they're going to take kindly to one or more of us being shot, if it comes to that?"

"I don't imagine they would. But let me play the devil's advocate here. Do we even know for sure there is a gun?"

Gordon hadn't thought of that.

"I mean," Angie continued, "we only have Jessica's say-so for it, unless you can tell me that someone else actually saw the weapon with their own eyes."

"No, I can't do that."

"I'll talk it over with Bill, then, but I think he'll feel the same way. We'll all keep our eyes open, and if you see something definite let me know."

"Eyes wide open," Gordon said. "Less than 24 hours to go now. We'll have to hope for the best."

"We'll have to hope."

EVE WAVED GORDON OVER when he returned to the tent area. She was with Nora and Sam, and Nora, who was generally not too demonstrative, seemed more animated than usual.

"We were interrupted when I was going to show the pictures earlier," Nora said. "But I think there's something here."

"Couldn't you tell that when you were taking them?" Sam asked.

"Not really. I'm focusing on getting as many shots as I can of the people and the environment, so I'm not really thinking of what's going on with the people."

"Can you show us?" Eve said.

"Let's go where there's some shade and privacy. It's hard to see the screen in the bright sun."

They moved into the forest behind the campsite and sat down. Nora had two cameras around her neck. She took the one with the telephoto lens first and called up an image on the viewfinder.

"These three were taken at the barbecue Sunday night," she said. "I was a ways back and shooting with the long lens, so they probably weren't aware of me. At one point, Tyler went away for a few minutes, and that's when these were shot. If you remember, Tyler was sitting across from Brandi and Mason was right next to her. Here's the first one."

They leaned forward to get a better look. The image showed Brandi and Mason in close-up. He was leaning over and whispering something into her ear. It was hard to know what to make of the expression on her face, but it seemed to convey at least some sense of interest.

"Then this was taken a few seconds later."

In the second shot, Mason was now sitting upright and laughing. Brandi was smiling.

"And then this one a few seconds after that."

In the third photo, Brandi was still smiling, and Mason was looking at her intently.

"What does that expression on his face look like to you?" Nora said.

They looked at it for several seconds, and Eve finally said, "If I didn't know better, I'd think he was in love with her."

"I could go along with that," Sam said.

"That may be putting it on too high a plane," Gordon said, "but it certainly looks like sexual interest. Do you have anything taken afterward?"

Nora shook her head.

"I didn't even remember this until I went back and looked through these photos. The way I work, I probably figured I had them covered and moved on to get some different people."

"Well," Gordon finally said, "these pictures don't prove anything, but they point to something we should be looking out for, wouldn't you think?"

The others nodded. Nora pulled the strap of her other camera over her neck.

"These are some pictures I took at Keener Flat. I was using the wide-angle lens and getting some shots of Bill and Shirley putting dinner together while you guys and Angie were looking for Tyler. I didn't even realize what was in the background until I looked at them this morning."

Nora had framed the shots so that Bill and Shirley were in the foreground at the right and one of the tents was in the background on the left. In the first two frames, it was only the tent behind them. In the third frame, Brandi and Mason were walking into the image from the left. In the fourth, fifth and sixth frames, they had stopped in front of the tent and were apparently talking and making hand gestures. They were far enough in the background and the light was dim enough that no detail of their faces registered on the small screen.

"It doesn't exactly look as if he's paying condolences," Eve said.

"They do seem to be having a discussion," Sam said.

164

"Ah, to be a fly on that tent," Gordon said. "But it's too late now. The pictures are only suggestive, but they suggest something we haven't been considering until now. If both brothers are in love with the same woman, that would be another motive for doing each other harm."

"As if half the Schroeder fortune wasn't motive enough," Eve said.

THEY WENT BACK TO CAMP, and shortly afterward Brian and Emily returned from a walk upstream. They had discovered a beaver pond a quarter of a mile away, and Brian was waxing enthusiastic about having seen such a wonderful scene of raw nature.

Emily was clearly underwhelmed.

Gordon, however, was listening intently. A pond suggested good fishing, and perhaps slightly larger trout than would usually be found in a stream this size. He realized that since the first night of the trip, he and Sam had been entirely intent on keeping an eye on the Linfield twins. Fishing had barely crossed their minds.

News of the pond made him realize how much he had missed the chance to fish. After the brief conversation with Brian and Emily, Gordon went back to his tent, took out his fly rod, and began to assemble it. Sam walked up as he was beginning to thread the line through the ferrules.

"What do you think you're doing?" Sam said.

"Getting my rod ready, just in case."

"And just in case you decide to go fishing, who's going to keep an eye on those troublesome twins?"

"I have it all figured out. There should be enough time after dinner for each of us to get in half an hour of fishing at the beaver pond. We can each take a turn while the other stays at camp and keeps an eye on things. It'll work."

"You're not still thinking of catching a Golden Trout are you?"

"Not likely here. But I'd like to be able to say I got in at least *some* action."

Sam shook his head, after which he fetched his own rod and began putting it together. A coin toss resulted in Gordon getting first crack at the beaver pond.

IT BEGAN INNOCUOUSLY ENOUGH, as such things often do. Mason, Tyler and Brandi were at the same table for dinner, with Nora making up the fourth. As Nora later recounted it, it was a glum and uncommunicative group, and her attempts to get a conversation started were going nowhere.

Toward the end of the meal, Mason, looking at one of the other tables, reached for his water bottle and knocked it over, the contents spilling on Tyler's plate.

"You did that on purpose," Tyler snapped.

"Oh, come off it," Mason said.

"You're denying it?"

"Of course I'm denying it. Why would I want to do that?"

"For the same reason you do everything else. To piss me off."

"Get a grip, Tyler. You're not that important."

"Yes I am. If you didn't have me to pick on, what would your sorry life be like?"

Mason rolled his eyes, looked at the sky, and muttered something that sounded like "Moretti, Moretti, Moretti."

"That does it," Tyler shouted loudly enough to get the attention of all the other campers. He stood up, turned his waterlogged plate upside down on top of Mason's plate.

"Fuck you, Mason. Fuck you to hell and back."

Mason jumped to his feet. "That was disrespectful, bro."

"Yeah? Well, respect has to be earned."

Mason put his hands on Tyler's chest and gave him a hard shove, sending him backward several feet.

"Am I starting to earn it?" Mason said.

Tyler responded by lunging at his brother, but by now Bill and Gordon were up, and they got between the twins before any blows could be exchanged.

"Calm down, for God's sake," Bill said. "Look, I know everybody's been under a strain, but let's try to keep things under control."

Bill and Gordon were holding the brothers tightly enough that things actually were under control, at least for the moment. Mason and Tyler realized it and relaxed in their respective grips.

"Now shake hands and make up," Bill said. "Nobody's trying to hurt anyone else here, so let's go forward with that idea in mind."

Gordon looked over at Sam, who shook his head slightly. Despite what Bill had just said, they knew better.

THE BEAVERS WERE NOT in evidence at the pond, but it looked to Gordon like a lovely fishing hole. The beaver dam had caused the 20-foot-wide stream to expand to 50 feet, and backed the water up another 120 feet or so. There was no sign of fish feeding on the surface, so he decided to fish a Hare's Ear nymph under an indicator, eight to nine feet below the surface.

He went to the top of the pond, where the Awatos was flowing into it, figuring that trout would be waiting below the inlet for the current to wash food their way. He cast to the entry point and let the current carry his fly and indicator downstream. After a drift of 12 to 15 feet, he saw the indicator twitch slightly on the surface and raised his rod. There was a fish on the other end of the line.

It was a nine-inch Brook Trout, dark green and speckled with red spots. He brought it in quickly, removed the hook from its lower lip and released it back into the pond. A second cast yielded another, this one ten inches long.

"Having fun?" Eve said.

He hadn't heard her approach and was a bit startled, but he quickly turned to her and said, "As a matter of fact, I am."

"All right if I sit and watch?"

"It's not exactly must-see TV, but go ahead."

"What are you fishing for?"

"Whatever's in here. Probably mostly Brook Trout and Rainbows." He paused. "I was hoping to catch a Golden Trout this trip, but that doesn't seem to be in the cards."

"Why not?"

"They're mostly in the high-elevation lakes. We won't be hitting any more of those."

"Don't let me stop you," she said.

He cast again, without result, then twice more. Nothing happened. He wondered if she was bringing him bad luck. He moved down the edge of the pond and made a cast into the middle of it, about 20 feet above the beaver dam. The current was nearly imperceptible here, and his indicator drifted toward the dam at a rate of a foot every two or three seconds. Halfway to the dam, the indicator jerked under the surface, and Gordon set the hook.

This was a bigger fish than the previous two, and it took a few minutes to land. As he caught glimpses of it in the water, he could see that it wasn't a Brook Trout and figured it was probably a Rainbow. Only when he got it close to the bank and knelt to net it did he realize what he had.

The bright orange-red stripe over the golden lower half of the body. The spotted tail. The green upper half with no speckling. It was an unusually large Golden Trout, 13 to 14 inches long.

Eve was by his side and had her hand on his shoulder as he was lifting the net from the water.

"It's beautiful," she said, looking at the fish.

"A Golden Trout after all. Go figure. Not many people have even seen one."

Writhing in the net, the fish had dislodged the hook from its mouth. Seeing that, Gordon lowered the net into the pond and released the fish, which had been untouched by human hand.

"Whatever you're doing," he said to the fish, "go back and keep doing it."

As they watched the trout swim off into the depths of the pond, they heard the gunshots.

THE PLAN WAS FOR ME to stay behind in camp and keep an eye on both brothers while Gordon hiked upstream to fish the beaver pond. It wasn't bad as plans go, but there was one aspect of it we hadn't considered. What was I supposed to do if the twins split up and went separate ways?

Which, of course, is exactly what happened.

After dinner, people scattered to the four winds. I was concentrating on the brothers, so I didn't really see who went where or did what. I was trying to sit out in the open at the campsite and keep an eye on two different people, all the while doing my best to appear not to be doing what I was doing. That is hard work. At first, I played with my fly rod, as if I were getting it set up to go fishing. But it was already set up, and you can only do the same gestures so many times before it begins to look fake. Then I pulled my pack out of the tent and made a pretense of going through it — more than once, actually — until that became unsustainable. Just as I was trying to think up a new bit of business, Mason set out on the path leading upstream to the beaver pond.

He and Tyler had been keeping a distance between themselves after the dinner table outburst, and as I checked Tyler, I realized Brandi was no longer with him. In fact, with Mason gone, it would be just Tyler, Angie and me in the campsite.

I had to make a quick decision, and I decided to follow Mason, concluding that Tyler was safer in camp with Angie than Mason would be on the path to the beaver pond. Where everyone else was, I had no idea.

So I grabbed my fly rod and shouted out, "Hey, Mason! Wait up!" and began to jog toward him.

It was pretty obvious that he didn't appreciate my overture, but I pretended not to notice. As I got near him, I said: "I'm heading up to the beaver pond to fish with Gordon. Mind if I tag along with you?"

He looked at me as if I were cold mutton and finally said, "It's still a free country, I guess."

I took that for a yes, and off we went.

We were walking along a beautiful mountain stream on a delightful late summer evening, and I noticed no details of any of the landscape. That's how intent I was on watching Mason. I tried to ask a few small-talky questions. The responses were monosyllabic — at least in those cases where a grunt wouldn't suffice.

Mason kept stopping to look at the stream nearly every minute, apparently hoping I'd take the hint and keep going. But when I need to, I can be very good at not taking hints. A few minutes into the walk, I realized the poor guy was just going out to get his fix in a bit of privacy and was probably getting more and more agitated as I stuck to him. I couldn't think what to do, other than keep going to the beaver pond and turn things over to Gordon.

The first shot hit the trail ahead of us, kicking up dirt, pebbles and a small tuft of grass. I heard it clearly enough, but only with the second shot did I grasp what was going on. The second shot hit the trail a few feet farther ahead than the first, but we had also kept going after the first one.

The trail was just a couple of feet from the creek on our left, and there fortunately was an overhanging bank and a small pool there. I gave Mason a shove with my left hand, and he did a belly flop into the water. With my right hand, I threw down my rod just as the third shot sheared off some bark about ten feet from the ground on a tree to my right. I followed Mason into the creek, though I went in more elegantly, feet first. I grabbed his arm and pulled him up against the overhanging bank with me. The shots had come from the edge of the forest that followed the stream up from the campground. I figured we were out of the shooter's line of sight now, and sure enough, there were no more shots.

It felt like hours but must have been no more than a minute before we heard people running up from what seemed like all directions.

SAM AND MASON had been drawing close to the beaver pond when the shots rang out, so Gordon and Eve were first on the scene. The others ran up from wherever they had been, and in two to three minutes the entire party was on hand. Later, Gordon would wish that he had paid more attention to who had arrived when, and from what direction. It was a small consolation that no one else had noticed.

The entire group then walked back to the camp, where Sam and Mason were prepared to go into their tents and change into dry clothing. Bill stopped them.

"That shooting incident has changed everything," Bill said to the group. "Jessica was carrying a pistol for self-protection on her hike, and this morning, she found it was missing."

"You can't possibly suspect us!" Emily almost shrieked.

"Yeah," Tyler chimed in. "What about the guy who was at the lake yesterday?"

Bill raised his hand and quieted everyone.

"I'm not saying I suspect anyone. In fact, there's nothing I'd like more than to rule everybody here out. But in order to do that, we need to subject everybody to a pat-down search and a search of their personal belongings."

"Do you have a warrant?" Mason asked.

"We don't need one, for two reasons ..."

"So you think you're above the law?"

"Please let me finish, Mason. In the first place, all of you signed an agreement prior to the trip, stating you would abide by Blanchard's rules, which specifically include no firearms on the trip, and which allow us to take any reasonable measures necessary to enforce those rules. In the second place, we're not law enforcement. We're not going to arrest or prosecute anyone. All we're trying to do is maintain the safety of our paying customers."

"So who searches you and Angie?" Mason continued.

"Any man you all choose can subject me to the same search we subject you to," Bill said. "And any woman you pick can search Angie."

"And what if we refuse to be searched?"

"That's right," Emily said. "I know I don't have the gun, and I'd rather no one went through my intimate belongings."

Shirley stepped forward next to Bill, turned to the group, and bellowed in her best teacher voice:

"Cut it out!"

The group instantly went silent.

"Can't you all see how serious this is? None of us is going to get a wink of sleep if we don't do as Bill says. We need to do the search for the good of the whole group. And I'll volunteer to go first. Hell, I'll even let Bill search me."

"No, no," Angie said a bit too quickly. "That's all right."

"So who's searching you guys," Mason said sullenly, knowing he'd lost the argument.

"I nominate Gordon to search Bill," Sam said.

"And I nominate Eve to search Angie," Gordon said.

No one objected, and it looked as if they had a reluctant consensus. Bill stepped up and spoke in a low, level voice.

"Before we do the search, there's one more thing. I'd like to go around the group, left to right, and have everyone say where they were and who they were with when they heard the shots. We need to cover that point while it's still fresh in our minds."

The answers proved interesting but inconclusive. Gordon and Eve were together at the pond and alibied each other. Sam and Mason were together, being shot at, and were likewise in the clear. Brian and Emily said they were together, just downstream from the camp, but as a married couple, the alibi they provided each other was less strong than the others.

That left the other six accounted for only by their own tales: Bill had been tending to the horses. Angie had been washing up the dinner dishes. She thought Tyler was in the camp, too, but didn't see him when she heard the shots and looked up. Tyler said it was because he had just slipped into the woods to relieve himself. Brandi was in her tent, lying down briefly after dinner. Jessica had gone for a stroll downstream, but hadn't seen Bill and Emily, nor had they seen her. Shirley had just started upstream toward the beaver pond and said no one else was in sight when she heard the shots. And Nora had gone up the hillside behind the camp to take landscape photos of the meadows from above.

With that out of the way, the searches commenced as planned. As everyone had packed lightly for the trip, the effort didn't take long and was completed by twilight.

Jessica's gun wasn't found.

Bill and Angie gathered everyone around the campfire, which Gordon and Sam had set up after being searched. He lit it and the flames quickly engulfed the wood, bringing light and warmth to the cool night.

"Thank you for your cooperation," Bill said. "Now that we all know that none of us is packing heat, we can relax and enjoy the campfire. Tonight, let's hear from Tyler and Brandi."

BRANDI WENT FIRST. She had, it turned out, grown up in Burbank near Los Angeles. Her father was a firefighter, who ended up on disability after being injured on the job, and her mother was an elementary school teacher, so she had to fend for herself more than some other kids. After high school, she wanted to get out of Southern California, so she applied to several colleges in Northern California and was accepted at San Francisco State, where she'd gotten a degree in English a year ago. In her senior year, she became more interested in art, and spent a lot of time in studios at the school and around San Francisco. That was where, at the beginning of the year, she had met Tyler. She had been impressed that he hadn't asked her to pose for him because he didn't do that sort of painting. She was thinking of going back to school and getting a degree or a certification that would lead to a job in nonprofit management, preferably something to do with the arts.

Tyler, for his part, seemed uncomfortable speaking in front of the group. He told the story of his background, referring to his wealthy grandfather only as an "East Bay real estate man," and downplaying the extent of his own prospects. He went on at length about his painting, but in a rambling way that threatened to lose the audience. To help him out a bit, Shirley finally asked a question:

"How come you didn't bring your painting materials along on the trip?"

"Well, I wanted to spend some quality time with my brother," he said, which, given the scene at dinner, fell flat, "and I don't paint landscapes."

"If you don't paint landscapes and you don't paint nudes, what *do* you paint?" Shirley persisted.

"I do abstract works that push the boundaries of color and texture," Tyler said.

No one wanted him to continue down that road, so the questioning stopped. After a few words from Angie about the last day of the trip coming up, the campfire circle broke up.

The two talks had left Gordon puzzled. Brandi had come across as much more mature, focused and articulate than Tyler. He understood that the woman is usually the smarter half of any couple, but even with that starting point, the chasm between the two seemed nearly unbridgeable. Perhaps, he concluded, she was young enough to naively see Tyler as a project who could be improved.

Something else was on Gordon's mind, and he sought out Jessica as soon as the group broke up. The moon was coming up behind the mountains to the east, and he said he wanted to ask her a question away from the group. They walked down to the Awatos, listened to its trill and murmur, and heard a fish rise to an insect against the opposite bank.

"Is it about the guy I was running away from?" she said.

"No. Not at all."

"Because if no one here has my gun ..."

"We can't be sure of that," Gordon said. "If the shooter was one of us, they could have stashed the gun somewhere before coming down to the creek or even tucked it away along the trail on the way back."

"So you think ..."

"I'm trying not to think anything, but it's possible the gun is still somewhere in this circle of people. So let me ask you what type it was."

"It was a 9 mm automatic, a small one. The man at the sporting goods store said it was 'popular with the ladies.' I wish I hadn't brought it."

"How many shots does it fire?"

"The magazine holds eight cartridges."

"Was any ammunition missing, or just the gun?"

"The ammo was all there. Before starting out, I loaded the gun from another box and brought a full sealed box of cartridges as backup. That box wasn't touched."

"Which means," Gordon said after a pause, "that if one of us has the gun and my math is right, the shooter still has five shots left."

I DREW THE FIRST WATCH that last night and took up my station after everyone had turned in. I carried a folding camp chair up the hill and put it under the shade of a couple of trees in the forest that overlooked the campsite. The same forest, come to think of it, from which the shooter had taken pot shots at us when we were walking along the creek.

Now there's a thought to keep a man awake and alert.

The luminous dial of my watch showed that it was 10:30. Bill was supposed to relieve me at 2:30, and our pack expedition is scheduled to arrive at the end of the road, Donovan's Station, no later than three o'clock tomorrow afternoon.

Four hours left on the watch, and sixteen and a half hours of babysitting the homicidal heirs before our job is up. And not a minute too soon, if you ask me.

It was chilly, but in the early going, my parka kept me warm. The moon was only one day off from full, so it cast plenty of light on the valley and the encampment. If anyone left their tent or came into that area, I should have been able to see them quite clearly, and they couldn't see me. I was feeling pretty secure until it occurred to me that if someone outside the group was keeping an eye on us, that person would have seen me coming up here and would know where I was.

All the more reason to stay wide awake.

There was a movement in the camp area. I leaned forward, as though being a foot closer would help me see what was happening 150 feet away. A figure had emerged from our tent, and I quickly identified Gordon by his walk. He was heading my direction, and I don't mind saying I appreciated the company.

As he drew close, I hissed, "Over here."

Gordon sat down on the pine needles to the left of my chair.

"Hope you don't mind the visit," he said. "I just remembered there was something important I forgot to tell you."

"Don't tell me you've figured out this situation."

"No, but almost as important as that."

I waited silently.

175

"I caught a Golden Trout tonight."

"You're kidding."

"I kid you not. In the beaver pond on a #14 Hare's Ear nymph, eight feet under the surface. About 13 or 14 inches long. We'd just released it when we heard the shots."

"We?"

"Eve was with me."

"Of course she was. And why is an interesting question, but not as interesting as why there was a Golden Trout in this creek."

"I asked Angie about that. She said there are five streams that come together at the top of this valley to form the Awatos. Four of them are spring-fed from melting snowmelt escaping through the side of the mountain at some point, but the fifth drains a small lake several hundred feet above this valley. And there are Goldens in the lake.

" 'The fish must have come down here just for you, Gordon,' Angie said. 'It's probably a sign of some sort.' "

"Do you believe that?"

"I believe that the fish came down from the lake. The sign part I'm not so sure about."

"Well, congratulations on the fish. That was one of the things you wanted from this trip."

"The other is to finish this job up right." He had picked up a small stick and was making grooves in the earth under the pine needles. "I wonder if we're not being played here."

"What do you mean?"

"Tyler's disappearance and reappearance were a bit too neat for my taste. And his story was so preposterous I can't believe even he wanted us to believe it. And all the so-called murder attempts don't add up. They don't seem serious enough. Not even tonight."

"I beg to disagree," I said. "From where I stood, with bullets hitting all around me, it seemed plenty serious."

"Firing a gun with people around is always serious, but let me ask you a couple of questions. The shots were coming from the forest. How far from the trail was that?"

"A good 50 to 60 feet."

"And how close to you did the shots hit?"

"Within 10 to 15 feet."

"So not very good shooting. Which is what you'd expect even from an expert firing a handgun at that distance. Handguns are a close-range tool. If someone really wanted to shoot Mason or you, and if they had any idea what they were doing, they'd have come a lot closer."

"Then we would have seen who it was."

"But it probably would have been the last thing you saw. My point is, it's almost as if someone is trying to scare them by creating an illusion that the twins are in danger without actually hurting them. But if so, why?"

Neither of us had an answer for that, and after a minute Gordon continued:

"So what I'm concerned about is whether all these close calls are drawing us away from looking for where the real attempt is going to come."

"It would have to be tomorrow," I said.

"It would. And I'm hanged if I can see what it would be. Any ideas?"

"None," I replied, after a suitable pause.

Gordon stood up.

"Well, you're going to have some thinking time the next few hours. If you have a brainstorm, let me know."

He stood up, said farewell, and walked back to the camp. I watched him all the way back to our tent, then checked my watch. Eleven o'clock.

Only 16 hours left until we reach Donovan's Station.

"WHERE HAVE YOU BEEN?" Eve said, as Gordon crawled through the tent flaps.

Gordon was brought up short. With Sam on watch, he hadn't expected anyone else to be in the tent. She switched on a small flashlight, and it illuminated the tent well enough that he could see she was lying atop Sam's sleeping bag under a blanket that was not quite drawn all the way over her bare shoulders.

"It's a bit chilly in here," she explained.

"Perhaps you should put on your parka."

"Later. We have some things to sort out first."

"Like how to protect Tyler until tomorrow afternoon?"

"Don't play dumb, Gordon. You can't pull it off."

She pulled the blanket down a bit, enough to show some cleavage and make it clear that on the top half of her, at least, there was no clothing under the blanket.

"I don't think I'm imagining that there's been a bit of chemistry between us, Gordon. Tonight's the last chance to do something about it. End the trip with a good memory, and no strings attached."

"It's a big leap from chemistry to biology."

"Not as big as you're making it, though I must say it's unusual to see a man who can play hard to get."

"Aren't you forgetting that I'm getting married a week from tomorrow?"

"I'm trying. But that's all the more reason. You probably could use one last fling before you settle down. Most people could."

"Look, Eve, you're a very attractive woman, and back in the day I really would have jumped at this, but I really don't think ..."

"And you can always invoke the 200-mile rule."

"The 200-mile rule?"

"Anything that happens more than 200 miles from home doesn't count. Calories. Gambling. Sex. Sloth. None of it matters when you're that far away."

He looked at her for several seconds, then averted his eyes.

"You know," he said, "I believe we're only 195 miles from San Francisco as the crow flies. I'm afraid it *would* count."

THAT EVENING CONVINCED ME it was a good thing I never decided to pursue a career as a night watchman. I wouldn't have lasted a week. I don't have the nerves for it and am too easily distracted.

Once Gordon went back into the tent, I began to pay attention to my surroundings. For someone with an active imagination, that's not necessarily a good thing.

The forest is not a quiet place at night. There are all sorts of noises, grand and subtle. Once or twice during my shift, the wind kicked up, rattling through the treetops above, dislodging leaves and branches. At least it shut up the animals, which seemed to be moving about among the trees as though the forest was a shopping mall on Saturday afternoon.

One of the gusts of wind came up shortly after Gordon left. I drew my parka around me more tightly and listened as I kept an eye on the campsite. The tents shimmered in the wind, but all else was still. When the wind died down to nothing, almost as quickly as it had started up, the silence in that little valley was utter and absolute. I might have been the only living creature in it.

Behind me, in the forest, a twig snapped.

It didn't sound that far away, and I flicked on my flashlight as I turned to see if I could get a good look at what caused it.

A doe and two fawns were walking through the woods about 20 feet behind me. It's hard to say if my flashlight startled them more than they startled me.

I'd been at my post less than an hour and already had a bad case of the nerves.

I switched off the light, turned to face the campsite again, and tried to get back into my normal breathing pattern. As I sat there, I realized turning on the light had been a mistake for several reasons. If, instead of the deer, it had been the Charles Manson look-alike, the light would have given him a perfect target if he were inclined to shoot. If he or someone else was watching the camp from elsewhere in the valley, I probably tipped off my location and the fact I was keeping watch.

With the flashlight off, I moved the folding chair over about 30 feet to the right. Just to be safe. I sat down and began scanning the campsite slowly, from left to right. Nothing was out of place until I reached the end of my turn radius.

Someone was walking toward the camp from the edge of the woods, right by the trail that led to the beaver pond.

In a second or two I had figured out it was a woman, and in another second or two, I had concluded, based on size and outline, that it was Brandi. She was striding purposefully toward the tents. There may have been something in her right hand, but I couldn't tell for sure. At this distance, I couldn't see that kind of detail.

I made a spot decision that I needed to check this out and started downhill toward the camp. I figured that if I cut in between our tent and the Reeds' (numbers 2 and 3 in the semicircle) I could intercept Brandi before she got to hers, No. 5. I moved more swiftly and quietly than I had thought I could, but thanks to the high elevation, I was breathless when I got to the tents. I came out from between them just as Brandi passed by.

As I stepped out from between the tents, Eve popped out of ours. I wasn't expecting that.

I looked at Eve for a second, then turned to Brandi. She had gotten on her knees, preparing to go into her tent. She was holding her right arm awkwardly, as if she had something in her hand and was using her body to conceal it from my sight.

"Brandi!" I hissed in a loud whisper.

She pretended not to hear me and went headfirst into her tent. Anything she might have been carrying would be out of sight before I got there. I turned back to Eve. Even by moonlight, I could see enough of her face to tell she was a bit shaken and enough of her shirt to tell it was only halfway buttoned and there was no bra underneath. She quickly regained her composure.

"Good evening, Sam. Gordon's still up if you want to talk to him."

And with that, she walked quickly to her tent and hopped in, leaving me speechless.

As a matter of fact, I did want to talk to him, so I got down and clambered into the tent.

"What happened?" he said.

"I was about to ask you the same thing."

"You're on watch, so something had to happen to bring you down here. You go first."

I inhaled deeply and took a long time exhaling. My breath was starting to come back.

"I was keeping an eye on things," I finally said, "and I saw something move to my right. At the edge of the forest, where the trail heads up to the beaver pond. Someone was walking toward the campsite, and I saw it was Brandi. It looked like there might be something in her hand, so I started down to intercept her."

"You made the right call."

"Thanks. She just beat me to the spot between this tent and the next one when Eve popped out of here. It startled the living daylights out of me. Before I could turn back to Brandi and stop her, she'd shimmied into her tent."

"That was bad timing," Gordon said, after a brief silence.

"In more ways than one."

"Could you see what was in her hand? Do you have any idea what it was?"

"I couldn't see anything for sure. But I do have an idea."

"The gun."

"The gun. If it was one of us that shot at Mason and me, she or Tyler could have anticipated there would be a search and ditched the gun just off the trail."

"Figuring they could come back later. Yeah. It makes sense."

"So what do we do?"

"I don't see what we can do until morning. You'd better get back to your watch."

"In a minute, Gordon. But you haven't answered my question. What happened?"

"Nothing happened."

"Given how Eve looked coming out of our tent, that doesn't cut it as an answer. You don't have to tell Elizabeth, but you owe me an explanation."

Gordon took a deep breath before answering.

"She was waiting inside when I got back from our chat. She suggested we take our friendship to another level."

"And you weren't tempted?"

"Of course I was tempted. Don't be ridiculous. But I told her I didn't think it was a good idea, and she accepted that. She put her shirt back on and left."

"With the shirt only halfway buttoned."

"Cut her some slack, Sam. She didn't have to go very far, and I don't think she was expecting to run into anyone."

I'd been watching him as he spoke, and, despite what I'd seen, I believed him.

"Well, maybe the leopard *is* changing his spots," I said. "I'm starting to think you may actually be ready to get married."

"Ready or not, it's happening a week from tomorrow. Now get back to your watch before we're all butchered in our sleep."

Saturday August 28

AT SOME POINT AFTER MIDNIGHT, I realized that since coming back from our tent, I had been scanning the valley and the campsite with a regular motion and with nothing happening for so long that I had almost fallen into a trance. I've never tried meditation, but I imagine it might be something like this. Except in meditation, as I understand it, you're not generally on the lookout for a villain with a gun.

It's hard to describe the feeling of desolation in a place like this. When there was no wind and no animal noise — and that was getting to be most of the time by now — the silence was so profound it would give anyone the jitters. After a while I checked my watch, which read 12:28. Two hours left on the shift.

Having cleansed my mind somewhat, I decided to put it to work. First, I kicked myself for missing two things that any competent sentry ought to have seen. One was Eve moving from her tent to ours. That obviously happened when Gordon came up to talk to me, but I ought to have been keeping a fixed eye on the camp while the conversation was going on. I didn't.

The other was Brandi going into the forest. It's possible she slipped away in the general milling around before bedtime and before I assumed my post. In that case I suppose I get a pass. But if she came up to the woods while Gordon and I were talking, that's two strikes against me.

But I did see Brandi heading back, and I would have intercepted her if Eve hadn't popped out of our tent like a whack-a-mole. And although I couldn't swear to what was in Brandi's right hand, my gut told me it was Jessica's missing gun.

So I ran with that idea for a bit. If I was right about Brandi picking up the gun, that could mean only one of two things. Either she'd fired the shots and hidden the gun on the way back to camp, or Tyler had been the shooter, had hidden the gun, and sent her out to get it when it may have seemed as if no one would be looking.

The second possibility made a bit more sense. Gordon said earlier that Tyler couldn't have the gun because he hadn't heard about it. But Brandi had. If she thought Tyler was in danger from Mason, she might have pinched Jessica's gun and given it to Tyler for self-defense. He could have taken the shots at us, ditched the gun before we got back to camp, and sent Brandi out to get it after bedtime. After his disappearance and lame story about it, he probably wouldn't want to get into a situation where he had to do any more explaining.

On the other hand, Brandi could have stolen the gun and pulled off the shooting with or without Tyler's collusion. For that matter, Jessica could have made up the story about the gun being missing in the first place. She could be an agent of Nick Moretti's, hired to do a hit on Tyler. But then why shoot at Mason and me? Or maybe Nora has been shooting more than photos.

By the time I'd reasoned things out that far, my recently whitewashed mind had become as cluttered as a graffiti-covered wall. I had to admit I wasn't going to think this matter through to a satisfactory conclusion tonight. The problem with this caper is that there's too much theory and not enough fact. Gordon and I (and possibly Eve) would have to put our heads together tomorrow morning to figure out how to make sure everybody gets through tomorrow afternoon in one piece.

So I tried to put all the speculation out of my head and concentrated on keeping watch in the routine way I'd been doing earlier. As might be expected, the monotony of the routine, combined with the lateness of the hour, had a soporific effect. The last time I looked at my watch, it was just after two o'clock, and I remember thinking, "Only 12 hours and change until we're safe at Donovan's Station."

And then I apparently fell asleep, because that's how Bill found me when he showed up to take over the watch at 2:30. As I said earlier, I was never cut out to be a night watchman.

EVERYONE WAS ALIVE AND WELL when breakfast was served, but long before that, Gordon was up and talking, in low tones, with Bill and Angie as they prepared the last breakfast of the trip. He explained how Sam had seen Brandi, possibly picking up the missing gun, but had been unable to intercept her before she got back to her tent.

"I think there's a pretty good case to be made for doing another search," Gordon said, "but obviously that's your call."

Bill and Angie looked at each other. Gordon thought he saw her shake her head slightly.

"I don't know about that," Bill said. "You saw what the reaction was to the idea of a search yesterday. Which, by the way, turned up nothing. How sure is Sam that he saw a gun?"

"I haven't talked to him this morning, but last night he wasn't a hundred percent."

"Even if he was a hundred percent," Bill said, "there's a 30 to 40 percent chance he'd be wrong, given the light and the distance."

"It doesn't seem like enough to justify the invasion of privacy," Angie said.

"Except everybody's privacy was invaded last night," Gordon said. "Aside from the gun, if it's there, you shouldn't find any surprises."

"Listen, Gordon," Angie said, "I know you mean well, but look at it from our standpoint. These people are our customers, and when we search their belongings, we find things they never meant for someone else to see."

"Like the white powder in Mason's pack," Bill said. "I'm not with the DEA, so I pretended it was sugar, but you know that's why he objected loudly to the search."

"And one of the women," Angie said, "had quite the selection of ... well, lots of women have them."

"Not to mention the condoms in the zippered compartment of your shaving case," Bill added, looking at Gordon.

He blushed. "I'd forgotten those things were even there."

"So you see," Bill said, "we need a really good reason to go through people's sometimes-embarrassing things. And may-have-seen-it-by-moonlight isn't a very compelling reason."

"So no search. But would you mind if Sam asked Brandi, if he can get her aside, what she was up to last night?"

Bill and Angie looked at each other again.

"If he can do it discreetly," Angie finally said. "I don't want her complaining to us about it."

"And you might want to ask yourself if it's really necessary," Bill added. "We have less than eight hours before the trip is over, and the forecast is for good weather. What are the odds of anything bad happening?"

"Higher than I'd like," Gordon said.

THE MOOD AT BREAKFAST was surprisingly convivial. Until it wasn't. But at the outset, there was a genuine camaraderie, arising from the shared experience of all the excitement on the trip so far. With only a few hours left, the campers were like the survivors of a shipwreck, who had come into sight of land.

While the others ate, Bill and Angie outlined the plans for the final day.

"We really don't have far to go," Bill said, "so usually on this day, I'll lead a one-hour field tour of the meadow, pointing out some of the biology and geology. That'll be about a half hour after breakfast."

"Bill's too modest to say so," Angie added, "but all summer long the people who have gone on this tour have come back with high praise for it. You learn a lot of neat stuff with just a little time and a little walking. You don't have to decide now, but think about it over breakfast."

Bill then launched into a description of the ride facing them that day.

"We'll ride through this valley for about two miles, then the river goes into a canyon as it drops down into the next valley. So we'll be going over a ridge and coming down the other side into Lower Awatos Meadows.

"When we get there, you'll be surprised at how much the river has grown. There are a lot of little tributary streams and springs between here and there. In the lower meadows, the Awatos is over a hundred feet wide, and the current can be pretty fast in places.

"The lower meadows are what geologists refer to as a hanging valley. At the bottom end, the valley stops at a cliff, and the Awatos tumbles in a waterfall 140 feet below into the canyon that takes us to Donovan's Station.

"A couple of hundred yards above the falls is Oakley's Ford. The river widens out to 150 feet or more there, and it's rarely more than a foot deep, running over a nice gravel and pebble bottom. It's easy to cross on foot or horseback. We'll stop on this side of the ford for a quick lunch.

"After lunch, we cross the ford, and the trail runs along the north side of the river. On the far canyon wall, it zig-zags with several switchbacks to the foot of the waterfall. There's a beautiful pool there. If it's warm and you want to stop for a quick dip, we'll do that. We'll probably stop briefly there in any event. After that, it's a fairly easy three-mile ride to Donovan's and the end of our trail.

"Any questions?"

No one said anything for several seconds, then Emily raised her hand. Bill nodded at her.

"That trail down the side of the canyon wall by the waterfall, with several switchbacks. How does it compare to the trail up to Keener Flat?"

There was a group intake of breath. So much had happened since Emily's meltdown on the trail up to Keener Flat that the group had largely forgotten about it.

"I'm talking about the terror factor, in case I didn't make myself clear," Emily added.

"Well, the trail's plenty wide enough for the horses," Bill started to say.

"Wider or narrower than the Keener Flat trail?" Emily asked.

"About the same," Bill said.

"And is it a sheer drop-off, like the other trail?"

"Not so much, because the next leg of the trail is always below."

"But looking down, does it seem like a straight drop?"

Angie came to Bill's rescue.

"The trail's on a cliff wall," she said, "but let's cut to the chase here. It's a safe enough trail, but at the same time, some people do get apprehensive about riding on it, and we want you to end the trip on a happy note. When we reach where the trail begins to follow the cliff, we can dismount, and you can take a look at it. If you don't feel up to riding it on horseback, you and I can lead the way on foot."

"No, that's all right," Emily said. "I don't want to be any trouble. I'll ride the horse."

"Are you sure, honey?" Brian said. "It'd be better to walk than to hold things up for everybody."

"Honest to God, Brian," Emily said, her voice rising as she rose from the table. "You take the biscuit. You really do. You bring me along on this trip where people are disappearing and being shot at and we're riding on trails where my vertigo is going to kick in. And you don't think of me at all. You just think of the convenience of everybody else. Screw you!"

She threw the half-cup of her lukewarm coffee at him, slammed the mug down on the table, and stalked off to the tent.

Brian remained glued to his chair, his face turning a crimson-purple while the coffee stain on his shirt front gradually spread.

It was utterly silent in the valley. There was no wind, no birdsong, and no one in the group was about to say anything.

Finally, Brian stood up.

"I apologize for the scene," he said. "I guess I really put my foot in it. I'd better go and try to make it right."

He followed Emily into the tent.

Shirley, who had been sitting at the next table a few feet from Gordon, turned to him.

"So, Gordon," she said in a low voice. "When did you say you're getting married?"

"A week from today."

"Well, you just got a sneak preview of what you're in for."

A MEETING WAS NECESSARY, and fortunately for Gordon, Sam and Eve, things broke the right way. Everyone else wanted to go on the meadow hike with Bill. Figuring that Tyler and Mason would be safe with all the other people around, and with Nora documenting everything photographically, they felt as comfortable as it was possible to feel about the situation. When Bill started the group walk downstream, the three of them hiked upstream toward the beaver pond.

"It's almost over," Eve said, when they sat down on the grassy bank.

"Six or seven hours," Sam said.

"A lot can happen in six or seven hours," Gordon said. "Does anybody here think we're going to have a smooth, uneventful ride to Donovan's Station?"

No hands were raised.

"So what do we have to watch for, and where?" he continued.

"I think Emily pointed the way this morning," Eve said after a pause. "The ride down the narrow trail to the foot of the falls is an accident waiting to happen. And if she pitches another screaming fit, that could provide a diversion."

"I agree with that," Sam said. "I think that's the most likely pressure point. But I don't think we can let our guard down anywhere. We have to be on them every minute until the trip is over."

"You're both right, I think," Gordon said. "And we really don't know what the scenery is like anywhere along this trail. It could provide someone with an opportunity."

"The best thing to do," Eve said, "is for one of us to stick like glue to each of the people. I take Brandi and you guys each latch onto one of the brothers."

"Are we really looking at Mason?" Sam said. "After all, he and I were the ones shot at last night."

"But we don't know by whom," Eve said.

"That's right," said Gordon. "It's a long shot, but we can't rule out the possibility that any of those three has the gun."

"Or none of them," Sam said.

"I think we need to at least make one more try to pin down the gun," Eve said. "Sam, do you think you could approach Brandi and ask her about her nocturnal ramblings?"

Sam sighed. "I suppose it has to be done," he said, "but I'm not sure how to go about it. That's not the sort of question that generally comes up in small talk."

"If all else fails," Gordon said, "go direct and see if you can catch her off balance. If you just ask straight out and don't lead up to it, she doesn't have time to come up with a story."

"I'll do what I can," Sam finally said.

"Why don't you head back to camp now?" Eve said. "You might be able to get her by herself when everyone comes back from the guided tour."

Sam looked at Gordon, who nodded slightly. Sam stood up.

"All right then," he said. "See you in a few."

When Sam had disappeared around the first bend, Eve spoke first.

"About last night, Gordon ..."

"What about it?"

"I wasn't expecting the answer I got. I hope you didn't think I was impertinent."

"Not at all. I was flattered by the visit. And its object. You were just a couple of years too late."

"Look. If we're all working together to see that those kids make it to Donovan's Station alive, I just want to be sure there are no hard feelings and no awkwardness between us."

"Not at all on my part. I never see any harm in asking, as long as you take no for an answer. And if you never ask, the answer's always going to be no."

She looked at him for several seconds, flashing a faint smile.

"Damn," she said. "You and I think alike, Gordon."

AS HINTS GO, the one about getting back to camp early was as subtle as a baseball bat to the knees, but the walk gave me a chance to think about how I should approach Brandi, assuming I could even get her alone without being too conspicuous. I decided that if the opportunity presented itself, I'd raise the question of what she was doing last night directly, but in a sort of golly-I-was-just-kind-of-wondering way and see how it played out from there. She seems to find me non-threatening, so I figure it's best to keep it that way.

Angie was by herself when I returned. She had just finished loading the last of the cookware onto the horses. When the field trippers returned, we'd be taking down our tents, then heading out pretty soon. I wasn't sure how I was going to get quality time with Brandi under those circumstances, but I decided to keep my eyes open and hope for a chance.

Sometimes you get lucky. When the group returned from the meadow tour, Brandi broke off from it and went down to the river to wash her hands. I suddenly decided mine could use a little cleansing as well and walked down to where she was. Everyone else was so intent on taking down the tents and getting ready to hit the trail, that I don't think anyone but Gordon and Eve, who returned at the same time, noticed.

Brandi was lying on her front on the grassy bank at the edge of the stream, her arms extended toward the water and her hands in it. She could probably see her reflection in the water and looked almost like a forest nymph. I came up a couple of feet to her right, dropped to my knees, and stuck my hands in the water as well.

"I see we have the same idea," I said.

"Hi, Sam," she said. We were on a first name basis. That was good. "Bill had me hold some plant he found out there, and it was sticky."

"You don't want to be riding with sticky hands," I said. Getting no response to that quip, I decided to be direct.

"Brandi, I have to ask you a question."

"What?"

"Last night when I was on watch, I saw you heading back from the woods with something in your hand. I tried to cut you off before you got back to ask if everything was OK, but then Eve popped out of the tent."

"Your friend works fast, doesn't he?"

I let that pass, but filed it away for future use. "Anyway, I dropped the ball then and just wanted to be sure. Was everything all right, I mean that you were off by yourself in the woods?

She looked up at me with a bemused expression, then broke into a laugh.

"You're so sweet, Sam. Everything was all right but my bladder, and I was just coming back after taking care of that. Thanks for caring, though."

"And you were carrying?"

"Toilet paper."

I put the odds of her telling the truth at three-to-one against, but was stumped for a follow-up question. So I just said, "Sorry. But I had to ask."

"That's all right."

I said nothing, partly because I had nothing to say and partly because I hoped she'd keep talking. My luck held.

"I'm going to be so glad when this trip is over," she said. "It's really wearing on me."

I kept quiet and nodded my head.

"It was supposed to be a bonding trip for Tyler and Mason, but it's been anything but. Mason is such a — a *snake.*"

The venom with which she said that took me by surprise, but I kept quiet and was rewarded. She sat up, looked back toward the camp, saw that we were alone, and turned back to me. In a half-whisper, she said:

"Sam, I need to get this out or I'll go crazy. If I tell you something, will you promise you won't tell anyone else?"

"Promise," I lied.

"Mason's been baiting Tyler something awful, and it's been driving Tyler nuts. Once we started out on the trip, Mason began to tell Tyler, whenever they were alone, that he was sleeping with me, too."

I gave her a quiet, and, I hope, sympathetic look. She went on.

"It's not true, of course, and I don't *think* Tyler believes it. The problem is, he might not believe I'd do such a thing, but he knows his brother would. I think that may have been why he disappeared in the storm. To get away from Mason and clear his head."

"Not because Mason mentioned Moretti?"

"That, too, maybe. Mason would use anything to get at Tyler."

"Sad," I finally said. "Have they always been like this?"

"You know, I said to Tyler once, 'As far as Mason is concerned, you only did one thing wrong in your life. Being born.' It seems to go back that far."

"I wish there was something I could do."

"You've done a lot by listening. And in four or five hours, this trip will be over. Hopefully that'll be the last I see of Mason, except when it's legally necessary."

From the direction of the camp, we heard Bill's voice shout, "Ten minutes."

"We'd better get back," she said, standing up. "Thanks, Sam."

I let her go back first and followed a minute later. Gordon had just about finished taking down our tent, and Brandi had gone into hers to do her final packing. I quickly pulled Gordon behind our horses and gave him the rundown on what she had said.

"Do you believe her about last night?" he asked.

"Not really," I said, "though there's a chance she could be telling the truth."

"Me, neither," he said. "But if she's even half telling the truth about Mason, it's amazing things have turned out as well as they have." He paused a minute. "And that would provide an explanation for why Tyler had the knife out when he was approaching the tent. If he thought Mason was in there with Brandi ..."

"You think Tyler would have killed him?"

Gordon considered the question for a moment.

"He might have killed them both," he said.

AUTUMN COMES EARLY in the High Country, and this seemed to be a day when the summer was thinking of checking out. It was sunny, and the sky was a deep blue, but it hosted a great many white clouds that danced overhead in a cool breeze blowing from the northwest. It was pleasant enough, but the morning augured a day in which the high temperature might not reach the mid-70s.

The trail was still wet down enough from Wednesday's storm that there was little dust as they rode along. Toward the southern end of Upper Awatos Meadows, they came across a grove of aspens, literally quaking in the wind and beginning to show the slightest hint of fall color.

From there, the river ran through a gorge on their right, and the trail went over a slight ridge before descending into the Lower Awatos Meadows. Bill and Angie stopped the procession at the summit of the pine-covered ridge so that everyone could look at the valley below and down the western slope toward the Central Valley. The usual Valley haze wasn't present, and the level of detail that could be seen on distant mountains was uncommonly high.

As they sat on the summit, pine needles dislodged by the breeze rained down on them. An occasional pine cone fell as well, and one hit Emily on the shoulder, provoking a shriek more of surprise than pain. Gordon focused on the Awatos, rolling through the valley. It was clearly a bigger river than it had been where they camped, and at the bottom of the valley, it ran over a number of rocks and boulders, generating rapids and white water, clearly visible even at a distance.

As they rode into the valley and down its side, following the river on their right, the valley gradually became narrower as it neared the falls. By the time the group reached the ford, it was only a few hundred feet wide. The river was essentially flanked by stretches of grass 50 to 100 feet wide that ended abruptly at the mountains on either side of the river. The river ran over Oakley's Ford in a lazy current no more than a foot deep the length of the crossing, then immediately below the ford it narrowed and picked up speed and depth as it headed for the falls.

The sound of the cascade was faintly audible in the distance as they sat down to lunch. Gordon joined Tyler, Mason and Brandi on the grass while Sam sat a distance away with Eve, keeping an eye on the entire group. Bill came by with sandwiches.

"I was worried that the ford might be running a bit high on account of the storm Wednesday, but it's back to normal now. For this year. After a dry winter, it's about two-thirds as wide and mostly a couple of inches deep. You could walk across it in flip-flops then if you wanted to."

"It looks to me," Brandi said, "as if someone's walking across it barefoot now."

They all turned. Sure enough, a young man was walking across the river, holding a pair of hiking boots in his left hand and a staff in his right. He appeared to be in his late twenties, of medium height with light brown hair and a scraggly beard. Unlike the hiker they had met at Sunrise Lake, he put out a sense of friendliness and conveyed no impression of threat or malice.

"Hello," he called out, as he came out on their side of the river. "They told me at Donovan's that I'd probably run into you folks."

"You just starting out?" Bill said.

"Left first thing this morning. I'm hoping to be at Blanchard Meadows by Labor Day."

"Sounds about right if you're walking," said Angie, who had just joined them. "You're traveling pretty light for a weeklong trip."

"That's the idea. Charles Pittman's the name. I want to see if I can live off the land for a week — just the plants I can pick and the fish I can catch. The way the first mountain men used to do."

"Why?" Mason said.

"Why? Because I want to live as self-sufficient a life as possible. We've all gotten too caught up in material things we don't need. I want to get away from that for a while, maybe as a test run for doing it more thoroughly later on."

He had sat down and begun putting on his socks. The gleam in his eyes showed he was caught up in his ideas.

"What if the fish aren't biting?" Brandi asked.

"I have some dried food and dehydrated meals as backup, but I'm hoping I don't need to use them. If I do, well, the worst case is I arrive at Blanchard Meadows a bit hungry."

"It can't be a very expensive trip," Gordon said, as Charles finished tying his boots. "It sounds like your biggest investment is a California fishing license."

"Fishing license? I don't need a fishing license. That's an unlawful state intrusion into my right to fish public waters. I have a right to resist unlawful authority."

"And the warden probably doesn't get up here too often," Gordon murmured softly.

Charles stood up. "Well, nice meeting you, but I've got to get going if I want to get to the upper meadows in time to catch my dinner. So long."

He strode off, and when he was out of earshot, Tyler turned to the others.

"I can't believe that. Why would you want to do what he's doing when you could take a trip like ours?"

"I'm trying to remember why we took this one," Mason said.

MASON GOBBLED HIS SANDWICH and excused himself early, heading off toward the horses. Gordon was pretty certain of the reason, but figured Sam could keep an eye on him. Brandi walked down to the river a moment later, leaving Gordon alone with Tyler. Gordon knew what was coming.

"Can I ask you a sports question?" Tyler said.

"You bet."

"When we get back, I want to put a bet on one team to win the Super Bowl at odds. What do you think of that?"

"I think it's all right if you look at it as a flyer that you're doing for fun. As an investment, it's pretty low percentage."

"Even if you bet on a good team?"

"It's hard enough to bet one game intelligently. A full season is next to impossible to predict."

"The Niners were 18-to-one to win it all just before we left. They came real close last year, and I'm thinking if the odds hold, I'll bet on them this year."

"It's as good a bet as any, which isn't saying much. As long as Steve Young stays healthy, they've got a chance."

"I think so, too. I'm going to make that bet."

Gordon concentrated on not rolling his eyes, and when Tyler took a bite out of what was left of his sandwich, Gordon leaped at the chance to change the subject.

"It's been quite the trip," he said, "especially for you, what with getting lost and all. Now that it's almost over, how do you feel about it?"

"I don't know," Tyler said. "I guess I'm a bit disappointed. I was hoping Mason and I could find some common ground, but it just didn't happen. Things actually got worse."

"I'm sorry to hear that."

"At least we know better than to try again. I think Mason wants me dead."

"That's a harsh thing to say."

"You don't know him the way I do." Tyler looked around and saw that they were pretty much alone, so he lowered his voice and continued. "In fact, I think he's trying to kill me on this trip."

A chill ran down Gordon's spine.

"Do you have any reason to believe that?" he asked.

"I've known him for 25 years. That's reason enough."

"But really, the trip is almost over. What could he do in the next couple of hours?"

"I don't know, but I'm taking no chances. I'm telling you so someone will know if anything happens to me. And I'm protecting myself. I have the gun in my saddle bag."

"The gun? You mean Jessica's gun?"

Tyler nodded. "Brandi pinched it because she was afraid of Mason. I don't know where she hid it that it wasn't found in the search last night, but she gave it to me this morning and said I should keep it until the end of the trip."

Gordon felt as if a dam had burst inside his brain and a roaring torrent of ideas was running through his head, competing for attention with each other. His first impulse was to think through what Tyler's admission meant in terms of explaining what had happened, but he knew he had to stifle that thought and focus on getting the gun.

"Tyler. Listen to me. That's not your gun, and you need to give it back now."

Tyler shook his head. "Nope. I'll give it back when we reach Donovan's Station, but not before."

"Tyler, you're being a thief."

"I'd rather be a thief than a dead man. You don't know my brother, Gordon."

Gordon looked frantically for Bill and Angie, and all he saw was Bill getting on his horse and turning to the group.

"All right, everybody," Bill said. "Mount up and let's roll. We're on the last leg."

"Don't worry, Gordon," Tyler said. "I really will give it back to Jessica when the trip's over."

And all Gordon could think of to do was to follow him back to the horses.

I HAD JUST MOUNTED MY HORSE when Gordon came up to me and made a gesture for me to lean over.

"Tyler has the gun," he whispered into my ear. "Keep an eye on him."

And then he was gone. It wasn't what I wanted to hear, coming into the last couple of hours of the trip, but I suppose I needed to hear it. As things turned out, I didn't get much of a chance to think about it.

We started across the ford single-file, at a deliberate pace, with Bill leading the way, Eve second, Tyler third, and me right behind Tyler, sticking to him the best I could. Brandi was right behind me, and Mason was a few slots back, with Gordon on his tail.

No sooner had we started across the ford than Mason pulled out of his place and galloped forward to pull even with Tyler on Tyler's left. I heard everything that went on between them, and it later turned out that I was the only one who did. Or who admitted to it anyway. I have a sneaking hunch Brandi heard all or most of the conversation, or argument if you prefer, but she denied it and there was no way of proving otherwise.

As Mason pulled up alongside Tyler, he leaned over and said, "So, Tyler, we have a bit of unfinished business to clean up."

"We have a lot of unfinished business," Tyler said. "Leave it for the end of the trip, or for our lawyers."

"No, this is between us, and we need to deal with it now."

"Why now?"

"Because I didn't appreciate your shooting at me last night."

"I didn't fire those shots, Mason."

"Oh, right. It must have been the tooth fairy."

"Are you calling me a fairy?"

"I didn't intend to, but if the shoe fits ..."

"Fuck off, Mason."

"Though now that you mention it, that might explain why Brandi's looking elsewhere for fun."

"You son of a bitch," Tyler said, and reached over to the saddle bag on the right side of his horse. He jammed his hand into it, rummaged around for several seconds, and sat up with a bewildered look on his face.

"Is this what you were looking for?" Mason was holding a pistol in his left hand, and his body was turned so that it shielded the gun from everyone but Tyler and me.

"I see you recognize it," Mason continued. "You still want to try to deny you shot at me last night?"

"It wasn't me," Tyler croaked.

Mason shook his head.

"You're such a loser, Tyler. You can't even lie convincingly. Everybody knows your story about being lost in the storm was a crock. You can't lie, you can't paint, and now I've got your gun and done your girl. You might as well die."

Tyler looked at him, terror in his eyes.

"Oh, don't worry," Mason said. "I'm not going to kill you. At least not now. But I do want you to know what it feels like to have bullets flying right past you."

He raised the gun, pointing it at Tyler.

I've had a lot of time to think about that moment since it happened. In the movies or on TV, someone in my position always thwarts or distracts the bad guy with the gun and saves the day. But that's make-believe. Every time I've thought about it — and that's been a lot — I kicked myself for not doing *something*. Anything. I could have shouted. I could have jumped off the horse and tried to grab Mason. I could have thrown something at him.

I did none of those things. I sat there in a state of mental, emotional, and physical paralysis. I went to see a shrink about it a few weeks later, and she assured me that paralysis is the normal response to the shock of being confronted by imminent danger. Intellectually, I suppose that's good to know. Spiritually and emotionally, I know I'll regret to my dying day that I couldn't react.

Then Mason fired the gun, all hell broke loose, and I felt as if I were seeing everything unfold in front of me in slow motion.

Bill turned abruptly to see where the shot had come from.

I could hear someone (I presumed Gordon) riding up from the rear.

Without even thinking, I began to get off my horse.

Behind me, I could hear Brandi stifling a gasp, and moaning, "Oh, no!"

True to his word, Mason had fired a shot past Tyler. How far past, it was hard to say, but Tyler wasn't waiting for seconds. He had released his right foot from the stirrup, and with his left foot, kicked himself off the horse in Mason's direction.

Mason wasn't expecting it. Tyler grabbed Mason's left arm with his right. Mason squeezed off another shot that went wild to his left, but he was off balance, and went slowly over the left side of his horse. As he and Tyler both came down on opposite sides of the horse, their two arms extended over the saddle like the top of a wishbone.

The force of the drop separated their arms, and Mason lost control of the gun, which went several yards through the air before landing in the river. Gordon pulled up alongside me and dismounted. Eve had gotten off her horse and was splashing furiously toward where the gun had landed. She had two million reasons for doing that, but, again, in hindsight, it probably wasn't a good idea, since it showed the boys where the gun had landed.

Soaking wet, Tyler and Mason got up and raced her to the point. Mason had the best angle and got there first, turning his back toward Eve to screen her out as he bent over to pick up the gun.

Tyler wasn't far behind, and launched himself at Mason, wrapping his arms around his brother as they both went down into the river again.

Only the gun had landed at the edge of the ford, and the tackle threw both of them into the deeper, faster water below the ford. Locked in a death grip, and seemingly oblivious to their situation, they were being swept downstream toward the 140-foot waterfall.

By the time Bill, Gordon, Eve and I got there, just seconds later, they were so far downstream that going in after them would have been pointless suicide. All we could do was watch them being swept to certain death.

And then fate or some mysterious force intervened. Halfway to the falls, they broke apart and suddenly seemed to realize the peril they were in. They began flailing around, separated, and two separate currents took them past a large, nearly flat rock just before the falls. Each of them was able to grab it, on opposite sides, and stop their fatal drift.

"There's still a chance if we act fast," Bill said. "Let's go."

THEY GALLOPED MADLY across the ford, and rode down the trail alongside the opposite bank of the river until they were even with the rock.

By the time they got there, Tyler and Mason had somehow pulled themselves up to its flat surface. It was only an inch or two above the water, and about six square feet, but it held them both. With the gun having been lost in their struggle, they sat there eyeing each other warily and gasping for air like two spent and punch-drunk fighters at the end of the ninth round.

"Sit tight, and for God's sake, stop fighting," Bill shouted. They were close enough to the waterfall at this point that it wasn't clear if they heard him over its roar.

Angie, having gotten the rest of the group across the ford, rode up.

"What do we do?" Gordon said.

Bill reached into his saddlebag and pulled out a tightly wound length of rope.

"This is a hundred feet, and it looks to me like they're about sixty from shore. I'll tie a knot and we'll pull it around my waist. Then I'll try to wade out and bring them back one at a time."

"Let me go after them," Gordon said.

Bill shook his head. "I'm in charge. I need to do it."

"I agree you're in charge, but I'm the biggest and probably strongest member of the party. And I'm pretty sure I have more experience wading in fast rivers than anyone else here."

Bill didn't immediately respond, and Angie jumped in.

"I'm in charge, too," she said, "and I agree with Gordon. Let the athlete do the physical rescue. But for crying out loud, let's do it now before they start fighting again."

"All right," Bill said after a few seconds.

As Bill prepared the knot, Gordon went to his saddle bag, took out a pair of running shoes, and tied them on. He took out pullover rubber slippers with cleated soles, sliding them over the shoes.

"The cleats give you better traction on a slippery river bottom," he said. "Old fisherman's trick."

They looped the rope over Gordon's body, tightening it around his waist. By now, everyone had reached that section of shore.

"Brian," Bill said, "You and Sam help me hold the rope. The other end can get pretty heavy when there are two people on it."

"Let me in, too," Jessica said. "I want to help."

"Right behind me, then. You ready, Gordon?"

"Ready as I'll ever be."

He jumped into the river. Even next to the bank, the water was knee-deep and moving at a pretty good clip. He almost lost his balance but managed to stay upright.

"Try to give me about a foot of slack," he said, and began moving slowly toward the rock.

Ideally, he thought, he would have had a staff to help him keep his balance, but he needed both hands free to deal with Tyler and Mason when he got to the rock. He moved slowly, making sure of his footing with each step.

As the water climbed to the level of his waist, he found it more and more difficult to get firm footing and keep his balance. His legs, strong from years of running up and down basketball courts, were beginning to ache from the strain. It took all his resolve to keep going. The water was icy cold and numbing his body, and he was breathing hard, trying to suck in oxygen at the high altitude.

The thought came into his mind: I can bring one of them back, but will I have the strength to come back for the other one. And the answer came back: I have to.

He was about six feet from the rock now, and the water was up to the bottom of his chest. If not for the tension of the rope, he wouldn't have been able to stay upright. He called out to the brothers.

"I can only take one of you at a time," he said. "One of you needs to get up on your hands and knees and be ready to reach out and grab my hand when I get there. When I pull you to me, wrap your arms around my body. They'll pull us back, and I'll come back for the other one.

"Who goes first?"

"You might as well, Mason," said Tyler. "You always do."

"Don't be a shit about it," Mason said. He got on his hands and knees and, with his left hand on the rock extended his right arm, ready to reach out when Gordon got two steps closer.

As Gordon began taking the first step, what happened next unfolded so quickly he could hardly be certain he saw it. With Mason precariously balanced on one arm, Tyler swung his right arm and cut Mason's legs out from under him. Mason went into the water several feet from Gordon, but for all the chance of grabbing hold of him, the distance might as well have been measured in miles.

The strong current propelled Mason down the river. He tried to get his feet on the bottom but couldn't. He flailed and tried to grab hold of another rock but couldn't. In only a few seconds, he was swept over the lip of the falls.

His scream as he went over could be heard only a second before the rumble of the cataract drowned it out.

Gordon watched him go in horror, then turned back to the rock. There, he saw another nightmare in the making.

In swinging at Mason's legs, Tyler had apparently lost his own balance and slid over the edge of the rock. He was holding onto the part of it nearest the falls with both hands, but, it appeared, none too steadily. Gordon was probably three steps away from him yet.

"Why did you do it, Tyler?" Gordon said.

"Do what? I didn't do anything."

"I saw you cut Mason's legs out from under him."

"You can't prove a thing. And I can't hold on much longer. Stop talking."

As Gordon took the first step toward the rock, a thought crossed his mind. If he were to get hold of Tyler and bring him safely back to the river bank, the only beneficiary of the action, other than Tyler himself, would be C&A Insurance, which wouldn't have to pay out two million dollars to a San Francisco gangster. Why was he doing this?

But the deep and primal belief that every human life is worth saving kicked in, and Gordon regretted the thought. He took another step toward Tyler, barely got his foot planted on the river bottom, and took a deep breath.

"Almost there," he said.

And Tyler made a fatal mistake.

He extended a hand toward Gordon before Gordon had got close enough. The other hand by itself was unable to maintain its purchase on the rock and slipped off.

As Tyler let go of the rock, Gordon made a frantic lunge in his direction, reaching out with his right hand. It grazed Tyler's arm but couldn't grab onto it.

Gordon lost his footing and went face-first into the river. When he came up, he could see the current relentlessly taking Tyler to the falls. He'd never forget the look of terror and disbelief on Tyler's face.

Tyler was so petrified he didn't even scream as he went over the edge.

Gordon was now being swept downstream himself, but the rope was pulling him back toward shore so that he was getting closer to the river bank at the same time he was getting closer to the waterfall.

He could hear Bill shouting, "Pull! Pull!" at the top of his lungs and was trying to calculate whether he would reach the river bank before he reached the waterfall.

He was so absorbed in that calculation that he didn't see the boulder until he hit it ribs-first.

The pain was worse than anything he had previously experienced.

Adding insult to injury, the blow knocked the wind out of him, and he ducked briefly underwater, swallowing some of it before he resurfaced. When he did, he tried to cough, but it hurt too much.

Barely conscious, he abandoned his will and his life to the four people pulling on the rope. He closed his eyes, drifted off for several seconds, and came to again when his back hit something soft, sending another jolt of intense pain through his body.

It was the river bank, ten feet above the falls.

Someone reached under one shoulder and someone else reached under the other. He looked up and saw Bill and Sam on either side of him. As they pulled him out of the water, the pain was so intense, he screamed and briefly passed out. He came to, lying on his back on the grassy river bank, in agony and gasping for air.

The first thing he saw was Eve kneeling over him, her face silhouetted against the bright blue Sierra sky.

"Gordon," she said. "Are you all right?"

It took everything he had to answer, and the words came out one at a time.

"I — can't — breathe."

Interlude: Wednesday September 1, 1999

From the San Francisco Chronicle

The body of a young man retrieved from the Awatos River yesterday has been tentatively identified as Tyler Linfield, 24, one of the twin brothers swept to their deaths over Awatos Falls Saturday afternoon.

Linfield and his brother, Mason, were the grandsons of Fred Schroeder, a land developer who built out much of the East Bay following World War II. Herbert McCabe, attorney for the Schroeder trust, confirmed that the brothers had been scheduled to inherit the bulk of the trust's assets on their 25ᵗʰ birthday later this month.

They had gone on a five-night guided pack tour that left Blanchard Meadows on the east slope of the Sierra last Monday. Just hours before the trip was to end, and under circumstances that are still unclear, they fell into the Awatos River and were swept downstream and over the 140-foot Awatos Falls at an elevation of nearly 8,500 feet.

The body of Mason Linfield was pulled from the pool at the base of the falls, but no trace of Tyler was found until yesterday morning. A fisherman hooked what he thought was the bottom of the river at Frenchman's Camp, a mile downstream from Donovan's Station.

Only the "bottom" began to drift downstream, and Tyler Linfield's body rose to the surface. Other anglers in the vicinity helped guide it to shore.

Headwaters County Sheriff Steve Bullock said the circumstances surrounding the tragedy are still under investigation, but that it appears the brothers got into an argument, jostled each other into the river, and were unable to escape its swift and unforgiving current.

They briefly were able to grab hold of a rock just above the falls, Bullock said, and one of the members of the party, attached to a rope, attempted to rescue them, but they were swept over the falls before he could get to them.

Bullock identified the would-be rescuer as Quill Gordon, 40, of San Francisco, a former standout basketball player at Cal. He was injured in the rescue attempt and transported to Mercy Valley Hospital by medical helicopter.

Hospital officials said he was released yesterday morning after treatment for cracked ribs, a dislocated shoulder, multiple contusions, shock and hypothermia.

The twins were the only children of Schroeder's daughter and only child, Laura Schroeder Linfield, who died in a fall from a zip line in Costa Rica in 1995. Their death before claiming the estate has created a buzz in San Francisco legal circles as to how the vast fortune will be distributed.

There will be no probate, as the estate was held in a trust administered by McCabe and his law firm. McCabe declined to say what would happen to the money.

"There were provisions for this sort of eventuality, of course," McCabe said. "All I can say is that to the best of our ability, the estate will be distributed in accordance with the wishes of Laura Linfield, and it will be done privately, discreetly, and with the utmost integrity."

Epilogue: Friday November 26, 1999

"IT WASN'T THE HONEYMOON I'd always dreamed of," Elizabeth said, "but it certainly was a honeymoon to remember."

We were sitting in a booth at a legendary seafood restaurant near the Financial District, waiting for Eve Bredon to show up. Herbert McCabe had called the meeting and reserved a booth for six. Gordon, Elizabeth, Nora, McCabe and I were already seated, and Nora had made the mistake of asking if Gordon's wedding and honeymoon had to be canceled, which led to Elizabeth's comment.

I was best man at the wedding, of course, and Gordon had given me a short and sanitized description of the honeymoon. I looked down at the table and focused on the tines of my fork, hoping Elizabeth wouldn't add too much more information.

"We had to cancel Hawaii because he was in no shape to make the trip," she said, looking at Gordon. "We went up to a little place in the Wine Country, where it was warm and pleasant. But mostly we just stayed in the room, where I kept Gordon supplied with steady doses of painkillers."

"You must admit," he said, "I was a model patient."

"You were quite docile, darling, but not much fun. And it really was too bad that you spent the honeymoon sleeping in the chair."

He hadn't told me about the chair. I shifted my attention from the fork to the soup spoon.

"I couldn't lie down," he said. "I might never have been able to get up. In any case, a do-over was clearly called for, and now that I'm my old self, we'll be taking a second honeymoon to Hawaii between Christmas and New Year. A *real* honeymoon."

"Couldn't you have postponed the wedding?" Nora asked.

"We didn't want to do that," Gordon said. "Too many people were coming from too far away. I felt that as long as I could stand up for 20 minutes, we should go ahead with it."

"He was a real trouper," Elizabeth said, "and he put on a bit of a show." I could sense her looking at me, and I blushed slightly at my part of it.

You see, Gordon was totally stoned on painkillers to get through the ceremony. When the time came for him to put the ring on Elizabeth's finger, I deftly removed it from my coat pocket and extended it toward him. He looked straight ahead, lost in another world altogether.

So, I gave him a gentle nudge in the ribs with my elbow.

I should have known better. His ribs were so tender he wouldn't have wanted anyone even breathing on them, and he let out an involuntary, high-pitched squeal.

The microphone overhead carried it to every corner of the church, and some people laughed. How does that old saying go? When you slip on a banana peel, that's tragedy. When the other guy does it, it's comedy.

"But he eventually got the ring on," Elizabeth continued. "Even if it was the wrong finger. I switched it before the reception."

I looked toward the *maitre'd* and sighed with relief.

"Eve's here," I said.

"Excellent," McCabe said. "Then we can order and get down to business."

Eve kissed her son and daughter, who looked to be about 7 and 5, goodbye, handed them over to a man I presumed was her husband, and headed toward our booth. The kids momentarily threw me until I remembered it was the day after Thanksgiving and school's out.

"I WANT TO MAKE IT CLEAR," McCabe said after the waiter had left, "that even though the expedition didn't end the way I hoped it would, I blame no one for that. The Linfield boys were bound to come to a bad end sooner or later, and it happened sooner. Gordon was on top of things all the way and risked his life to save them at the end. Sam did a stellar job pulling Mason out of the line of gunfire. I couldn't have asked for a more conscientious execution of the duties I asked you to take on."

"That's a generous appraisal," Gordon said. "I'm still asking myself if I couldn't have done better."

"I call that attorney's remorse," McCabe said. "It happens a lot when a lawyer loses a trial, and it doesn't do any good. Put it behind you as fast as you can."

"Easier said than done."

"In any case, there are a few loose ends. One of them is that I understand, Gordon, that your medical insurance didn't cover emergency transportation by helicopter."

Gordon nodded.

"I took the liberty of contacting the helicopter company," McCabe continued, "and was astounded to find out how much such an evacuation costs."

"So was I," Gordon said.

"Thirty thousand, in case the rest of you are wondering. I took the matter up with my partners, and we all agreed that since you were injured in the service of our clients, the estate should reimburse you for the cost."

He reached into his inside coat pocket, took out a business-sized white envelope, and handed it to Gordon.

"Thank you," Gordon said. "I really wasn't expecting this." After a pause, he added, "Are you sure this is legal?"

"I'm not at all sure it's legal, but we think we can get away with it, and it's the right thing to do."

"Well, thank you again."

McCabe turned to Nora, who was sitting at his left, on the inside of the booth.

"And Miss Robinson, thank you for returning that contract. Are you absolutely certain you're all right with it?"

"Absolutely. The terms were quite generous."

He took another envelope from the inside coat pocket and handed it to her.

"Then thank you. Do you mind if I enlighten the others?"

"Not at all."

"Miss Robinson shot a number of photographs on that final day of the trip. They were most helpful in documenting what happened and also quite chilling. Given the notoriety this case has generated, I wanted to be sure they didn't end up in a newspaper or magazine."

"Or on the internet," I said.

"That's right. I'm still not used to thinking about that. To be safe, the estate is purchasing all publication rights to the images to ensure they never get distributed to a wider audience."

"I wasn't planning on trying to sell them," Nora said.

"I understand that. But who knows what could happen in a few years? This way it's settled, and you've been compensated."

"Thank you," she said softly.

"And now," McCabe said, "I want to hear Gordon's explanation of what he thinks happened on that trip."

All eyes turned to Gordon. He was his usual, healthy, confident self now, and although he didn't openly show it, I think he was enjoying the attention.

"I've had a lot of time to think about it, while I was recovering from the injuries and since," he said. "We'll never be able to prove anything, but I have a scenario that fits the facts and makes sense.

"I think that when Tyler proposed the trip, he was genuinely putting out an olive branch to Mason. Mason went along for the ride, partly because he figured he could amuse himself by needling Tyler, and also because he'd met Brandi and been attracted to her. My sense of it is that at the outset, no one had any criminal ideas.

"That first night at Cliff Lake, Mason and Tyler started up the path to the top of the cliff, and I'm guessing he spontaneously came up with the idea of putting the ball on the path in front of Tyler. It couldn't have been premeditated because he wouldn't have known about the terrain until we got there, and it was probably the kind of nasty prank he used to play on his brother when they were growing up.

"He most likely expected Tyler to fall down on the path, but instead Tyler went over the edge of the cliff. It was just dumb luck that he went over where he'd hit the water instead of the ground below. But Tyler going over the cliff, instead of just falling on the ground, caused the situation to escalate. What was intended as a prank instead looked like a murder attempt, and that colored everybody's reactions from there on.

"The next night was the bear attack on Mason's tent. He assumed, as did the rest of us, that it was Tyler who stashed the salami in there, and he was wrong. But that assumption drove the rest of the events.

"Wait a minute," Eve said. "If Tyler didn't do it, who did?"

"Brandi," I said. "She sat in the background quiet and unassuming, but after Tyler took that fall into the lake — which had to be terrifying to her — she was the one pulling the strings."

"I think Sam's right," Gordon said. "But Mason didn't know that. After the bear incident, he doubled down on taunting his brother. When they were talking just before the storm, I wouldn't be surprised if he hinted he was getting Brandi's favors, or was close to getting them. Then he mentioned Nick Moretti — and he could only have known about Moretti from Brandi — and that set Tyler off.

"Like most gamblers, Tyler was impulsive and given to fantastical thinking. All I can deduce, though it wouldn't make sense to a normal person, is that he decided to break away from the group and spy on Mason and Brandi. The storm gave him the opportunity, and he took it."

"I'm curious, Gordon," Eve said. "Do you think there was anything between Brandi and Mason?"

"If you mean did they sleep together, I suspect not. But those pictures Nora shot on Sunday and Wednesday of the two of them together are suggestive. Mason was smarter than Tyler, and so was Brandi. Even though Mason was a piece of work, she might have been just a bit attracted by that intelligence."

"She's still young enough to find the bad boys attractive," Eve said. "It's more than plausible from Tyler's point of view."

"You know," Nora said, "that might explain something. If she was feeling a flicker of attraction for Mason, that may have made her overcompensate in protecting Tyler."

"I think that's very likely," Gordon said, "but it's only speculation. I'm 99 percent sure, though, that she was the one who fired the shots at Mason and Sam, though I don't think she was trying to hit them. Just scare them."

"Which she thoroughly did," I said.

"In any case," Gordon said, "to wrap this up, I think Tyler was planning on seeing whose tent Mason was sleeping in Wednesday night. But he probably passed Keener Flat when it was still dark and cloudy and missed the campsite. By the time he realized he'd gone too far, it was too late, so I'm figuring he found a quiet place to bed down off the trail and followed us to Sunrise Lake, where I caught him trying to go into Brandi's tent the next night."

"Can I ask a question?" Elizabeth said. "You said that Tyler proposed the trip, but given Brandi's role in the proceedings, isn't it possible she put him up to it in the first place?"

I hadn't thought of that, but as soon as I heard it, the idea made sense. I could see Gordon thinking the same way.

"That may be true," he said. "But, again, I don't know how we'll ever know. However it started, Brandi's interventions just escalated things between the two brothers, until it ended the way it did." Gordon took a sip of his red wine. "Kind of ironic, isn't it? Brandi had a boyfriend who was going to be worth four hundred million in a few weeks, and by going over the top to protect him, she lost him and ended up with nothing."

"Not so fast," Eve said, as the waiter arrived with lunch.

SHE EXPLAINED FURTHER as we dug into our meals. My sole, grilled in butter, was perfect.

"There was that life insurance policy of Tyler's," Eve said, after we had all taken a couple of bites.

"How did that go," Gordon asked.

"After the body was positively identified, we had no choice but to pay Moretti. I'm afraid C&A Insurance wasn't as happy about my job performance as Mr. McCabe was of Gordon's. But at least they realized it was a once-in-a-lifetime situation and they didn't fire me.

"I did, however, have to sit in on the meeting when Moretti came to collect. He looked quite debonair with his silver hair and navy pinstripe suit, and I'll never forget what he said when we handed him the check.

"He took that two-million-dollar check out of the envelope, looked at it, and sighed. Then he said, 'You know, Mr. Linfield owed me two and a quarter when all was said and done. But sometimes a businessman has to take the payment he can get, rather than the one he's entitled to.' The shark."

We ate in silence for a moment, then I said, "But you were hinting at something about Brandi."

"Yes. Well, as I think I mentioned before, Nick Moretti was the principal beneficiary of the policy, but there was a secondary beneficiary, as well. Moretti got two million, but Brandi was in line for five hundred thou."

"And you'll pay it?" McCabe asked.

"I don't see where we have any options. We've been stalling while we investigate some of the things Gordon was talking about, but there's really no evidence-based reason for denying the claim. I've been told that unless a smoking gun turns up by the end of this month, we'll pay it in December, call it the cost of doing business, and move on."

"Curiouser and curiouser," McCabe said.

"So, counsel," Gordon said, "do we get to find out what happens to the Schroeder fortune?"

"Do you really want to know?"

"All of San Francisco does."

"I suppose I've skirted enough ethical rules on this matter that one more isn't going to make any difference. But first, I need another glass of wine."

AFTER THE WINE ARRIVED, he made us promise not to speak a word to anyone else of what he was going to tell us. We agreed, of course.

"The whole Linfield trust is a mare's nest," he began. "That was one of the reasons I was hoping we could keep Tyler and Mason alive until September 27th. Their inheriting the money might have been morally repugnant, but it would have been legally clean. The mess that was left behind when they both died will be a long time in cleaning up."

And highly lucrative, I thought, though I didn't say so.

"When the will creating the trust was drawn up 11 years ago, I don't think Laura Linfield really gave much thought to what would happen if Mason and Tyler both died before they came of age. It seemed like such a remote possibility. But then the whole Schroeder family is living proof of the fact that death can come suddenly and unexpectedly to anyone at any time.

"In any event, a will has to provide for such an eventuality. She picked a dozen charities and nonprofit organizations to distribute the assets of the trust to, mostly environmental and animal welfare organizations. And after she signed the will, I doubt that she gave it another thought.

"Well, a lot of things change in eleven years. Three of the organizations listed are, so far as I've been able to tell, entirely defunct. Three others have merged with other organizations, leaving a question as to whether a distribution to the new entity satisfies the original intent of the will. And two others are under investigation by the state attorney general's office, which raises still further questions.

"The bottom line is that we could be looking at years of investigation, executorial decisions, and petitions to the court before a dime of the estate is ever distributed to any of those groups."

He took a swallow of wine.

"I hope all of you are keeping your wills up to date."

None of us said anything for a full minute, and I used some of that time resolving to take a new look at my ten-year-old will.

"Thank you for letting us know," Gordon finally said. "That's quite an amazing story."

"But that's not the end of it," McCabe said. "I was saving the best for last. Best in story terms, anyway."

We all turned to him.

"At the end of last month, we received a communication from an attorney representing Brandi Baine. She is pregnant and inquiring as to whether the will governing the trust made any provision for an heir or heirs unknown. Of course it does. That's a standard consideration in any competent will. Laura was quite adamant that there be a very generous provision in such an unlikely event, because continuation of the family line was very important to her.

"We deposed Miss Baine, and she agreed to take a DNA test to determine who the father is. The results aren't back yet, but I don't hold out much hope that they'll absolve the estate of responsibility. If she's right about the father, as I expect she is, that's where a quarter of the estate will go, and the will provides for generous support for the mother or mothers until the 25ᵗʰ birthday of the heir or heirs."

"So Tyler's kid is set to inherit $200 million?" I asked in disbelief.

"A lot more than that if it's properly invested for 25 years," Gordon said.

McCabe raised his hand.

"We don't know that Tyler is the father," he said. "In the deposition, she admitted to having relations with Mason the night Tyler was missing from the pack trip. Either of the twins could have been the father, and from the standpoint of the estate, it doesn't matter."

"But," I sputtered, "she told me there was nothing going on between her and Mason."

"I'm sure she did, Sam. But it's been my experience that people tend to be a bit more liberal with the truth when they're not under oath. When I asked her why she entered into relations with Mason, she just shrugged and said, 'I guess when a woman's feeling emotional, she can get a bit confused.' "

Elizabeth finally broke the ensuing silence.

"Would it be out of order to ask whether the presumptive heir is a boy or girl?"

McCabe had a third of a glass of Chardonnay in front of him, and he downed it in two gulps.

"Boys, plural," he said. "She's expecting twins."

Author's Note

FATHER RONALD KNOX (1888-1957) was a Roman Catholic priest widely known in his time for his Christian writings and BBC radio broadcasts. He also was a distinguished mystery writer during the Golden Age, a founding member of the Detection Society, and a friend of Agatha Christie, Dorothy L. Sayers, John Dickson Carr and other leading writers of the day. He even proposed a Ten Commandments for mystery writing in an attempt to make the genre less improbable than it otherwise might have been. His novels of the countryside, *The Footsteps at the Lock* and *Double Cross Purposes*, both featuring insurance investigator Miles Bredon, loosely inspired this book.

Charles McDermand, biographical information unknown, was an outdoor writer in the first half of the 20th Century. His book *Waters of the Golden Trout Country*, published in 1946, describes his fishing and camping experiences in the High Sierra backcountry during the 1930s. It is a beautiful elegy to a fishing experience that no longer exists, told in a style of fishing writing that also no longer exists.

Readers of this book would be well advised not to run off to an atlas in search of the locations where *The Slaves of Thrift* occurs. I took places I've encountered in the western mountains between Southern California and Canada, mashed them up with other places from the same wide area, and even added a spice mix of details that I plain made up. My aim was to create a fantasia of an enchanted wilderness that works on its own terms, even if it's more idealized than the reality of this crowded world.

Acknowledgements

Many thanks to the people who helped with the construction of this book. That would include editors Lauren and Dan Wilkins, Deborah Karas for her work on the compelling cover, and Nancy Ruiz DePuy, who took my scribblings on graph paper and turned them into the elegant map at the front of the book. And thank you, Linda, for your suggestions and assistance with formatting.

Thanks as well to those who provided technical assistance with the story elements. That would include Karen Horton, who helped with understanding horses; Ed Banks, who advised on the ins and outs of insurance policies; and Rob Allen, who answered several questions about wills and estates. Any errors in these areas are mine, not theirs.

Finally, a special word of appreciation goes to Judy Parrish, who gave me her late father's copy of *Waters of the Golden Trout Country*.

About the Author

MICHAEL WALLACE is a former daily newspaper editor and public relations and publications consultant. He is a native and lifelong resident of California and an avid fly fisherman and devoted reader of mystery novels of all stripes. He and his wife, Linda, live on California's Central Coast. His email, Twitter and Facebook addresses can be found at the website quillgordonmystery.com.

Made in the USA
Columbia, SC
20 January 2024